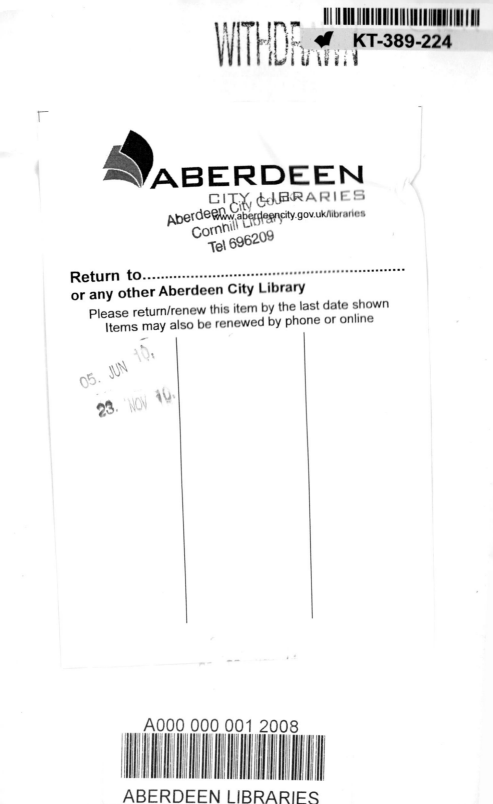

WITHDRAWN KT-389-224

ABERDEEN
CITY LIBRARIES

Return to..
or any other Aberdeen City Library

Please return/renew this item by the last date shown
Items may also be renewed by phone or online

05. JUN 10.

23. NOV 10.

SCARLET SASH

Recent Titles from Garry Douglas Kilworth

SOLDIERS IN THE MIST
THE WINTER SOLDIERS
ATTACK ON THE REDAN
BROTHERS OF THE BLADE
ROGUE OFFICER ⋆
KIWI WARS ⋆

⋆ *available from Severn House*

SCARLET SASH

A Zulu Wars novel

Garry Douglas Kilworth

This first world edition published 2010
in Great Britain and in the USA by
SEVERN HOUSE PUBLISHERS LTD of
9–15 High Street, Sutton, Surrey, England, SM1 1DF.

British Library Cataloguing in Publication Data

Kilworth, Garry.
  Scarlet Sash.
  1. Great Britain. Army. Regiment of Foot, 24th (2nd
  Warwickshire) – Fiction. 2. Zulu War, 1879 – Fiction.
  3. Historical fiction.
  I. Title
  823.9'14-dc22

ISBN-13: 978-0-7278-6890-9   (cased)

All Severn House titles are printed on acid-free paper.

Severn House Publishers support The Forest Stewardship Council [FSC],
the leading international forest certification organisation. All our titles that
are printed on Greenpeace-approved FSC-certified paper carry the FSC logo.

Mixed Sources
Product group from well-managed
forests and other controlled sources
www.fsc.org Cert no. SA-COC-1565
© 1996 Forest Stewardship Council
FSC

Typeset by Palimpsest Book Production Ltd.,
Grangemouth, Stirlingshire, Scotland.
Printed and bound in Great Britain by
MPG Books Ltd., Bodmin, Cornwall.

This novel is dedicated to the memory of
David Rattray
a brilliant oral storyteller whose accounts of
the Anglo-Zulu Wars still enthral me.

Acknowledgements

My thanks go to Ian Knight, not only for his invaluable work *Companion to the Anglo-Zulu War* and others, but also for his kind assistance with this novel. Also thanks to David Rattray for his *Guidebook to the Anglo-Zulu War Battlefields* and others. Appreciation too for Ian Castle's several books on the subject. Finally, as ever, I found myself ringing my friend Major John Spiers for unwritten (or at least difficult to unravel) answers to various general questions on the quirks and singularities of the British Army, which have developed mysteriously over the centuries.

The Iron Wind
(Zulu Battle Chant)

We are the boys of Isandlwana
who face the iron wind.
A furnace wind,
like the Saharan Simoom
or Haboob of Khartoum,
bringing madness on its breath.
No shield can turn it,
no mask,
no magic cloak.
Warriors are whisked away
like broken straws.
Sometimes
it takes our heads clean off.
We are the boys of Isandlwana
who run at the fiery rush,
into the bulleting blast,
for wind is only wind
and tomorrow will be calm
and quiet
and utterly still.

Prologue

A company of the 2nd Battalion of the 24th were moving cautiously through the scrub of Perie Bush, north of Kingwilliamstown. Somewhere amongst that hilly, rocky ground, covered with brushwood so thick that visibility was down to a few yards, were Gaika tribesmen armed with spears and old muskets. The trouble for the men of the 24th was that the natives were dark, the bush was dark, and sometimes you did not see the enemy until you trod on him. The area was covered by six shiny brass muzzle-loading guns, a battery situated high on a nearby hill, but these could not be fired into dense brush country where troops were skirmishing, for fear of hitting one's own.

Ensign Sebastian Early had started with twenty men at his back. He was now alone. Once they had entered the tangled growth of the bush they had become separated. Seb did not doubt that his soldiers were somewhere around, but hidden from him and each other by the dense vegetation. His heart was beating fast. Redcoats were not used to this kind of warfare. They preferred open landscapes, nice neat lines striding forth with bayonets fixed and reassuring friendly guns pounding behind them, clearing the way ahead. This was ugly close-quarter stuff, death waiting to leap on you from each leafy corner. It was dry, brittle warfare, with the smell of hot dust irritating your nostrils, and any man who was not scared as he stepped cautiously through the maze of thorn bushes and dwarf trees was a fool.

Revolver in hand, Seb stopped in the shade of a thorn. There had been a change of light to his left, which he had caught out of the corner of his eye.

'Corporal Edwards?' he whispered. 'That you?'

There was a sharp explosion just yards away and a ball whistled by Seb's head. He whirled and fired at a shadow. Two shots. Nothing. A shout came from far off, followed by the sound of more firing. A spear came out of the sun and embedded itself in the ground a yard to Seb's right. He peered into the dark scrub and fired again, three times, at a piece of darkness that had detached itself from the shade. There was a thump, a groan, and then thrashing sounds. Heart racing, he ran to the spot to find a native looking up at him with wide white eyes. Eyes that swam with fear. Seb stared down at the man who had been shot through the shoulder and was seeping blood into the grey dust.

'You're out of it,' muttered Seb, turning away. 'No more battle for you, chum.'

Just then three Gaikas came running at him before he had time to lift his revolver. There was a commotion behind them. Soldiers were chasing them. Only one of the Gaikas was armed. He carried a knobkerrie. This was struck out at Seb's head as he passed. Seb instinctively blocked the blow with his pistol arm. The knobkerrie caught him on his elbow causing him to yell in pain. The revolver fell towards the ground, but was held dangling on its lanyard. Seb gathered it up, reeling it in like a fish on a line. His eyes were watering with the pain. The hardwood club had caught him right on the point of the bone. His hand was uselessly numb. Four soldiers ran past him, one of them glancing sideways to make sure the officer was not badly hurt. Two of them stopped to fire their Martini-Henrys at the retreating Gaikas, who were dissolving into the bush.

In a short while, one of the soldiers came back, the one who had given Seb a quick look.

'You all right, sir?'

'Yes,' replied Seb through gritted teeth. 'There's a wounded native over there, behind that thorn.'

The soldier, a private, went to look. A moment later there was a loud scream. Seb ran round the shrub to see the redcoat staggering backwards, a spear protruding from his chest. It had been thrown with such force the point was showing through his back. Seb was horrified and stared around in vain, looking for the thrower. The enemy was nowhere to be seen. Nor was the body of the wounded native. This had been dragged away, or had dragged itself. There were snaking marks in the dust, along with a dribble of body fluids. Seb knelt by the private, who was now on the ground, blood bubbling from his mouth.

The dying man looked up and said, 'Oh, sir . . .' then his eyes misted over and his jaw dropped.

Seb stood up. All around him now were the sounds of fighting. He left the soldier, who was beyond help, and ran towards the battle. Mercifully he found himself on an open patch where soldiers had gathered and were firing at about thirty of the enemy, dark figures who were zigzagging as they ran away. Some of them were grabbing at invisible things around their heads. 'Catching stones' they called it. A belief they could snatch bullets out of the air with their hands.

A lieutenant stood by the kneeling redcoats, directing their fire.

'Peter,' cried Seb. 'Have you seen my men?'

'Some of them are here, with me, Sebastian,' replied his comrade. 'Everyone's scattered. It's this bloody bush country. You stick with us now.'

Seb nodded, fired one shot, then began reloading his revolver.

Guns opened up on the ridge behind them, now that the enemy was in the open. Seven-pounders. Their rounds landed amongst the retreating enemy, who now numbered about fifty as more and more emerged from the bush. Further troops appeared on Seb's left. Suddenly the natives stopped and turned, running back to fire with their ancient muskets into the soldiers, then away again, leaving two redcoats wounded. As they ran the Gaikas began going down under the intense fire from the Martini-Henrys. At least ten bodies tumbled on to the rocky ground, to be left by their fellows.

Gaika horsemen now charged out of the bush behind the soldiers, firing into their backs. There were about twelve mounts. They wheeled away and arced towards the warriors on foot, following them to a river, a glittering silver strip in the sunlight. The redcoats then raced after the horsemen, hoping to reach them before they crossed the river.

One of the Gaika riders was on a white horse.

An officer on the flank suddenly shouted, 'There's Sandili – I see Sandili.'

There was great excitement amongst the troops. Sandili was the leader of the Gaikas who had been causing so much trouble raiding farms and settlements in the Transkei. Seb took the officer at his word and urged his redcoats on. It would be a great feather in all their caps if they got Sandili. Every time a white horse was captured by the British they inspected the stirrups to see if one was shorter than the other: a sign that it was indeed the mount of the Gaika rebel leader.

The chase was however fruitless. The lieutenant who had become so excited by Sandili's presence did manage to reach the river while some of the horsemen were leaving it on the other side. He fired across the water, emptying his side arm. Several of the riders dismounted and returned his fire. Suddenly the lieutenant staggered back, his helmet flying off. He fell to the ground. By the time his men reached him he was dead. There was a hole in his forehead just above the right eye.

Seb gathered his breath as he stared down at the officer. He knew him, of course. Lieutenant Youngblood. From Worcestershire? Or Leicestershire? One of those. Youngblood had fought his last battle, out here on the African continent, in a dirty little corner of the Transkei. It was not the most glorious of deaths, to be sure. However, much would be said of his bravery, in some church back home in England, as well as out here in Africa. He had died a hero's death, chasing rebel Kaffirs across countryside which suited the local enemy's method of warfare. His brother would be proud, his sisters would speak of him in soft quiet voices, his father would gravely accept the condolences of his friends at the club, his mother would never cease to grieve.

Seb noticed, as he stared down at the body, that Youngblood was wearing a red sash on his left shoulder.

One

There is a town situated on the banks of the Klip River in the uThukela District of kwaZulu-Natal, South Africa. It was founded by the Boers but the British took it over. Lady Juana María de los Delores de León Smith, the Spanish wife of Sir Harry Smith, the Governor of Cape Colony, had the distinction of giving this community its new name. Naturally her Spanish *nombre* was far too long and elaborate for the small settlement standing between Johannesburg and Durban, situated in the shadow of the Drakensberg Mountains, so they called the place 'Ladysmith'. It was here on the outskirts of this town that the death of Captain Alan Charterman Brewer occurred: a fatality embedded with several strange circumstances.

'So, Colour, you broke down the door – alone?'

Lieutenant Peter Williams, the new Provost-Marshal of Lord Chelmsford's army in South Africa, had been given as an office a stone hut once used by a Boer family to house their pigs. Lord Chelmsford had, after all, only left a small garrison at Ladysmith, the main force being at Helpmekaar to the east. The interior of the hut had been thoroughly cleaned, the walls scrubbed, a layer taken from the dirt floor, but the smell of pig still lingered. Lieutenant Williams of the 24th Warwickshire Regiment felt his nose twitching every few minutes and looked longingly through the doorway at the warm fresh air outside. His sergeant assistant stood in that doorway much of the time, breathing through his mouth.

Colour Sergeant Murray of the 90th (Light) Infantry, a man in his mid-forties, dark and heavy of brow, with a skull like a bull, shook his greying head.

'No, sir, not alone. It was too heavy, ye ken. Thick as a mine prop and locked solid. I ordered one or two men to give me a hand, like. We had to use the veranda bench as a battering ram. Got it down in the end, though,' he added, proudly. 'Took a bit of hammerin', sir, but we burst through the bugger.'

'One or two men?'

'Well, half a dozen. I dinna ken the exact number, sir.'

'And what was the first thing you saw?'

'The captain, slumped forward in a chair, under the window.'

'Which was barred, it being the duty officer's quarters?'

'That's right, sir. Bars up at the window. Shutters down.'

Williams had already inspected the shutters. They were intact. No bullet holes. He was not shot from the outside, that much was certain. The bars themselves were embedded in mortar and stonework. There was no other way out of the room, except perhaps through the thatched ceiling which also formed the roof. However, the thatch was intact and bore no signs of being tampered with.

'Describe exactly what you saw, if you please, Colour.'

'Och, both arms was dangling like, one either side of the chair, sir. The revolver was lyin' on the floor, down under the captain's right hand, just where he'd dropped it after shooting hisself. His head was sort of thrown back, like, lollin' on the back of the chair. Mouth open, eyes open, a *horrible* look on his face as if he'd seen a ghost.'

Williams did not correct the sergeant by saying he was not to assume the handgun was dropped by the dead man or that he had shot himself. The revolver could have been placed where it lay by another hand. Instead he asked him about the position of the corpse's legs.

'Straight out, but open. In a sort of V shape.'

'Any signs of a disturbance in the room.'

The colour sergeant raised his eyebrows.

'I didn't touch the place, then you was called for, sir.'

'So no one actually inspected the body, to see if the captain was indeed dead?'

'Ah well, yes, I did that, sir. Put my cheek to his mouth, to see if there was breath there. And the corporal, he lifted the captain's wrist to see . . .'

'Which one? Which wrist?'

The colour sergeant juggled a bit with his hands, then said, 'Definitely the left one, sir. Aye, the left. The corporal's intentions was to check for a pulse, but he dropped the hand immediate like, it being cold as ice so he said.'

'Where was the officer who was relieving Captain Brewer?'

'He stayed outside, sir. When I called to him that the duty officer was dead, he sort of panicked like. He scurried off to find you, sir.'

Williams said, 'I don't think you can assume you know the nature of Lieutenant Jameson's emotions, Colour.'

'Sorry, sir?'

'You said he panicked and *scurried* off.'

'I'm just saying what it seemed like, sir.'

'We'll leave that. Can you describe the dead man's injuries – as you observed them at that moment?'

'Well, it was obvious when I went round to his front that he'd been shot in the chest.'

'How many times?'

The colour sergeant blinked rapidly.

'Once, I think, sir – och no, I tell a lie, *twice* it was, one hole bigger than the other . . . it's a horrible thing, sir, for a man to kill himself on Christmas Day. Well, I mean, I suppose his family will have to be told what day it was? They probably raised a glass to him, in his absence. Proud that their son was serving Queen and country in a foreign land. I know mine do for me, on Hogmanay. What makes a man shoot himself like that? No letter, is there, from his wife? The regiment hasn't had a sniff of mail for weeks now. What gives a man like that the blue devils, eh? He wasn't one of those officers – beg pardon, sir – who the men hate, you know. They quite liked him – well, apart from him not being quite up to the knocker in battle experience, but nobody held that against him . . .'

The colour sergeant was clearly quite upset by the sudden death of his officer and was trying to make sense of it. This was not the job of an army policeman. It was work for the padre.

Peter knew there was a letter, an old one, and it was from his wife, telling him she was leaving him for another man, a captain in the Guards. Brewer had also built up quite a large bank of creditors, mostly gambling debts but some heavy tailors' bills and there were two sizeable invoices from a purveyor of handmade shotguns in Norfolk.

All in all, there was plenty there to depress a man, if he needed an excuse to shoot himself. But – but in truth, *many* officers had debts. It was in the nature of the service. If you had no private income you had to rely on an officer's pay. Captain Brewer had held a brevet rank, which meant he only received the pay and allowances of a lieutenant. Peter himself, as a lieutenant, received 5s 3d a day, which did not go far when one was required to keep up the standard of dress and sportsmanship required of a commissioned officer. One could build a long enough line of creditors without having a wife to take care of, though in this case there had been a wife, until very recently anyway.

'Thank you, Colour, you've been a great help.'

'Will you be needing me again, sir, as we're not long for marching out against the Zulu?'

'I may need to talk to you again, yes. And you know, Colour Murray, it's not completely out of the question that there might be a trial yet, of some kind. Please be ready to make yourself available.'

'It's a very sad thing, sir, this suicide business. There was Private Jenkins, you know. Put his rifle in his mouth and pressed the trigger with a stick. Nobody knows why he did it. He was ill, like. Had a bit of a fever. But no cause to top himself . . .'

'Yes, thank you, Colour.'

The thickset Scottish senior NCO looked unhappy. Williams knew the men of the 90th were edgy. All the regiments were on edge. Lieutenant-General Lord Chelmsford was eager to teach the Zulu some hard lessons in warfare. Peter Williams, and everyone else, knew that the British government wished the whole of South Africa to be formed into a Confederation which would rein in the Boers and the Zulu nation. At present the Zulus were an independent kingdom, supposedly friendly, but who knew what was in the mind of King Cetshwayo? A recent border raid by Zulus in which two of their runaway wives had been recaptured and executed had given Chelmsford and Governor Bartle Frere the excuse they needed to invade Zululand.

Cetshwayo had received an ultimatum: willingly disband his army – a huge force of thousands of disciplined warriors – or be forced to do so. There was a host of other demands, some minor, some major. This, despite the fact that the independent Boundary Commission had found in favour of the Zulus and their right to their own land. No self-respecting king, virtually an emperor, was going to submit meekly to the demands of these white ants that were overrunning the landscape. War was now inevitable and mobilization had begun on both sides.

Williams stared through the open doorway, his nostrils still taking offence at the stink of pigs in the air.

Brewer did have two wounds in his chest and two rounds had been fired from his revolver. Lieutenant Williams had once been shot in the arm, in a skirmish with some Bantu. It hurt. It hurt like bloody hell. Williams could not imagine any man, after having shot himself once in the chest, having the strength of mind and spirit to do it again. The pain, the agony of that first round smashing through bone and ripping his organs asunder, would surely have rendered Brewer unconscious. Even supposing that consciousness remained, it would take superhuman effort to lift the weapon the second time and pull the trigger, while such terrible pain raged through body and brain. Even were such an action possible, *twice* in the same place? Surely the second time he would have blown his own head off, just to be absolutely sure?

'Thoughts, Sergeant?'

Sergeant Jackson, wearing an identical red sash to the one around the lieutenant's shoulder, turned and shrugged. They had both been seconded to the posts of army policemen by their colonel and neither enjoyed the position. Jackson enjoyed the camaraderie of battalion and company. Williams wanted to be in his proper place in the line when the regiment went into battle. This was what they had joined the army for, despite the dreadful pay and a job held in disdain by most civilians. Apart from their red sashes they were identical to the other soldiers of equal rank in their regiment. It was like being told, 'Oh, and by the way, you're not one of us any longer. You're now to be set apart and – oh yes – despised by the other troops as law enforcers, meddlers, interfering bastards and sods to be avoided.' At the bar, in the tavern, they were ignored by all except their closest friends. Even the senior officers who had appointed them loathed them. Policemen tended to get in the way when there were important issues at stake. Policemen were forever asking questions, even as soldiers were in the firing line, during attack or defence: bothersome as mosquitoes.

'Probably suicide, sir,' said the sergeant at last, unfolding his arms and deigning to enter the stink. 'I would say.'

'Just because we want it to be suicide, Sergeant, doesn't mean we should leave it at that. Lord knows I would like the damned idiot to have pulled the trigger on himself – but twice?'

Again, the sergeant shrugged. 'Sorry, sir, you asked my opinion and I give it. That's to my way of thinking. Door locked *and bolted*. Window shut tight. Bars. What did the murderer do? Dig his way out, then fill in the tunnel? Sorry, sir, I think he did for hisself, pain or no pain.'

'What about the roof? You don't think a man who was a thatcher in civilian life . . .?'

The sergeant's face showed a glimmer of interest. Even if you were ostracized; even if you were banished from normal society; even if you were a pariah – solving a puzzle was always a most satisfying exercise. 'Everyone thought *this*, but we two thought *that*, and hey, you know what, it turns out we were *right*.' You could walk tall and ignore the sneers on the faces of your former comrades.

'We could look at that, sir. Yes, definitely. I could go through the men's records. Don't need to look at all of 'em, 'cause a few are Welshmen, see? Slate roofs in Wales. Start with any Norfolk men. They're the ones most likely to be handy with the reeds. Then we could – what's that word you use, sir? When you talk hard to 'em?'

'Interrogate.'

'Right, then.' The sergeant rubbed his hands together as if anticipating a delightful party. 'Right, we could interrogate the buggers.'

Williams gathered up the papers from the empty ammunition boxes he had been using as a desk.

'Well, don't get too excited, Sergeant. You know we've been forbidden to use the garrotte.'

'Sir?'

'It was a joke, Sergeant. I'll see you here tomorrow morning, eight sharp. All right?'

'Understood, sir. Oh, and sir, I checked with local residents and army personnel near the duty officer's quarters, to see if anyone heard any shots?'

'And?'

'One or two people did hear shooting, but when there was no further commotion, did not get up to investigate. A woman said she thought someone was shooting a cat or a stray dog.'

'What time would that be?'

'Middle of the night. Nobody's quite sure.'

Williams went out into the hot summer sun. At least the pigsty had been cool. Out here it was hot, though because of the elevation, not sweltering. There was a lot of banging and clattering going on nearby too – a fort was under construction – and it filled Williams's head with noise. He made his way along the main street in the general direction of an alehouse known as Yarpy's Yard, where he was to meet his old school friend Ensign Sebastian Early.

In many regiments in the ever-expanding empire belonging to Great Britain, Ensign Sebastian Early would be called a second lieutenant, but the 24th were old-fashioned and were determined to cling on to the traditional form of the rank until they were actually forced to relinquish it in favour of the new.

Peter and Seb had joined the 24th together, but Williams's advancement had been swifter due to the offices of an aristocratic cousin, while Seb was a mere local board school headmaster's son. Both had lived in the village of Much Wenlock, Shropshire, close to the Welsh border. The 24th had been raised in Warwickshire and the great majority of the men were English, but the regiment had collected a lot of Irishmen and a lesser number of Welshmen.

Seb bore no resentment at Peter's advancement, he had said so himself many times, due to the fact that he knew he himself was of superior officer material and would jump over his friend to a captain's rank before the war was out. Peter had laughed at Seb's confidence, but told him not to volunteer for the Forlorn Hope in order to do so. 'I don't want to have to be the one to tell your father you went in the vanguard because you were jealous of *me*.' It was a joke, of course, but Peter always felt slightly awkward about their respective ranks and hoped Seb came to his lieutenancy soon.

Seb was standing at the bar when Peter entered. The young ensign had the ever-present sketch pad by his elbow, a pastime which Peter had no interest in, but pretended to for his friend's sake. They were both excited by and interested in wild beasts, but their individual approaches to the animals of Africa were quite different: Sebastian liked to draw and paint them, Peter enjoyed shooting them.

'So?' said Peter, beating the dust from his shirt and nodding at the pad. 'What have you been recording for the Royal Society today?'

Seb had about as much chance of impressing members of the Royal Society as he had of growing golden horns, but he eagerly opened his pad and showed Peter a picture of a small antelope.

'Klipspringer,' he said. 'Smart little fellow, isn't he? Caught him leaping from rock to rock just north of the town. I mean, he's hardly a lion or leopard, but interesting just the same.'

'And he stood still and posed for you?'

'Of course not. He was jumping about all over the place. But he stayed around long enough for me to do a rough sketch of him. I filled in, later.'

Peter made a weapon of his finger and made a clicking sound. 'Dead little fellow now.'

'Oh, come on, Peter,' cried Seb, 'he's not much bigger than a cocker spaniel – you can do better than that.'

Peter laughed. 'Quite right. Just funning. Hey, I like the flame tree in the background.'

'No, you don't,' replied his friend, 'you're just flattering me in order to get me to buy the drinks.'

'How well you know me,' sighed Peter. 'Well then, off you go, my fine artist, call the man.'

'Squareface,' said Seb to the barman, 'and a dash of water.'

The Boer barman's hand went to a rectangular bottle with GIN written very simply on the label.

'How's the South-East, this hot afternoon?' said Peter, using Seb's school nickname.

'Hot,' replied Seb, grinning. 'And how's Lord Chelmsford's great detective? Solved the riddle of the sphinx, have we?'

Peter picked his glass up from the bar.

'I'll give you riddle of the sphinx, young Seb – chin-chin.'

The pair threw the clear firewater down their throats and visibly shuddered with pleasure.

Two

'So – how are the preparations for war going?' asked Peter of his friend. 'Tell me what I'm missing out on.'

Seb wondered whether to make light of the great hustle and bustle, but then decided Peter actually wanted to know the details.

'Oh, I don't know – not a great deal, Peter, unless you want to turn quartermaster and spend all your time purchasing wagons, oxen and other livestock. I'm told we have nearly eight thousand bullocks, horses and mules, along with six hundred or so wagons. We need, of course, a huge supply train. There's not much out there in the Drakensbergs to sustain an army of over sixteen thousand men.'

Peter whistled as he stuck up a finger for the barman to refill the gin glasses. 'Are those the figures? Sixteen thousand?'

'More, I should think,' replied Seb. 'Not for me. I'm on duty in an hour.'

'Have a lemonade, then?'

'Oh, all right. Anyway, rounds of ammunition go into the millions, so I'm told.'

'No wonder we need all those carts and wagons.'

Seb nodded. 'I suppose. Now what about you? How's this case going – the suicide of poor old Brewer?'

Peter needed no second bidding to go into the case with his friend. He looked down into Seb's eyes, the ensign being considerably shorter in stature, and recounted the morning's interviews.

Seb listened intently to the unfolding.

Sebastian Early was a fairly intense young man. This last year, 1878, had seen his twenty-third birthday. At five feet six inches he was small when compared with many of his brother officers, though fairly well matched by the soldiers of the 24th, themselves tending to come from hard but short mill-worker or farmer stock. Like all his brother officers, and indeed virtually every soldier in the battalion, he sported a moustache. He had fairish hair, and muddy-brown eyes that fixed on your features when you were talking to him, as if studying the movements of your facial muscles. He was honest, loyal and, like many Victorians, packed with integrity – but he had a flash temper which often flared when arguing one of those unanswerable and unimportant questions associated with politics or women. Religion he never debated, having realized at an early age that an atheist will always argue from the point of view of logic and the religious man from the standpoint of faith, and since the two are completely incompat- ible argument is fruitless.

Senior officers, those concerned with promotion and progres- sion through the ranks, tended to ignore him. He was not a 'fine figure of a man' as, say, Lord Cardigan had been. There was no lion in his bearing. More of the lynx or civet cat. He had no booming voice. He had no modish style of dress such as some officers like Mad Henry adopted, like wearing thigh boots, a straw hat or chamois-leather gloves. He did not even own an endearing idiosyncrasy, like Lieutenant Harford and his obsession with bugs and beetles, which might make him stand out from others. This is not to say he lacked charisma completely. Sebastian Early was not one of those washed-out, faded young men who say and do nothing out of the ordinary. He was a cheerful man, popular with many of the junior officers, having a good sense of fun and a natural humour. He just did not appear to senior officers to be hiding a field marshal's baton in his knapsack.

'But, Peter, that's not the only case you're investigating, is it? What about that major of the 90th? What's his name, Parkinson? Aren't you looking into the theft of his gold half-hunter?'

'Ah,' said Peter, becoming animated, 'now that's a strange one. The thief had to be a soldier, because the theft took place at midnight in the camp confines. There were no natives in the camp on that evening, it being some sort of festival for them. And the thief was wearing shoes or boots. How many Zulus or Bantus do you see shod that well? The strange thing is the footprints don't match.'

Seb raised his eyebrows. 'There was more than one man?'

'No – that's what I'm saying. Only one set of prints, but the left foot is smaller than the right, and made less of an impression in the soil outside the window. It was as if the man had two different legs, the right from Sergeant Major Keay,' a large Highlander with legs like tree trunks, 'and the left from Archie Cox,' a thin, reedy lieutenant with pins like willow staves. 'Most strange. It's got me stumped.'

'Unless the thief was doing it on purpose – you know, wearing odd footwear to throw any investigations off the scent?'

'Possibly, but it doesn't seem very likely, does it? You'd want to be in your normal footwear, so you could make a quick exit from the scene of the crime. I would. Why encumber yourself with a shoe that doesn't fit? I mean, it's going to be hell's own job to unravel this one. I thought about someone with a correcting boot, someone perhaps with a club foot, but the surgeons say there's no such soldier.

'Parkinson is as mad as fire about his damn pocket watch. "Where's my gold half-hunter, Williams?" Every time he sees me it's the same question. You'd think a major's timepiece more important than the murder of a commissioned officer, to hear him talk. He obviously loved it, though, for he described it so fondly you would have thought it was a hound or child.'

'Described it?'

'Yes – as I said, it's a half-hunter, you know, without the flip-lid that the hunters have. And according to Parkinson, hunters and half-hunters come in two styles – the *savonette* and the *lepine*. On the first one the small seconds dial is at ninety degrees to the winding stem, usually at six and three. Lepines, however, have the seconds dial directly in line with one another, at six and twelve. Parkinson's watch is in the savonette style. Fascinating, eh?'

'Fascinating,' repeated Seb, without any visible effervescence.

'Also, the major's watch has a rampant lion engraved on the back, so it shouldn't be hard to identify.'

The 'No, indeed,' came out with even less fizz.

Seb threw back the remains of the lemonade and then straightened his red tunic.

'Well, time to be off. See you later, Peter?'

'In the mess, for dinner? Fine. I should be on my way too.'

They both moved towards the doorway, Peter with his long legs reaching it first. Putting on his white helmet he turned at the last minute and said, 'Oh, by the by, my sister Gwen sends her fondest regards . . .' His sentence was cut short by a loud cry from the street.

'Stop that man! Thief!'

A figure flashed by on the outside.

Peter's instincts were sharp and he leapt through the doorway into the street. No doubt he intended to chase the runaway. At that moment though there came the sound of a shot. Seb was shocked to see Peter flung forward on his face and when he stepped outside, Peter was lying in the mud. Blood was seeping through a hole in his back. His arms were outstretched and his face buried. Seb grabbed his friend's hair and lifted his head out of the dirt so he could breathe. But there was no life in the man. Seb turned him on his side. The bullet had gone through his heart and had torn a huge hole in his breast. A large pool of blood had appeared in seconds. Peter was dead.

'Jesus Christ!' screamed Seb. 'Oh, Jesus Christ, Peter!'

A man appeared above the pair. He stood over them, looking down, his face a ghastly colour. There was a rifle in his hand.

'He – he just jumped out. I was shooting at the Kaffir. He just appeared like that.' The shooter, a Boer, snapped his fingers. 'God man, I didn't mean to hurt no one – not him, anyway. I was firing at the Kaffir who stole my saddlebags. I just rode in from Pietermaritzburg. Jesus, what the blazes was he doing, leaping about like that? I had a bead on the black, when he just threw himself in the way . . .'

The Boer was obviously distraught, but Seb could say nothing to relieve the man's feelings. His grief at the sudden death of his friend had choked all words out of him. He simply sat in the mud with Peter's head on his knees, the tears flooding down his cheeks, while a crowd gathered around them. There was a numbness inside him. Every once in a while he glanced down at Peter's face, hoping to see some signs of life there, and then lifting his head again to the ring of faces.

The Boer was now pleading with onlookers, asking them if they had seen what had happened, asking them in fact to exonerate him from blame. 'It wasn't my fault. He came out of the bar like a bloody springbok. Jesus man, I wish to God it hadn't happened . . .'

For Seb the following hours went past in a dream. The body was collected and would be buried the following morning. Speed was required because the army was in a state of war. Lieutenant Peter Williams was not the first British officer to die in Africa. He would certainly not be the last. Men died every day, from action in the field and from disease. This was the army. This was Africa. If the spear or bullet did not take you, those colourful bastards the yellow or blackwater fever would. But the personal grief, of a friend, was not less felt because of these facts. Seb had grown up with Peter. They were like brothers. The pair of them had argued, fought each other with fists, fought others back to back, fished in streams for sticklebacks, chased girls, played hookey, lit fires in the forest and baked stolen potatoes in them, shared a last apple, lied for each other, taken punishment for each other, and sworn eternal friendship after blooding with a penknife. They had been bonded by boyhood. They would have died, one in place of the other, if given the choice. Seb was devastated.

Their friendship was known to their commander, Colonel Glyn, who came over to Seb after the quick military funeral the following day.

'A horrible accident, young Early. I'm sorry for it.'

'Thank you, sir.'

'I know you two were close.'

'Yes, sir. Very close. I am engaged to Peter's sister. I have no idea how I'm going to tell his family . . .'

'You would rather do that, than have me do it?'

Seb stared at the colonel. 'Yes, sir. I would.'

'I don't envy you the task.' The colonel lifted his helmet and scratched his head. 'I have other matters to attend to, of course. The general has given me the task of finding the army a replacement provost-marshal. Why my regiment, I have no idea. We provided the last one, after all. Why not the 90th? Or the Buffs? Or the 99th? Are the 24th the only damn regiment in Natal? Anyway, not your problem, young man. I shall write to the family in a more official capacity – a formal letter to say what an outstanding officer he was. That sort of thing.'

'Yes, he was.'

The colonel looked surprised. 'Was what?'

'An outstanding officer.'

The colonel's face took on a look of understanding.

'Quite. Now, I must . . .'

'I'll do it.'

Again the colonel looked taken aback, but before he could frame a question, Seb spoke again.

'I'll take the position, sir – if you'll let me. Provost-Marshal.'

The colonel blinked. 'Why would you want to do that? I have to force the post on people. Soldiers want to soldier, not mess around looking for thieves and blackguards. If they did – want to do the latter, that is – they'd have joined a police force, wouldn't they?'

'I want to do it.' The colonel clearly needed an explanation, so Seb added, 'I'm not likely to get promotion in the field, sir. I never get noticed out there, no matter what I do. This – this position gives me the chance to be an individual.' He let out a short laugh. 'No competition, you understand. If I do a good job, it might get me a lieutenancy.'

'Good enough reason, I suppose. Keen, eh? I like that in a man. A job's always done better if the man wants to do it. All right, it's yours. Now, the red sash . . .'

'I have it, sir. Took it off Peter's body.'

'Did you? Did you now?' murmured the colonel, gently. 'Well, my boy, wear it with pride. It's a mucky job, an unpopular one, but necessary, I suppose. You won't make many friends, you know, while you're in the position.'

'I'm aware of that, sir. Will I keep the sergeant?'

'The sergeant? Oh, Jackson? No, 'fraid not. He's needed back on the line, by his captain. I'll send you someone else. In the meantime, you can collect Lieutenant Williams' papers – his investigations and what not – from the orderly room. They're under lock and key. Can't have every rank and file reading private interviews. You might study them before coming to me and we'll see which ones are worth pursuing, eh? Talk it over, when I've got the time. Not much of that at the moment, I admit. Lord Chelmsford is champing at the bit. Now, are you all right, Early? Bad business, but the war goes on. Good that you'll write to the family. I like a man who takes his responsibilities seriously. Not like that bloody fool Harwood. Scorpions, indeed!'

With that the colonel walked away, out of the silent valley, back towards the British camp.

Three

After the funeral, Seb sat in his quarters and for many hours indulged in melancholy. He could not get the sound of spades on stone out of his head, the tools that had hacked at the hard rocky African earth while nameless multicoloured birds had shrieked in the bushes nearby. The *clink, clink, clink* as they dug the grave of his boyhood companion was still loud in his head. The ground had not yielded voluntarily. The sweating soldiers who cut the hollow oblong must have silently cursed the dead man. They had stripped to white vests, which had soon turned red, and yellow, with the dust. Little red-and-yellow men with sinewy arms, chopping a hole for an officer stupid enough to jump in the way of a bullet.

Seb felt he could not sink any lower in spirit than he was at that moment, as he went over and over the previous day's events in his head. Why had he not leapt after the runaway instead of Peter? Peter's reactions were swift, but Seb had always thought his own were superior. He was lighter on his feet. In their races as children it was Seb who almost always won. Peter had been the stronger boy, but Seb was the quicker. It should be him that was lying out there under that hard foreign ground with its burnt-ochre colours, not Peter.

For a while Seb tried blaming the Boer who had shot Peter. From Pietermaritzburg? Why hadn't he stayed there? Why hadn't he come to Ladysmith the day after, or the day before – or even just a few minutes either way? And the Kaffir who stole his saddle-bags? Both of them were equally involved in the death of Peter. Yet – yet, it had been an accident. A twist of fortune. Accidents are events locked in a precise time impossible to understand in retrospect. Just a second either way and all would have been well. If this, if that. If only. What a waste of a man. What a stupid waste of a fellow who might have changed the world. Certainly Peter's education and upbringing had groomed him more than Seb for greatness.

And what was Seb going to tell Gwen, Peter's sister?

Seb had told the colonel two lies after the funeral.

He had said he was engaged to her. He was not. They were good friends, very fond of one another, but there had been no engagement, neither understood nor spoken. Why had he told such a lie? Had it been to convince the colonel he was closer than he seemed to the family? That his interest in Peter's passing was deeper than was outwardly obvious? Something like that. He had wanted the colonel to see how badly this death had affected him. This was not just another soldier-chum, taken by the circumstances that surround war. This was family. Peter was as a brother to him and Seb wanted the colonel to understand that.

The other untruth was that Seb wanted the job of Provost-Marshal. That was an even bigger lie, with the same sort of reasons woven around it. His best friend had died in the post, therefore it was his duty to fill the void. He knew, even as he volunteered, that Peter would be laughing at him from the grave.

Seb, Seb, what are you doing? You know you love soldiering. This is not soldiering.

So now he was stuck with a job he did not want. He did not hate it, exactly, because he hardly knew what the work entailed. Peter had talked of it from time to time, but Seb had not listened with the ear of one about to take over. Seb also knew he would rather be following the colours on to a field of battle than untangling knotty problems concerning army crime. Quick promotion? He knew as well as the colonel, who had taken the lie without a blink, that he would be forgotten when promotions were in the wind. The post of Provost-Marshal was an oubliette that no senior official would bother to investigate unless it was absolutely necessary.

Late in the afternoon, in mellow light, Seb went to Peter's grave, to sketch and then paint it with the small palm-sized palette of five colours – a travelling artist's set manufactured by Winsor and Newton – in order to send it home to Peter's family. He found someone else there, performing a similar duty, a civilian friend by the name of Jack Spense. Jack had a wooden box camera on a tripod, taking a photo of the last resting place and surrounds of the unlucky Lieutenant Peter Williams.

'Oh, Seb, I'm sorry. Just . . .'

'I know, Jack. Came to do the same thing myself.'

They both stared at the grave, which had a simple wooden white cross bearing Peter's rank, name and regiment.

'Bloody shame,' said Jack, a willowy man in his mid-twenties. 'You expect it on the field – but out in the street?'

Seb was quiet for a while, then he lifted his head and wrinkled his nose. He stared hard at Jack. 'What's that awful smell?' he asked.

Jack lifted his arm and sniffed his own shirt. 'That? Oh, that's just collodion solution. Chemical I use on the plates. Spilt some on myself earlier today when I threw it away. The wind was in the wrong direction.'

Seb's eyes opened wider. 'It's burning a hole in your shirt.'

Jack nodded, seemingly quite undisturbed. 'Yes, I know – too much sulphuric acid. That's why I had to throw it away.'

Seb went back to his quarters, still feeling very upset. He tried to cheer himself by remembering good times: how excited the pair of them had been at hearing they were going to Africa.

'Africa, Peter – just think of it!' Seb had cried in delight, when their orders had come through. 'The hand of some higher power is in this somewhere. How else would we get such astoundingly good fortune?'

Peter, it was true, had been less enthusiastic, but certainly not unhappy with the thought of foreign shores. He had put his arm around the shoulders of his ecstatic friend and grinned, saying, 'Different skies, different stars – you'll like that, South-East.'

To Seb it had been the fulfilment of a dream. He had long been desperate to leave behind his slow dull life in a small English garrison town and set out for exotic climes. How wonderful it had seemed to him, to voyage to another country – another *continent* – where things were quite different. India or Africa would have been equally acceptable to him, or Singapore or Burma, or – to tell the truth – anywhere where the colours were brighter, the air clearer, the sky bigger. In such places the people were lighter of foot and had fire in their veins. They smiled more easily and did not seem oppressed by life as many were in Britain, where the population was weighed down by heavy dull weather and mills spewing out choking, poisonous fumes. Life seemed simpler east of the old country, though Seb realized *simple* was not necessarily *good*.

Africa was a land of marvels, from its myriad remarkable wild beasts and birds to its amazing vegetation and landscapes. He could not have wished for a better posting and he had not been disappointed. Even the light here in this beautiful land had a crystal quality. The colours of the birds sprang at him — vivid and startling — and the earthy smells, when it was dusty and dry, and especially just before it rained, were astonishing. He loved it.

Some did not. There were soldiers who hated Africa with venom. They criticized everything they saw, heard or experienced. When they were not on duty they lay on their beds and stared at the ceiling. God knew what flat minds they had. But Peter and Seb had enjoyed every minute of their off-duty time. The pair of them had explored as best as the army and battles would allow, and found everything fascinating. Even the African night skies were different, encrusted with new stars that shone with a far greater brilliance than English stars.

Now Peter was gone.

The maudlin mood returned quite rapidly and Seb sank into a state of melancholy reflection again. At ten o'clock there was a merciful knock on the door of his room and Seb opened it to find Ensigns Carpenter and Swale standing there.

'Come on, South-East,' said Carpenter. 'We're not going to leave you to mope tonight. You will take a glass or two with us.'

'Enough to drive away the maudlins,' added Swale. 'Nothing more, nothing less.'

Seb sighed. 'No, really, boys — I just need a quiet . . .' but they were inside the room in the next second, and one was helping him into his tunic, while the other was putting his cap on his head.

'Do as you're told, South-East, there's a good chap,' murmured Carpenter, patiently.

They dragged him from his room and out into the African night air, steering him towards the nearest tavern. Once they had got some porter into him, enough to loosen his brain a little, they changed to squareface, which resulted in a loosening of the legs. Younger than Seb, Carpenter and Swale were two good youths who would not desert a comrade when he was in the depths. They had known Peter, not as a friend but as a member of their battalion. They regretted his passing but they were aware that Seb had been very close to the Lieutenant Provost-Marshal and it behoved them to prise their chum from his room and soak his brain for a few hours. Carpenter always said to Swale that a decent brain-soaking got rid of most ills, physical and mental. Swale however was of the opinion that while certain ills were undoubtedly vanquished, others replaced them when the morning arrived.

All in all, from the point of view of the two younger ensigns, the evening was undoubtedly a success. Ensigns, and their cavalry equivalents, cornets, tended to be high-spirited youths. Not perhaps as loutish and outrageous as midshipmen in the navy, who were known to crop the ears of drunk, unconscious comrades with scissors, but certainly more larrikinish than full lieutenants. Seb not only had his brains thoroughly soaked, but it appeared they broke free of their moorings and floated about his skull. He took strong issue with a barman who refused to serve them with more gin which resulted in the three ensigns being catapulted through the swing doors and out into the baked-earth street. He started a fight with two young naval officers which his escorts had to finish. Then there was the incident with the scrawny jungle fowl which Seb stole from the backyard coop of a hardware store. With the bird under his arm he marched into the kitchens of the officers' mess and demanded 'the capon' be plucked and boiled, and dished up on the long dining table 'within seven minutes'. Finally the duty officer was called from his bed at around 2 a.m. to find three ensigns singing 'Adieu, Spanish Ladies, Adieu' in the shrubbery of a brigadier-general's garden.

After having rotten mangos thrown in his direction, fortunately not very accurately due to the unstable state of the throwers, this very sober and diligent officer had all three men taken into custody. He informed them they were confined to an empty bungalow which served as a guardroom. They escaped very unsteadily but easily ten minutes later to cause further havoc in the main street of Ladysmith. Chased by some nightwatchmen, they joined some Swazi youths in a game of cards in an alley and managed to lose their boots, belts and caps.

Fortunately they had given their names as Dibbs, Dobbs and Duddly (with two 'd's if you please!) to the duty officer, who though aware these were pseudonyms had not the energy or the patience to delve any further into their identifications. He knew of course, from their uniform facings alone, that the three ensigns were from his own regiment, the 24th, but in the light of day the humour of the situation struck him, gave him a good story to tell over a glass of whisky, and he let the whole incident waft away on the morning's warm breezes. He did later tell his listeners that if ever he recognized any of the ensigns again, they would feel the toe of his boot, and this was only right and proper.

★   ★   ★

Three days after the funeral, Seb was sitting in what had been Peter's office, but was now his own. Around his left shoulder he had tied a scarlet sash: his badge of office. It felt foolish, wearing this make-do insignia, but the office of Provost-Marshal was only semi-official. There was talk about an emblem which would be part of the uniform, but for the moment the job was a temporary one. No officer who wanted to get back to real soldiering wanted anything sewn to his coatee. It might look too permanent and result in him remaining in the post.

Seb had also managed to obtain some sweet-smelling herbs from a native and now the air in the old pigsty was at least breathable. He was presently sorting through Peter's papers, trying to make sense of some of the cases on his books. The three main queries were the murder, the theft of the major's gold half-hunter and a stabbing (though not fatal) of a private soldier.

The first two were of course still high in the air, but the third was bothering Seb (as it had bothered his predecessor) in that the soldier maintained he had been 'set upon' by three comrades, while those comrades in question swore that the private had turned the bayonet on himself and the wound was self-inflicted. All four men had stuck rigidly to their stories, despite several hours of questioning, and though three statements would seem to outweigh one, this was the split in the first place and they were natural odds. The three told the Assistant Provost-Marshal that the soldier had injured himself to get out of battle duties, and the wounded private said that two men had held him while a third had plunged the blade into his abdomen. There were no other witnesses. It was one man's word against another.

Seb sighed, wondering whether to question all four men himself, since the earlier questioning had been done by a sergeant. Like many new young officers, Seb was somewhat arrogant in his consideration of the rank and file. He did not have a high opinion of non-commissioned officers, thinking them rather ignorant and roughshod characters. The sergeant APM and the accused men themselves were all of a piece, so far as that was concerned. Perhaps it would take an officer with perception to sort the wheat from the chaff? As he was contemplating this action someone came through the doorway and saluted.

Seb looked up. A corporal stood before him. He was quite tall for the kind of man the regiment normally attracted. Those from the mines tended on the whole to be fairly short men, with muscle packed around their solid bones. Those from the cities and towns were also on the short side, but stunted with hollow chests. This man was above average height, lean and brittle-looking. Brown, with weathered features, he had a sort of pinched appearance below his broad, upward-sweeping brow.

Seb guessed his age at around thirty-five or so.

'Yes, Corporal?'

'Corporal Evans, 716, sir,' shouted the man before him. 'I been sent to you to assist the officer in the discovery of crimes.'

Seb looked down at his desk knowing his expression would reveal his annoyance. Peter's sergeant had rejoined the regiment proper and a corporal had been sent in the sergeant's place. Obviously so far as the colonel was concerned, since the last Provost-Marshal had been a lieutenant and warranted a sergeant, and the new PM was only an ensign, a full-blown sergeant was out of the question. It seemed a corporal was good enough for Seb, damn the colonel's eyes and liver.

'I see,' growled Seb, his head still down. 'Well, Corporal, do you have any experience in this kind of work?'

There was no answer. Seb looked up, angrily. The soldier must have seen the irritation on his face, because he said in a loud unnatural voice, 'Did you say something, sir? I'm deaf, you see. The guns did it. Artillery. Deaf as a post, unfortunately.'

'Oh, shit!' said Seb throwing his pencil down hard and leaning back in his chair. 'They send me an idiot!'

'Not an *idiot*, if you please, sir. Just hard of hearing. I'm thought of as quite bright, actually.' Seb had the grace to blush and the corporal added by way of explanation, 'I can read a man's lips, if I can look directly into his face when he's talking to me.'

'Forgive me, Corporal. It – it isn't you. It's the whole . . .' he waved his hand around the pigsty. 'It's this – this bloody job.'

'Know what you mean, sir,' yelled Evans. 'No offence taken. Not a *man's* work, is it though? Wasn't looking forward to it meself. But now I'm here, there's just the two of us, eh? Might as well get stuck in and get it over with.'

Seb sighed. 'I don't know how much you've been told . . .'

'Face, sir. Can't see the lips,' shouted Evans.

Seb lifted his head and mouthed very distinctly, 'Corporal, can you lower your tone? You're shouting.'

'Sorry, sir – difficult, you see. Can't hear myself speak. In my head, it's dead quiet, like.' This was said in a softer tone.

'I'm sure it is – now, look, I don't know how much you've been told but it isn't just one incident that has to be solved. We're to work together for the next century or so. Sorry to be the bearer of bad news. It grieves me as much as I'm sure it does you.'

Evans frowned. 'Oh, like that, is it?'

'Indeed. Exactly so.'

'We're stuck with it, eh?'

'Looks like it, Corporal.'

'Oh.'

Seb motioned for the corporal to take a chair and told him to remove his helmet. Seb then got on with his paperwork, ignoring his new assistant. In fact what he was doing was thinking hard. He needed a little space to absorb the fact that he now had a helper and was trying to work out the best way of dealing with their situation. After a while he sent the corporal off for two mugs of tea, while he wrote in his notebook. He always found that writing things, anything really, helped his thought processes. When the corporal returned with two steaming mugs, Seb spoke slowly and carefully to him.

'Corporal Evans, are you paying attention?'

'I've got you in my sights, sir.'

'Good. Now, you must understand we shall obviously be working very closely together, so it would be silly to have a stiffly formal arrangement, such as would be necessary in the regiment proper. We shall still have to observe the normal courtesies some of the time, of course, especially when there are others present, but I want you to feel free to engage me in conversation when you have something important you wish to impart. Is that fairly clear?'

'As a Welsh mountain stream, sir.'

'Excellent, because I want you to feel at ease. I am willing to regard it as quite acceptable for you to look on me as an ordinary person, rather than your superior officer.' Seb was trying to think how the general would treat his personal cook or clerk. 'We can't be too casual with one another, of course, because it would not look good to – to other officers. You will need to call me sir, on most occasions, when there are other officers – and yes, indeed, other soldiers from the regiment in the vicinity. However, if we are quite alone or in the company of, say, local militia, it would be perfectly acceptable to drop the "sir" occasionally.'

'What do I call you, then?'

'What? Oh, you don't call me anything. You just do not need to punctuate every single sentence with the word "sir".'

The corporal relaxed, spread out his legs in front of him, leaned back in his chair and grinned. 'Well then, that's fine, isn't it?'

Instinctively, Seb had waited for the 'sir' at the end of the corporal's sentence and had to check himself from a reprimand when he realized that he was waiting in vain, for had he not just said that it was unnecessary to observe the proper formalities when they were alone? This arrangement was not going to be easy for either of them, he thought, though perhaps it was going to be more diffi-cult for him rather than Evans. The thing to do was not allow the situation to deteriorate into a lack of respect for the Queen's commission. That would not be fair on the army or on others whose discipline had to remain tight. In fact, Seb was already begin-ning to regret his offer to relax protocol.

'Now – Evans – what did you do? I mean, before you joined the army?'

'Shepherd.'

Seb waited but nothing more was forthcoming.

'Yes,' he said, 'you were a shepherd. In the Welsh hills?'

'Not a lot of flat ground, where I come from.'

'Quite. But is there anything else you want to tell me about yourself?'

Evans frowned and shook his head. 'Not really.'

Seb said, 'Well, what about your father?'

The corporal leaned forward, looking interested. 'What about him?'

Seb was becoming exasperated. 'Well, who was he?'

Evans chuckled. 'He was me da, wasn't he? Had the same name.'

'Yes, but what did he do?'

'Shepherd.'

If this was an example of the corporal's 'brightness' Seb thought his new assistant was going to be worse than useless. He picked up his headgear and walked towards the door. 'Come on, Corporal, let's go and look at the scene of the crime – or suicide.'

Evans remained seated. Seb seethed inside, realizing he had not been facing his assistant.

He turned to the corporal. 'Up man. Let's go!'

'Right you are, then,' replied Corporal Evans. 'Where are we off to, eh? Quite exciting, this sort of work, eh?'

Four

S eb and Evans went out into the warm day.
      Seb breathed deeply and turned to his new assistant and felt
a sudden inexplicable need to be chummy for a moment.

'I like the climate here, Corporal. It's like perpetual summer
back in England. I used to dream of that as a boy. A summer which
lasted forever.'

'Not me, sir – I used to dream of winter.'

Seb grew irritated. Was this man deliberately trying to annoy
him by disagreeing with everything he said?

'Oh come on, man, as a shepherd you must have hated the
winter, outside in all that cold and rain?'

'Right, the cold and rain wasn't so good, but the short days
were. And I wasn't always a shepherd, see. I laboured around the
farm, too. Men like me were worked from dawn till dusk by the
landowner. Summer I used to go to my bed dog-tired after a
sixteen-hour day. Winter, the days were sometimes as short as eight,
or even seven, hours.'

This was of course a revelation to Seb, who had never done
manual work for a living, nor had been at the beck and call of a
farmer who might work him to death without a pricking of
conscience. He had not put his mind to such things. It discon-
certed him to learn such obvious differences in his lifestyle to that
of a farm worker.

Lamely, he said, 'Still – the sunshine feels good.'

There was a great deal of bustle in and around the buildings.
Preparations for war were being carried out with long strides and
great determination. Everyone had to be seen to be busy. Even the
collarless town mongrels were trotting from shade to shade, as if
taking part in these preparations. Out on the parade ground the
relentless marching was in progress. Sergeants were yelling, cor-
porals were yelling, the boots of redcoats were thumping down
hard on the earth, packing the world into an even tighter ball.
Here and there were riders, mostly field officers of foot regiments:
those of major rank and above. General Lord Chelmsford had a

distinct lack of cavalry amongst his troops, though there were local men of the Natal Native Horse riding back and forth. A field bakery wagon rumbled by the two men as they walked through this flurry of humanity.

Stepping neatly over a bullock turd, careful not to disturb the mass of glittering blue flies presently feasting thereon, Seb came to the duty officer's quarters, a small square white building on the far side of the parade ground. Seb walked around it, studying the exterior.

It was a rounded-roofed drab uninspiring piece of architecture: a mud-bricked box topped by a dome of thatch in a thick layer. There was the door at the back, thick and sturdy, and a window at the front, barred and shuttered. Studying it from the outside, Seb could not see how anyone could have committed a murder within and not left evidence of his being there. Unless, as Peter had thought, it had been an expert thatcher who escaped through the roof and patched the hole with infinite care before leaving.

He turned towards Evans. 'Go and find me a ladder, Corporal.'

Corporal Evans opened his eyes wide.

Seb said, 'Go on, do as you're told.'

The duty officer was not at home, but the door had been left ajar. Seb inspected the lock. This had been changed for a new one and the door had clearly been repaired where it had been damaged.

Evans returned a short while later with a ladder.

Seb put the ladder up against the building and climbed it to inspect the thatch at the top. There was a bird's nest right where the ladder touched the edge of the roof. A small indignant bird shot out, almost striking Seb in the face. It disappeared towards the skyline, twittering in annoyance at the disturbance. Seb studied the thatch and could not see any evidence of it being tampered with. That was not to say it had not been touched, for thatchers were talented men. Was it possible that someone had breached the thatch, then reset the reeds? A very skilled job if that was the case.

'Pass me that stick,' Seb called down, presenting his face to the man on the ground. 'Yes, that one by the fence.'

With the stick in his hand Seb began poking and beating the roof in various places, to see if there were any weaknesses.

It all appeared to be very intact. He climbed down the ladder and instructed the corporal to return it. When Evans got back from the errand, they discussed the building.

'Well,' said Seb, 'what do you think?'

Evans replied. 'This is where the officer shot hisself, isn't it?'

'My predecessor believes it to be murder,' Seb said, remembering to look into the face of his corporal. 'Captain Brewer had two bullet wounds in the chest, either one of which on its own would have proved fatal. Lieutenant Williams maintained that a man would have great difficulty in shooting himself twice in the heart.'

'Bloody near impossible, I would say,' confirmed Evans, starting to get louder in tone as he became more voluble, 'pardon my pidgin-Bantu, sir. Once would do it. I seen men shot in the chest. They do lots of things, like yellin' and screamin', thrashin' around or just groanin', or even staying quiet like, but one thing's certain, there's not the strength there to do nothin' positive like. It's all . . .' Here his previously excellent language failed him.

'Reactive? But perhaps, after a period of time? Say twenty minutes, or an hour, they might gather the energy needed? Just supposing they were still alive?'

'Beggin' the officer's pardon, but why bother? Why not just lay there and fade away, like?'

'Perhaps to banish the pain, once and for all?'

'By giving hisself *more* pain? Sir, you and the other officer, the daft one who got hisself shot by the Boer?'

Seb bit his lip. After all, the corporal was unaware that Peter was Seb's closest friend. 'Lieutenant Williams.'

Evans leaned over his commanding officer. 'Yes, Lieutenant Williams, that one. You and he, sir, are educated men, not like me, a blockhead shepherd from the Welsh hills. I expect you had a lot of schooling. You've studied books and the like, while I've watched sheep getting their wool tangled in gorse. You know a thing or two . . .'

'Get to the point, man.'

'An officer, he's bitter and full of gall, and wants to end his miserable life, plays with his gun, then shoots himself in the chest. Bang.' Evans was acting this out as he spoke. 'Suddenly, unexpected-like, a horrible, agonizing pain sears through his body like a river of fire. Unbearable, I'm sure. Bloody unbearable. He's never experienced pain like it before and it shocks him to the core with its terrible violence. So, does he do the same thing again, eh? Not on your bloody life he doesn't. No, no, no. He lifts the weapon to his temple and blows his bloody brains out – makes damn sure that

this time there will be no more pain, and wonders why the hell
he didn't do that in the first place.'

Seb ingested this piece of information with consideration, then
after mulling it over for a few minutes he said, 'Corporal, you're
not as stupid as you pretend.'

'Thank you, sir, I wasn't pretendin' nothing.'

'You have a strong imagination – almost a fanciful one. Neither
I nor Lieutenant Williams, who I have to tell you now was a very
good friend – we went to school together – neither of us has
thought to put ourselves in the place of the deceased man.'

'Looking after sheep does that for you – nothing much to think
about except what you dream up, so to speak. I'm sorry I called
your friend daft, sir. Didn't mean nothin' by it, you understand.'

'I'm sure he's been called worse by the other ranks. So, using
that imagination of yours, look at this building and tell me if you
can see a way out for the murderer.'

Evans did as he was asked.

Finally, he said, 'No, I can't.'

'Right,' said Seb, 'let's have a look inside.'

The pair of them went to the doorway. Seb rapped on the wood
with his knuckles, several times. No one came, no one answered.
He then pulled the door wide open. Seb went inside first, followed
by Evans.

'Good God!' cried Seb, shuddering, as something scuttled
between his legs. 'The room's full of spiders!'

Spiders, beetles, cockroaches, centipedes, one or two small lizards,
a whole variety of wildlife seethed inside.

'It's that bangin' and clatterin' you did, sir – on the roof. You
knocked 'em down from the thatch.'

'So I must have,' muttered Seb, grimacing. 'Well, they'll soon
disperse, I'm sure.'

They both stared around the busy square room. The structure
was simple and solid-looking. Evans began stamping around the
floor and when asked what in God's name he was doing, he replied
he was making sure there were no secret passages under hidden
trapdoors. At that moment the sound of foot rang hollow. He
looked up into Seb's face with an expression of triumph.

Seb shook his head. 'Drain,' he said. 'The roof leaks. I know. I've
done duty in here when it's been raining stair rods.' Seb pointed
to a small grille in the floor next to the wall behind the desk.

'It runs along the edge of the wall. A rat might get out that way, but not a man.'

Seb went to the window and reached through the bars to push open a shutter. There were some huts about twenty-five yards away, starkly obvious in the brilliant sunshine of the summer day. Seb knew these to be the quarters of the Natal Native Contingent.

Turning his attention back to the room he noticed the wardrobe in one corner. This was for the duty officer to hang his tunic in, but was rarely used since an officer would not like to be caught out of uniform with colonels and generals likely to call in at odd times. The wardrobe was the largest piece of furniture in the place. There was also a desk, a chair and a stove in one corner with a narrow chimney pipe.

'Have to be thin as a weasel to go up there,' said Corporal Evans, looking at the chimney pipe. 'Have to *be* a bloody weasel.'

Seb inspected every square foot of the interior and came to the same conclusion they had reached when studying the exterior. The only exit was through the roof. Yet now he could see the ceiling, that too looked untouched. While he stared at it, a cockroach appeared and disappeared again into its many folds and creases.

So the ceiling-cum-roof *looked* as if it had not been interfered with – yet Seb knew that the dexterity of mankind was deep, wide and astonishing. Michelangelo's *David* looked as though it had been sculpted by a god with extraordinary powers, yet it had been fashioned by a man. There were, he had no doubt, quite a few Michelangelos amongst British thatchers. They might call themselves Taffy, Jock or Jack; they might be unknown outside the shire; they would never be feted by kings or find eternal fame; but still their talent was nothing short of genius. A great thatcher, a legend among artisans, would be able to take the roof apart straw by straw until there was a hole large enough for him to crawl through, then replace those straws exactly so. A brilliant thatcher could escape from this room without leaving a trace.

'Who in hell are you? What do you want?'

A captain stood in the doorway to the room. He took off his helmet and wiped the sweat from his brow with a kerchief. His face bore the look of a man who has been on duty too long. A stringy individual with a sour-looking mouth and thin nose, his small dark eyes went from Corporal Evans to Ensign Early with no change of expression. Evans had opened the wardrobe door and was poking the back panels with his fingers. He had not turned round at the officer's question.

'You there!' bellowed the captain. 'Look at me when I'm talking to you.'

'Not well made, these things, are they?' shouted Corporal Evans over his shoulder, in a voice as loud as the one the infuriated captain had used. 'Not well made at all. Local carpenters, eh? We could show them a thing or two in Llandwyfyn, I can tell you. They might be able to make bullock carts, but they're crap at cabinetmaking.' He closed the wardrobe doors with a crash. 'Bloody terrible workmanship.'

The captain's face was almost purple when Evans swung round to see him standing within the room.

The corporal came to attention and saluted smartly.

'Is he mad?' cried the captain, appealing to Seb.

'No, sir, just deaf.'

'Deaf? What's he doing deaf?'

'Guns, sir,' shouted Evans, reading the captain's lips. 'Artillery.'

The captain winced at the shout but chose to ignore the corporal and whirled on Seb.

'What the hell are you doing in here? Are you my relief? You're half an hour early. Who are you?'

Seb pointed to the red sash on his shoulder. 'Ensign Early, Provost-Marshal – I'm investigating a crime.'

The captain's eyes smouldered. 'Get out!' he snapped.

A few days previously Seb would have obeyed such a command without a murmur. An ensign was more or less the lowest form of life amongst commissioned ranks. There was an equivalent, a cornet in the cavalry, but the cavalry was a cut above a foot regiment. A cornet would believe himself to be superior to an ensign simply because he sat on a horse and dashed about the countryside. A cavalry man was more flamboyantly uniformed, was extravagant in his movements and manners, and looked down upon the rest of the army. Seb was normally a cockroach to any cavalry man and a captain of foot. But here, at this moment, he was something else: he was the Provost-Marshal of Lord Chelmsford's army and therefore unique.

'No, sir, I shall not. I shall go when I'm ready to go and not before, if it please you. My assistant and I are – are sifting through the evidence of a possible murder. You, sir, are intending to obstruct the course of my investigations and it will not do. It will not do at all, sir.'

The captain's eyes started from his head.

'Ensign, you are speaking to a full captain!'

'I'm fully aware of that, sir, but I have a job to do and by God I shall do it.' Seb coughed nervously, before adding, 'Corporal, inspect that wardrobe once more, if you please. There may be some vital clue we may have missed.'

Corporal Evans made a face, shrugged, and did as he was told to do by his commanding officer.

The captain snarled. 'You have made a grave mistake, Ensign. Do you know who I am? I'll have your testicles hanging from the flagpole before tomorrow morning. Green facings, eh? 24th. Colonel Glyn, your commanding officer, is a particular friend of the Stenhall-Chases. You will report to him at three o'clock today and be prepared for a severe reprimand.'

Seb's heart was pounding with the knowledge of his own insolence as he continued to stare at the captain while saying over his shoulder, 'Are we satisfied with what we've found, Corporal?'

Only too late did he remember his assistant could not hear him and he had to abandon his audacious stance to turn and touch Evans on the shoulder. He motioned his assistant towards the doorway. Evans took the hint and left the building. Seb then came smartly to attention, saluted, and then turned towards the doorway. Behind him the captain suddenly became aware of the wildlife that had been introduced to the duty officer's quarters. Seb left him staring with revulsion at a six-inch millipede that flowed elegantly over his tabletop.

'Who was that?' asked Evans, as the pair walked away from the building.

Seb said, 'The Devil, unless I miss my guess, in the guise of one Captain Stenhall-Chase, of the famous Stenhall-Chases, doncha know. Well, actually I *don't* know, but my guess is they're gentry – aristocrats from somewhere or other. Probably Surrey or Hampshire. As to what he's doing here now, my guess is staff.'

'You're not gentry, sir?'

'Not in the slightest. My father's the headmaster of a parish school.'

'Isn't that gentry?'

'Only to shepherds,' replied Seb, a little unkindly, but Evans simply grinned and remarked, 'I get a shillin' a day in the army. I got tuppence as a shepherd. Even a private soldier's gentry to a Welsh boy stuck in the hills and valleys on a cold wet afternoon in February.'

At three o'clock sharp, Seb was standing in front of the officer commanding the 24th, Colonel Glyn. The colonel had been talking to his adjutant and now half-closed one eye as he stared into Seb's composed features.

'So, young Early, isn't it? What have you been up to, upsetting captains of the 99th?'

'Yes, sir, Captain Stenhall-Chase, I believe. I was merely trying to do my job, sir. The captain seemed to take offence at the slightest opportunity.'

The colonel nodded and seemed not unsympathetic.

'You'd better stay out of that man's way. He's a notorious snob, young Early. Comes from an old family. Father's an earl. Second son, though, so he gets the army not the estate. There's a third one who's the vicar of Haslemere, in Buckinghamshire. Powerful family. Now, consider yourself told off, young man, and get back to your duties. What were you doing in the duty officer's quarters, anyway? I thought we had agreed that Brewer committed suicide?'

'I feel there are aspects of the incident which still have not been resolved, sir.'

'Do you now? Well, my advice is to forget any unresolved aspects and keep the big picture in the frame. You have other investigations in progress, I'm sure. Go with those which have stronger evidence of foul doings. Aren't you supposed to be looking for a major's gold watch?'

'Yes, but . . .'

'Off you go, then, and find the blasted thing. That will be all, Ensign Early.'

Seb saluted and left the colonel's presence.

As he walked away, he muttered to himself, 'Old family? Who the devil *doesn't* come from an "old family". We all go back to Adam, don't we? What's so special about the Stenhall-Chases?' He stopped in midstride, straightened his tunic, and then said, 'And I'll be damned if I'll give up on poor old Brewer. He deserves a thorough enquiry, and I'm going to see he gets it.'

Five

The day following the inspection of the scene of the murder, Seb visited the Natal Native Contingent lines. The NNC was made up of battalions of African soldiers led by white officers, with some black officers. Mostly the warriors carried their traditional weapons of spears and shields, but each company had around ten rifles carried by their black NCOs. The firearms were out-of-date muzzle-loaders, usually Sniders or Enfields. Many of the Africans were of Swazi origin with grievances against the Zulu nation. The cream of these local fighting men were chosen for the plum job of mounted soldiers and were known as the Native Horse.

At first Seb could find no white officer, nor any English-speakers amongst the blacks there. Plenty of livestock roamed around the camp and in the huts: chickens, geese, pigs and one tethered goat. There were also tame parrots, dogs and a monkey or two. But white officers and NCOs seemed to be in short supply. Finally he discovered an African NCO with a good command of Seb's native language. The man was a broadchested soldier with a high forehead and hard brown eyes. He was fitting a feed bag on the nose of a dusty horse when Seb approached and he looked at the white officer warily.

'Yes, suh,' he said, simply. 'You come to arrest me?'

Seb was surprised. 'You know what the red sash means?'

'It mean you are a policeman, suh.'

'Well, you're better informed than some of the line regiment soldiers.'

'Suh, I do nothing wrong. It must have been one of my brothers.' He then gave Seb an extraordinarily wide grin. 'My brothers are wild men, suh, when they take to the drink.'

'No, this is nothing to do with you. I simply want to ask you some questions. Did you know an officer died in that building over there? The duty officer's quarters?'

'I hear about this.'

'What do they say – those who told you about it?'

The sergeant shrugged. 'He shoot himself.'

'Were you here that night? In the barracks?'

'I was here.'

'What were you doing at the time?'

'Me, suh? I talk with my friends.'

'And did any of you hear shots?'

There was no answer forthcoming.

'Think hard, man. I need to know the answer.'

A frown appeared on the sergeant's face. He looked nervously down the lines, as if hoping someone would come along to rescue him from this inquisitive policeman who was asking lots of questions. He was probably thinking he was going to get dragged into something which would all end in tears. As an African he naturally suspected those tears would be shed by him or one of his kind. The auxiliaries took a lot of the blame for the transgressions and mistakes of white soldiers.

'Well?' asked Seb. 'Come on, man, you're not in any trouble. This is just for my own interest. Did you hear two shots fired?'

'No, suh.'

Seb was disappointed. He looked at the position of the huts again, then at the DOQ building, and shook his head.

'Listen, you must have heard something. Are you telling me you heard nothing?'

'No, suh.'

Seb began to get exasperated. 'Well, which is it? You either heard the shots or you didn't.'

'We all hear them, suh. We think it is maybe the picquets firing. Or somebody shooting dogs. I look out the window, but nothin' there. That's all I know, suh. Nothin' else.'

'Why did you say you hadn't heard shots?'

'No, suh. I say I no hear *two* shots.' The man paused for a moment, before adding, 'I hear *three*.'

Seb was taken aback. 'Three? Are you sure?'

'Yes, suh. One big, two small.'

'Sma— you mean, different weapons.'

'Yes, suh. One big, one small, 'nother small – I think this is so. I look from the window. Nobody there. Some men go outside, thinking it is the picquets, but nobody there. All quiet again.'

'Three shots. Could they have come from different locations? One nearer than the others?'

The sergeant shrugged. He had told the officer what he knew. There was an end to it, so far as he was concerned.

'You all heard three shots?'

'Yes, suh. All, I think.'

'Thank you, Sergeant, you've been very helpful. Would – would you like me to speak to your captain about you? You never know, it might lead to some sort of advancement in rank.'

The brown eyes widened. 'No, suh. I am happy.'

He was one of those soldiers. Keep your nose clean and your head down and you will not get hit by any stray missiles. He did not want attention. He wanted to be left alone to do his job. Already a senior NCO, he had nowhere to go anyway. No one was going to make him an officer for assisting a policeman. Seb left him tending his horse and went back to the pigsty to think over what he had heard.

A short time later he had a visit from a white auxiliary officer, a major.

'You've been talking to my men?'

Seb looked up from the table he called his desk.

'Yes, sir, I have. Just one man, by the way.'

'What for?'

'Furthering my investigations.'

'Next time, you come and see me first, understood?'

Seb was getting used to this.

He replied as coolly as he could, 'Well, actually sir, no – it doesn't work like that. I'm entitled by my position as Provost-Marshal to interview who I like, without referring to the chain of command. After all, I might be asking questions about you in particular.'

The major went red in the face.

'Damned impudence.'

'Yes, sir, but necessary for the solving of a crime, I'm afraid. I'm sure you see that.'

'And – and was it about me, *in particular?*'

'No, on this occasion it was a set of general questions, but as you're here, sir, perhaps you can verify some of the answers. Your man said there were three shots fired the night Captain Brewer died. Can you confirm that?'

The major stared at him as if he were a garden slug, but finally answered the question.

'It could have been three shots, yes.'

'From different weapons?'

The major shook his head. 'Just three shots – that's all I remember, Ensign.'

'Oh, well the sergeant seemed to think there were two shots from a smaller weapon and one from a larger one.'

The major made a gesture as if to say, well, that's all I know, and moved towards the doorway.

Before he left, however, he turned back and said, 'You know, their ears are better than ours. The blacks. They can smell better, see better and hear better than we can. They're closer to the earth than us. Closer to natural things. Their raw senses are better attuned to the world out here than our civilized ones. If my sergeant said the shots came from different weapons, you can bet your life he's right.'

Here was a major, proud of his men. There were those who would rather die than lead a battalion of natives. Officers who thought that such a post was many steps down from leading soldiers of the Queen. But then there were men like the one-armed Colonel Durnford, beloved of his black troops. Men who loved Africa and Africans, who looked on such a command as a great privilege. Here was such a man, this major, and Seb was impressed by the pride he heard in the major's voice when he said 'my sergeant'.

Seb turned his attention back to the scattered pieces of paper on his desk top. His boyhood chum Peter had not been a good note-taker. In fact Peter's paperwork was appalling. Seb had found no coherent set of notes on the case at all. The first thing he did was get himself a notepad. On the first page he wrote and underlined the heading:

Captain Brewer.

Beneath this, he wrote:

1. *Thatch: possible escape route for a murderer?*
2. *Three shots fired, the first from a different weapon.*
3. *(From Peter's notes): No powder marks on victim's chest.*

What this meant to the investigation, Seb had no real idea. He was still stuck with the main problem. The door to the building had been locked and bolted. True, the key was missing and had there been no bolts it could be deduced that a murderer had locked the door on the outside and thrown away the key. But there were bolts. No one leaving that room could bolt the door on the inside after vacating it.

Seb was suddenly startled by the shout of 'Tea, sir?' and looked up to see Evans entering the room with two steaming tin mugs.

'Thank you, Corporal. What's that you've got under your arm?'

Evans glanced at the parcel as he placed down the mugs of tea. Then he took it and banged it down on the tabletop. It hit the wood with a clunk.

'A private left it. Said you'd sent for it. What is it, sir?'

Seb took off the paper wrapping carefully and exposed the contents of the package.

'Revolver, Corporal. This is the actual weapon that supposedly killed Captain Brewer. His side arm.'

They both stared at the shiny handgun, then Seb picked it up and checked the chambers of the cylinder. Incredibly, no one had bothered to unload it. There were three cap and ball cartridges in the five-round cylinder. This was a Beaumont–Adams percussion cap .442. It was gradually being replaced by the Webley Mk VI, but most officers in South Africa still carried a Beaumont–Adams. Its original designer was a man called Robert Adams, but one Lieutenant Frederick Beaumont of the Royal Engineers had improved upon the double-action revolver, allowing the user to fire it by cocking and releasing the hammer, as well as using the trigger.

Seb looked down the barrel.

'Been cleaned,' he said. 'Shame.'

'Not that you'd know what to do with it if it hadn't, eh, sir?'

Seb looked up at the Welshman. 'You never know what clues might be left on a murder weapon.'

'If you say so, sir, but I dunno what you might expect – murderers don't usually carve their initials on the butt.'

'Twelve rounds a minute,' said Seb, conversationally, turning the weapon over and over in his hands. 'With a quick reload.'

'I wouldn't know, bein' a common soldier, like. I rely on me Martini-Henry rifle, even if it does get too hot.'

'Effective range up to thirty-five yards.' He sighted along the barrel. 'Maximum range, one hundred yards.'

'Couldn't miss at a few inches, eh?'

Seb sighed. 'You'd think this weapon could tell us *something* about what happened, wouldn't you? It's very frustrating. Here is the actual gun that killed our victim, but it tells us absolutely bugger all except that two shots have been fired.'

'Makes you want to weep, eh? You knowing all there is to know about such a weapon, yet amounting to nothing in the end. It's a shame murderers *don't* leave somethin' of themselves on the butt somehow. We'd soon sort out a mess like this if they did, wouldn't we, sir?'

Seb plonked the handgun back down on the table.

'You have too much imagination, Corporal.'

On the 1st of January, Ensign Early and Corporal Evans decided to join the 2nd Warwickshire and other regiments up on the Biggarsberg Plateau, where Chelmsford's Central Column under the command of Colonel Glyn had finally come to rest after leaving Pietermaritzburg. Here the 1st and 2nd battalions of the 24th had fortified their position and were poised to invade Zululand, though small garrisons had been left at Greytown and the Tugela River ferry crossing. The Central Column was made up of nearly five thousand soldiers – redcoats, native auxiliaries and white militia.

There were two other main columns: the Coastal Column, commanded by Colonel Pearson with some five thousand men, and the Northern Column under Colonel Wood with two thousand.

There were also two columns of less importance. The first was headed by Colonel Rowlands, whose two thousand troops were to police the areas to the north. The other was under the command of Colonel Durnford, whose force of black soldiers numbered around five hundred. Durnford, with his fiercely loyal Natal Native Horse, was to patrol the Natal border to stop the Zulus entering by the back door in a counter-attack.

Seb and Evans joined a caravan of six ox-carts heading for Helpmekaar. The night before they left a local man had come to Seb's quarters to offer himself as a servant. Seb had until that point no intention of hiring any kind of manservant, black or white, but this man was particularly insistent.

'What's your name?' asked Seb. 'Look, I really don't need anyone.'

'People call me Sam Weary, sir, but that is a name given to me because of my great energy and does not illuminate my real character.'

'I see – ironic, eh?'

'Yes, sir, if that means full of iron and tonic. My full name is Samuel Becket Wandala, sir,' said the native. 'Sam is of the Xhosa' – when he said the word 'Xhosa' the *xh* became a click of the tongue – 'and Sam can help you, sir, very much. Sam is very good with cooking food and cleaning clothes. Just to try me, sir, and you will not find any regret in your decision.'

'Well, Sam Weary, you realize we're just about to go into battle?'

'Yes, sir, Sam knows that, sir, but he is steadfast in his determination to assist you. He has heard, sir, that you are the new army policeman. Sam can help you with any terrible crimes, sir, by listening to words you cannot hear, words you cannot understand. He speaks several of our native languages, sir, and can hear where you cannot. It would be best if you hired him so that you can learn of what his people are thinking and saying. All this would be very useful to you, sir, really.'

Seb thought about this offer and realized the man was probably right. It might be very useful to have a native on the team: someone who could give him an insight into a world which was normally closed to whites.

Seb stared into the face of the man before him and believed he saw intelligence and honesty in his features. Sam Weary was probably in his late twenties, was lean but strong-looking, with narrow shoulders. His muscles were small hard knots protruding from his jet-black skin. His hair was long and stiff with earth-dust, which gave him a wild appearance, but his face was gentle and embedded with large soft brown eyes. He wore a sailor's cast-off nankeen shirt, full of holes, a pair of flannel trousers and different-sized old army boots with the toes cut out so that they would fit his long slim feet.

'All right, Sam Weary,' said Seb at last. 'I will take you on. But no thieving from anyone, especially my fellow officers.' Seb knew the code well enough to be aware that Sam would not steal from his master: you did not bite the hand that fed you. However, there were often no such scruples when it came to the master's friends, to whom a native servant owed no allegiance.

'Sir,' said Sam, his face full of delight, 'you shall not have any worry from Sam regarding such terrible crimes. How should it be if the policeman's servant was himself a thief? Why, that would make a mischief of his master's calling. Sam is a Christian person, sir, who goes to the tin tabernacle with no such sins jingling in his pocket.'

'Tin tabernacle?'

'The church which was sent to us from your own generous land, sir, by the kind missionaries of Great Britain.'

Seb then realized Sam Weary was talking about the corrugated-iron chapels which were sent out to various parts of the empire in prefabricated kit form. They were built with roof trusses that lined up with the vertical posts in the wall panels. The one Seb knew of was a Methodist church, which had several Gothic embellishments made of wood attached to the galvanized iron roof. However, many different denominations used them as temporary places of worship, or in areas where it was difficult to find building materials. It must have been a good source of income to some North of England iron foundry.

'Well, good – so long as we understand one another.'

'Oh yes, sir. My smile shows you what is in my heart. You will not have any cause to concern yourself. Sam will work to the best of his ability and assist you in every way.'

'This is a very irritating habit, Sam, to talk of yourself in the third person.'

'Sir?'

'Never mind – just say "I" and "me" occasionally, instead of referring to yourself by your name.'

'Sam will try, sir.'

And so Sam Weary was with them, on the back of the ox-cart, heading towards Helpmekaar and the Central Column of Lord Chelmsford's force.

'I don't see why we need *him*, sir,' said Evans, nodding in the direction of the native servant. 'I can do what's necessary.'

'Can you speak isiZulu?'

'No,' admitted the Welshman.

'Then shut up.'

''Ow many tents have we got.'

'Two, Corporal.'

'I'm not sharin' with 'im.'

'You'll do as you're told.'

'He can sleep outside. He stinks.'

'So do you, Corporal, or hadn't you noticed?'

'It's a different kind of stink. His is buffalo stink.'

'And yours is what?'

Evans saw the funny side of his own argument, and grinned. 'Sheep.'

'You sort it out between you,' Seb finally conceded. 'I refuse to be a go-between to a corporal and a servant.'

They arrived at their destination in the light. Seb went off to report his presence to Colonel Glyn. Evans and Sam Weary were left to sort out the luggage and erect the two tents. They were directed to a site on the edge of camp, near a hollow filled with rocks. Both men began trying to erect the first tent in sullen silence. When it became apparent this would not work, for they needed to communicate during the operation, Sam Weary said, 'Please, sir, you must hold the pole while I must pull the canvas over.'

Evans, his back to Sam, carried on fiddling with some guy ropes, not answering.

'Corporal-sir! We must work together,' cried Sam.

Still no response from the deaf Welshman. Suddenly Evans, frustrated, threw the tangled guys on the ground and glared at them, as if it were their fault they resembled birds' nests. Sam went to pick them up and this time spoke directly into Evans' face.

'Why do not you not answer Sam's question?'

'What? Oh, perhaps it's because I can't bloody well hear you, see? You need to let me see your mouth.' Evans pointed to his right ear. 'Deaf! I can't hear you, see? And look here, Samuel Becket, whatever your name is. I'm not happy about this arrangement, see? I'd rather you slung your hook. So don't go getting uppity with me, all right?'

'Sam would like to be friends with you. We can assist the officer together.'

'Look, you – I don't make friends with foreign blacks. That's not to say I'm especially against them, see – I'm not all that keen on Englishmen either and back home we live next door to each other. My friends come from Cymru, see. I'm *acquainted* with one or two of the other kind from the British Isles, but my friendship is a precious thing, not to be wasted on *Sais* or *tramorwyr*.' Another thought seemed to occur to the corporal, as he added, 'Besides, you're the buggers we're fighting, eh? Fraternizing with the enemy, it would be.'

'Sam is no enemy, corporal-sir. Sam . . .' he suddenly remembered the ensign's advice, '*I am just an ordinary man who wants* to eat every day, not once every week. Now, please will you hold the centre pole, so Sam can pull the canvas over it? Then he will make you some tea, corporal-sir, which will make you calm and tranquil again. Tea is good for the nerves and Sam makes the best tea in all Natal. Afterwards he will cook you some eggs and pig meat. You will soon think of me like your *best* friend.'

'Oh I will, will I? Like bloody hell, I will.'

When Seb came back the two tents were up and the smell of cooking hit his nostrils.

'Good to see you two are hitting it off,' he said, rubbing his hands. Seb still had a schoolboy's taste, appetite and stomach. 'What's that you're frying there, Sam? Oh my, it smells good.' He glanced up towards a makeshift corral only fifty yards away, where over a thousand oxen were milling around, churning up the mud. The wind had changed and the smell coming from the corral was hugely offensive. 'Or it would be, if we weren't downwind from that lot.'

In truth there was no escaping the foul odour anywhere on the plateau. A pall of stink pervaded over the whole fortified camp. It could not fail to intrude, with so many animals present, not to mention the latrines and casual toilets of five thousand men. Horses and oxen vied for supremacy of numbers, followed by a lesser group of mules. Dogs ran under and out of the heavily-laden wagons and carts that, when on the move, needed manpower as well as animal-power to keep them rolling. However, the neat rows of bell tents stretching in lines away from larger ridge tents told of order amongst the chaos. Several starkly present wooden huts served senior staff with more solid walls to contain their whisperings and murmurings as they planned the coming invasion. And the Royal Artillery's shiny 7-pounder guns – an even neater row of six rifled muzzle-loaders – served to underline the gravity of the undertaking which the British had before them.

Thunderclouds were gathering above the plateau and Sam Weary glanced up nervously. The summer season saw many heavy rain showers. Some of them lasted an hour, some a week. Black, rolling cumuli nimbus threatened to engulf the Drakensbergs. Sam Weary quickly served the two men with his fingers, whose tough skin seemed able to withstand the heat of the sizzling fat running from the eggs and bacon. Evans grimaced as his fried egg was dangled then dropped from a grubby hand on to his tin plate, but Seb did not blink an eye. The officer was intent on dipping his bread into the spreading yolk as it broke on contact with the metal. Seb was far away somewhere. Often a dreamy soul, he bothered his senior officers quite a bit at times.

After the meal, Sam Weary asked, 'Was that very good cooking, officer-sir?'

'Oh yes,' replied Seb, always easily satisfied by a plain tasty meal of the fried variety. He smacked his lips. 'Very good.'

'Huh! There's nothin' to cooking bacon and eggs,' muttered Evans, as he read the servant's lips. 'Easy, isn't it?'

Sam Weary made some peculiar movements with his fingers in front of the Welshman's nose.

'Eh?' cried Evans in an overloud voice. 'What're you playin' at, boy? You making fun of me?'

Seb, sitting cross-legged opposite the two men, came out of his dream.

'What's the trouble, Corporal?'

'It's him,' fumed Evans, 'makin' obscene gestures in my face, he is. I'm not standing for it, sir. I tell you it's not right. I'm due some respect. I'm a non-commissioned officer in Her Majesty's army and shouldn't be put upon by black men like him, see?'

Seb said, 'What's this, Sam?'

'Sir, Sam was just deaf-signing to the corporal, to save him from looking at my lips. Sam . . . I meant no harm, sir.'

'What do you mean, *deaf-signing*?'

'One of Sam's daughters was born deaf and not able to speak with her mouth, sir. A nun-lady from the land of Belgium showed Sam's wife how to use our fingers to talk with her. Look,' Sam Weary made a shape with the fingers of his right hand, 'this means "Are you still hungry?" and this "Are you tired?" There are many, many such signs, sir. And if you wish to spell out a whole word, you can do so with the fingers. Each one of the five fingers is a,e,i,o,u. Sam thought the corporal-sir was able to do the same as the nun-lady showed us, at the tin tabernacle.'

'The corporal was not born deaf, Sam – he's deaf because of the guns. And unlike your daughter, he learned to speak before he lost his hearing. Evans? A thought just occurred to me. We might do well to learn this technique from Sam. It might help us while we're questioning reluctant witnesses. A sort of secret language. What do you think?'

'I think it's daft,' replied the huffy corporal.

'Sam thinks this is a very good idea, masters.'

Evans, staring at the moving lips, cried, 'You would!'

At that moment a terrible racket came from behind some nearby tents. The air was full of yells, most of which were oaths and swear words, and the sound of scuffling. Seb jumped to his feet and ran around the end tent to see what was causing the commotion. Evans and Sam followed him close behind.

There were at least twenty drummer boys, beating the living daylights out of each other. It was a junior brawl. The savagery was unbelievable. The whole bunch were punching and kicking, tangled together like a single beast, screaming oaths and shouting in pain as they were hurt. Seb waded in, grabbing tunics and tearing the boys apart, tossing the struggling bodies away sprawling in the dust. Evans was soon doing the same, ripping the milling children from each other. Tears were flowing down some sweaty dirty faces, others had expressions of triumph. The corporal then concentrated on keeping the parted combatants away from each other as the ensign reached the core of the fight, where two young blades, heads down, were steadily windmilling at each other.

He grabbed their separate collars and lifted them high and wide, away from each other.

Punches rained on his chest from the smaller of the two, whose eyes were still tightly closed and whose voice was as hoarse as a twenty-stone fish-seller's at Billingsgate market.

'YOU BLOODY BASTARD. I'LL PUNCH YOUR FUCKIN' LIGHTS OUT, YOU SODDIN' FUCKER!'

'Oh, you will, will you,' said Seb, shaking the boy like a rag doll to stop the hail of punches on his breast. 'Well, I'll thank you, sir, to keep your *bloody sodding* tongue still, unless you want to spend a night on the wooden horse. I've never heard such foul words.'

The boy's eyes opened above the bleeding nostrils and went very round when he saw who he was speaking to. Seb dropped the quiet one and held the noisy one well away from himself, after noticing that the blood was dripping off the youngster's chin and down his uniform. When he started choking Seb planted him firmly on his feet. The boy looked hot and bothered, as did they all, and he still glared up at Seb. His hair was matted with sweat and dust, his face red with the heat of anger and effort. The expression was twisted into a gorgon-like mask.

'I ain't in your battalion, sir.'

Clearly the child was still overheated enough to throw all caution to the winds and take on a fully grown-up officer.

'Nor you might be, boy, but you see this . . .' Seb pointed to the red scarf tied around his shoulder. 'You know what that is?'

A sullen, 'No,' came out.

'That, my young friend, is the scarlet sash of a provost-marshal. The Queen's representative of law and justice in this wild land beyond the reach of ordinary constabulary. I am the camp's policeman, and these two men with me are my assistants. Would you like me to march you up in front of your colonel for punishment?'

Common sense gradually entered the drummer boy's brain.

'Nnnno, sir. Sorry, sir.'

'You damn well will be, you little scruff.' Seb turned to face the other boys, who were all quiet now. 'What in the devil's name is this all about? Look at the state of you all. You're a disgrace to your regiment. Damn me, you're all from the 24th.'

'Diff'rint battalions, sir,' murmured one boy.

'And so you form mobs and go out looking to thump respect into each other, is that it?'

No answer. Heads were hung low.

'This won't do, you know. You're here to fight Zulus, not each other. What a waste of effort!' Seb remembered the excess of energy he had had as a boy of their age, which he expelled by thundering around the countryside after game. Not allowed a hunting rifle, he had made a club with which he chased rabbits and partridges through the harvest stubble, ineffectively attempting to knock them on the head. 'Go back to your tents and clean yourselves up. I'll let you off without punishment this time, but next time you'll be very sorry, understand me? I'll have your skins flayed from your backs to make drums with.'

'Yes, sir,' came the murmurs from young mouths, as the boys picked up their scattered caps and sorted them out between them, until they all had on the right headgear. They separated into their two battalions and the groups walked off in different directions, but even before they were out of earshot there were boasts such as, 'Did you see that corker I gave the big bugger with the warts . . .?'

'Language!' called Sam after them. 'Good Christian children will not go to heaven if they speak in such a manner.'

The three men went back to their tents.

As a provost-marshal Seb was in a peculiar, perhaps an ideal position for a keeper of the law. Any minor misdemeanours were dealt with by the regiment. Drunkenness, brawls, insubordination – all such crimes were effectively punished by various officers of the battalion, from the sergeant-major up to the colonel, depending on the seriousness of the nature of the thing. Punishments were harsh. Men were still tied to gun carriages and flogged. Men were still hanged. Seb himself in certain circumstances had the power to hang a man.

Essentially, though, Seb was there to investigate and root out malefactors, perpetrators of such terrible crimes as serious theft, murder and assault with a weapon. Thus he did not have the messy job of collecting vomiting drunks or using himself as a wedge to drive between large men fighting each other. The duty officer might have to do that, but Seb was normally exempt from such onerous tasks.

It started to rain and a deep growl rumbled across the sky from within the dark clouds. The smell of rain swept through the camp. Seb hurried back to his tent, while Sam and Evans had found something to agree about in the appalling state of youth today. It was not like that in their fathers' times. In those days one had respect for the accepted norms of social behaviour, and yes, for the older generation, etc., etc., etc. Seb thought the two men were getting on very well together.

Inside his tent he lit a lamp to study some papers he had acquired by stealth and cunning. Running his eyes over them he saw the name of the man who had preceded Brewer as duty officer the night he had died. A groan escaped Seb's lips.

'Oh no, not *him*.'

Of all the men in Lord Chelmsford's army, it had to be Captain Stenhall-Chase.

Well, the man would have to be questioned.

Seb looked through Peter's jumbled and rather erratic notes and could not see an occasion where his friend had spoken officially to Stenhall-Chase. Of course the two might have had a chat in the officers' mess about the murder. Maybe Peter had decided it was the way to deal with such a difficult officer? Or, indeed, possibly Peter had meant to question the man later, but had not got around to it before his tragic accident took matters out of his hands?

Poor Peter, it would be weeks before his family was informed. Suddenly Seb remembered something about Peter's mother. He recalled that she had once been obsessed with breathing-tubes for the dead. There had been a certain hysteria sweeping England at the time Peter and Seb had left for Africa: Gothic novels and so-called 'actual reports' had raised the anxiety about being interred alive. Stories had been circulating, in which claw marks had been found on the underside of coffin lids when corpses had been exhumed. People had been buried alive, so the stories went, although at the time it was assumed they had passed into the other world.

There was a state of suspended animation, readers of newspapers learned, which resembled death, but from which the victim eventually woke. Some bright inventor had come up with the idea of putting breathing-tubes between the casket and the surface of the ground. Also a cord in the coffin which was attached to a small silver bell on the surface. In that way, if a living man or woman was mistakenly interred, they would at least be able to suck down air and ring the bell to get disinterred. Peter's mother had insisted that all family members *had* to be buried with breathing-tubes installed, despite the fact that Peter had pointed out there was no food or water underground. Neither Peter nor Seb, who had been staying with his friend at the time, let Peter's mother see later newspaper reports of disaffected youths going round at night plugging the breathing-tubes with graveyard clay.

'I'll have to write another letter,' Seb told himself, 'to inform Mrs Williams that Peter had a breathing-tube and a bell.'

The fact that Peter's heart had been mashed by a large-calibre bullet would not have affected her desire to have the apparatus installed.

Six

The morning after Ensign Early had chastised the drummer boys for running riot in the camp, the boys had been collected together for punishment. Seb had not been the only one who had been disturbed by the gang warfare of minors. Their behaviour had come to the notice of senior officers, who demanded that some discipline be instilled in the youngsters by their NCOs. Thus the boys were gathered together in one long line and ordered to play tattoo after tattoo for five hours without pause or respite. Fifty drummer boys, all in one long line, beating out a rhythm in unison! What a sight and sound! It drew many a soldier from his tent, to marvel at what one could do with a set of hardwood sticks and a piece of skin stretched over a wide tube. Seb, watching and listening for a while, could have forgiven them anything.

By midday the boys' hands were chafed and raw. They were dropping one by one from fatigue. Finally the order was given to dismiss and they were either carried or dragged themselves to their tents to reflect on their mortal if youthful sins.

That morning Seb went to interview Captain Stenhall-Chase.

He made some enquiries and eventually found the captain about to mount a horse, a big bay which was probably his own private steed.

'Sir, could I have a word, please?'

The captain turned and stared at Seb, obviously not recognizing him from their earlier meeting.

'What is it, Ensign? Be quick. I have to ride south.'

Seb then remembered that the captain was in the 99th. That column was commanded by Colonel Pearson. Yet Stenhall-Chase had a staff appointment written across his arrogant features. He was probably carrying dispatches for Pearson from Lord Chelmsford, or something of that nature.

'I need to ask you some questions. Could you delay leaving, do you think? It shouldn't take more than an hour.'

It was then that Stenhall-Chase noticed the red sash on Seb's shoulder and his face clouded over.

'Oh it's you. Bloody nuisance. What sort of questions? No, dammit, I need all the daylight I can get.'

'Sometime later, then? I could join your column.'

'I doubt it. And it's not my column.'

The captain turned his back on Seb and mounted his horse.

'Sir,' said Seb, holding the bridle of the gelding, which also seemed anxious to be out of Seb's way. 'I'm going to have to talk with you, whether you like it or not. I have the authority . . .'

'You can stick your authority up your backside, Ensign,' said the haughty captain, 'it don't mean tuppence to me.'

He kicked Seb's hand free of the leather and urged his mount forward, leaving Seb in a cloud of dust.

Seb glared after the retreating rider.

'You arrogant bastard,' muttered Seb, under his breath. 'We'll see about you.'

He then marched straight to the hut which was used as a staff headquarters. A guard on the door looked at him quizzically, but then simply came to attention, snapping his rifle into his body. Seb walked into a room where a trestle table covered in maps was surrounded by senior officers. He looked around for Colonel Glyn, but his commander did not appear to be there. He recognized Lieutenant-Colonel Pulleine and was walking towards him, hoping to catch his sleeve and draw him away from the table, when he realized that Lieutenant-General Lord Chelmsford's eyes were on him, though the general continued to point to a map with his right forefinger and was saying, '. . . Pearson is taking the Coastal Column along this route, while Wood will continue with the Northern Column . . . Ensign, do you have a message for me?'

Seb realized he had been mistaken for a courier.

'Sir? No, sir.' Seb came to attention. 'Sir, I need . . . I'm the Provost-Marshal, sir.'

The eyes of a dozen staff and other senior officers were on him.

'Ah, yes – I see that now, unless my junior officers have taken to fancy dress.' The general indicated the red sash. 'Well, if it's not a message, what is it, then?'

Seb went all hot under the collar. For a moment he was at a loss what to do. Should he just murmur his apologies and leave? That would be the easiest and most sensible thing to do, with so much rank in the room, dripping from hat and shoulder. Also a general was not an easy man to converse with, if one was fairly low in the chain of army being. On the other hand, Seb had a job to do. Colonel Glyn thought the war took precedence over police work, and if Seb had been a normal member of the regiment, he would think so too. But he was no longer a soldier of the line. He was the Provost-Marshal. Such a position dictated that he walk a narrow field and not deviate from his goal.

'Sir,' he said, 'could I have a private word?'

His own voice sounded ludicrously loud to him. Looks of astonishment were on the features of colonels and majors. All faces then swung back in the direction of the general.

'A private word?' said the general, but not in any annoyance. 'How intriguing. Is it worth delaying these gentlemen who are anxious to be about their duties?'

'I – I believe so, sir.'

'Well, let's hope I am of the same belief.'

The general nodded curtly to the other officers and led Seb into an adjoining room. There he opened a box of cigars, put one between his lips and lit it, drawing in the smoke with a look of satisfaction. Clearly this was Lord Chelmsford's reason for taking a break. Seb had provided an excuse.

There was no offer of a cigar to Seb, who would have refused it anyway. He much preferred pipe tobacco.

'Thank you for seeing me, sir,' began Seb. 'I'm sorry to have interrupted your important meeting.'

'Oh, it's not *that* important, young man. We're just planning to wage a major war against another sovereign nation.'

Mild sarcasm. Generals were entitled to that, by nature of their high rank. Seb forced a smile to his face. 'Yes – yes, of course, sir. Well, the thing is, I'm investigating a murder. What I believe to be a murder. I mean, the death of Captain Brewer . . .'

'Of course, I know of the incident. I was told it was suicide.'

'On the surface, sir, it might seem so. But there are certain anomalies – I won't bore you with them here . . .'

'Please do, Ensign.' The general pushed some papers out of the way and sat on the corner of his table. 'I'm all ears.'

Seb drew a deep breath. 'All right, sir – I will. Both I and my predecessor in the post, Lieutenant Williams – you will have been informed of the accident which took his life, I'm sure, sir – we are, were, that is, we have both been disturbed by the fact that Captain Brewer was shot twice in the chest. Sir, I for one cannot believe a man would commit suicide in such a manner. A sensible man blows out his own brains. Even suicides feel pain. The pain of a bullet in the chest must be incredible . . .'

The general puffed out a cloud of smoke.

'I agree.'

Seb was stunned for a minute, then said falteringly, 'You – you do, sir?'

'Most definitely. And the further anomalies?'

'My former colleague's notes tell me that there were no powder marks on the shirt of the deceased officer.'

'Which indicates?'

'Well, sir,' Seb demonstrated with his right hand, 'if I were to shoot myself in the chest with a revolver, by bending my arm thus, the muzzle, as you can see, would be no more than an inch or two away from its target. In which case, it would leave powder marks. There were no such marks on the captain's shirt. Peter's . . . Lieutenant Williams' study of the body led him to believe the shot to be fired from at least three or four *feet* from the victim. Impossible for a man to do that to himself, unless he fitted up some sort of device.'

'Of which there was none in evidence.'

'None at all, sir.'

'And now to the nub, if you please, Ensign – my cigar is halfway through its journey.'

'Yes – yes, sir. Fact is, I want to question several people – an officer. Captain Stenhall-Chase. He was on duty immediately prior to Captain Brewer. The captain does not see the need to be questioned and refuses an interview. The captain's in the 99th and has ridden off towards the Coastal Column.'

The general raised his eyebrows. 'Does not see the need to be questioned? But you, young man, are the Queen's representative of the law in this lawless land – damn drummer boys running amok – deal with that by the by, if you will, Ensign? Where was I? Oh yes, Stenhall-Chase. One of my staff officers. Know the family. Good family. But not above the law. No one is, not even me. I can't go around murdering fellow officers either . . .'

'Oh, sir,' said Seb quickly, 'I don't mean to say the captain is the actual *murderer*.'

'No, no of course not, but you have to have all the information you can gather. Evidence. I will get word to the captain that he is to attend an interview at some time. Can't say when, Ensign – you understand that? Now, is that it? Can I go back to my war?'

'Yes, sir. Sorry to intrude.'

The general stubbed out the butt of his cigar in a tin lid that was obviously there for the purpose.

'Good. Now, Ensign, I want you to do something for *me*.'

Seb's expression became attentive. 'Of course, sir – you're the general.'

'Yes, I am, aren't I?' came the return, pregnant with satisfaction. 'Well, what I want from you is surveillance. I need you to keep a close eye on someone.'

'What, sir – spy on the enemy?'

'No, not the enemy, exactly, though naturally I don't trust him, or I wouldn't ask you to watch him. There's a Boer by the name of Zeldenthuis – Pieter Zeldenthuis. One of our scouts.'

Seb was aghast at this duty. 'But – but, sir, I'm a policeman . . .'

'That's right.' The general left the room and rejoined the other officers, who were having coffee.

Seb left the room by a separate exit, which led to the outdoors, not having to re-enter the room full of high rank. His mind was spinning. Spy? He was being asked to spy on a fellow soldier? Well, not a Queen's soldier, admittedly. The Boers had not exactly joined the invasion force in great numbers. They found it hard to choose between hating the Zulus and hating the British. They were equally despised.

This Pieter Zeldenthuis was obviously one of them. But what was Seb supposed to look for? Surely a Boer would not actually side with the Zulus? That was ludicrous. Perhaps he was looking after Boer interests with regard to the British? The Boers had always felt they were first in the land and that rightly they should be governing it. The British had come in later and simply taken over. The Boers, pushed ever northwards into the Transvaal, surely wanted to regain their sovereignty over the whole of South Africa? Perhaps Zeldenthuis was an insurgent of some kind?

Seb was also lost as to how to go about such work. All his principles were against sneaking around, secretly gathering information about a person. All the teaching of his superiors and elders – father, brother, tutors, cousins, family friends – was that such activities were vile and unmanly, certainly ungentlemanly. One did not carry tales, tell tales, snitch on another fellow. In fact, one did the opposite: one took punishment one did not deserve rather than reveal the identity of a comrade – at school, in private life, in the regiment. You took the punishment and felt you had done the right thing by not tattling on another fellow, even if you did not particularly like the chap. Indeed, even if you hated him.

Now here he was, having received a direct order from a general, the commander of his army no less, to break that code.

Seb's Uncle Jack was a spy, of course, had been since the Crimean War, but though the whole family loved Jack, they did not mention his chosen work within the army. They spoke of him as a 'military man' or 'infantry officer', Jack being attached to the 88th or Connaught Rangers, but his spying and saboteur activities were not for dining-room conversation. So following in Uncle Jack's footsteps would not be regarded as a good career move by Seb's parents.

'What is one to do?' asked Seb of himself, as he hurried through the lines of tents. 'Orders have to be obeyed.'

There was no time like the present. He found the Natal Native Contingent camp and began to make enquiries. Eventually he tracked down Pieter Zeldenthuis, who was feeding his horse with hay. Zeldenthuis wore tan clothes with a broad-brimmed hat and knee-length riding boots. He looked tough, with tree-bark skin, as if he had been left out in the wind and rain like new wood, to season. He seemed quite a bit older than Seb, perhaps in his thirties, but there was a boyish slant to his features. When Seb approached his head came up and he nodded and smiled.

'Howzit, bru?'

'Hello,' replied Seb. 'Going for a ride?'

'Ag, no, just feeding and watering the brute,' answered Zeldenthuis, in clipped accents. 'What about you, soldier? Out for a walk, or did you want to speak?'

'Ah, yes. You see, I'm the new Provost-Marshal—'

'What's that mean amongst you *rooineks*?' interrupted the Boer, in an amused tone. 'You like a junior field marshal?'

'No, no. I wish. I'm an army policeman.'

The Boer threw his hands up. 'Whoa, boysie – what have I done? You come to arrest me, or what?'

Seb felt he was continually on the back foot.

'Nothing like that. I came to see you on a private matter. You see, I like to paint wildlife a bit – nothing grand, of course . . .'

'Of course.'

Seb began to get irritated. 'What's that supposed to mean – repeating my phrase?'

'Well, a British gentleman would *never* boast about his skills with anything – brush, pen, *firearm* – his modesty would not allow it. I expect your Joseph Turner, the English painter, told people he was just dabbling in oils. So of course you would not tell me you were a *good* painter. Are you a good shot, Mr Provost-Marshal? With the rifle or handgun?'

Seb was not going to be bullied into boasting. 'Fair.'

'Ag – not good, just fair.'

'It's the truth. I'm not a sharpshooter, but I can hit an ordinary target when I need to. What about you?'

'Me? I'm brilliant. I can hit a bumble bee in flight with a shot from the hip, you know?' He laughed. 'There's the difference between us. I'm bloody fantastic at everything, while you're just *fair*. Which makes me wonder why you lot are in charge here. How come you rule the world and you're just *average* at everything, while all we've got are a few thousand acres of farmland and we're bloody brilliant?'

Seb finally saw the funny side of this fellow.

'Perhaps we secretly know we're best, and we know everyone else knows it, so we don't need to talk about it?'

'Or maybe average is adequate, if you want something hard enough – maybe talent without desire falls short, eh? So, you're a Sunday painter? Don't look at me like that, it's not your profession, is it? That's soldiering, and policing, so it's got to be a pastime. Why do you come to me? I'm no artist, boysie. I'm just a Yarpie with a horse and gun.'

'I was told you know the country well. I'd like to paint a caracal, if you could find me one.'

'Show me a Boer who doesn't know his own country.'

Which was precisely why Seb had used this excuse.

'Could you do that, sometime?'

'Not a lion, or a cheetah?'

'No, everyone does those. I want something different.'

'You ride?' asked Zeldenthuis.

'Of course.'

'Right, let's go down to the Buffalo, now, *rooinek*.'

'I'd prefer it if you didn't call me a *redneck*. I've been out here a year now and my neck's as brown as yours. Where will I get a horse?'

'One of my boys will let you borrow one. What's your name?'

'Sebastian – call me Seb.'

'And the other half?'

'Early – as in early dawn.' Seb hesitated and then added, 'My friends call me South-East.'

Zeldenthuis began to saddle his horse.

'I'll hold that in reserve. I'm not your friend yet. Don't know that we ever will be friends. Seb will do for the time being. I'll get you that mount, then we'll see what the Buffalo River has to offer in the way of wildlife. Personally, I prefer to shoot it when I see it, but if you want to paint it, that's your business. You can pay me two English pounds every time I take you out.'

'Two pounds?' cried Seb, incredulously. 'That's almost eight days' pay.'

'I'm expensive. Two pounds and a glass of squareface. Now, let's get you that nag, eh?'

The horse that Zeldenthuis acquired for Seb was actually no nag. It was a skittish piebald that almost danced its way over the ground. They stopped off to pick up a Martini-Henry rifle for Seb, since it would have been foolishness in the extreme to leave the camp and head towards Zulu territory without adequate arms. Soon, though, they were on their way to the Buffalo River. Seb was slightly nervous outside the boundaries of the camp, even though he had already whetted his fighting spirit in South Africa in the previous year.

It had been in the Perie Bush, north of Kingwilliamstown. A company of the 1st Battalion of the 24th had fought on hilly, rocky ground, covered with thick shrub. The enemy at that time were Gaika tribesmen. Somehow he had survived that encounter, but it had served to make him as cautious as he should be in open country. There was nothing to stop small parties of Zulus crossing the Buffalo and waiting in ambush. War *had* been declared, after all.

As they neared the river's edge the wildlife increased, especially the bird life. Seb's heart soared. This was what he joined the army for, to be permitted to travel to places where the colours and the variety of life were immensely superior to that of his own country. Oh, yes, part of it was the excitement of being in the uniform of an army that was feared and admired throughout the world.

And yes, he loved his own country, for its pleasant greenness and placid countryside – but this! – this was thrilling beyond anything. The land was vast, the sky was vast, and both were packed with birds and beasts of infinite shape and pattern. The tints and shades swam in his head: earthy ochres, bright brilliant primary hues of feather, vivid stripes and spots, subtle shadows that melted into a background of vegetation and dusty landscape. You could almost breathe the colours, take them down into your lungs, into your bloodstream, feel them racing through your arteries.

'Do you like to paint?' he asked the Boer, as the horses picked their way along the stony track with their sure hooves.

'Never tried it,' came the answer. 'Never wanted to.'

'You should. At least, you should do *something* creative. Perhaps you should try writing about this wonderful farmland you think so much of?'

'Ag, I'm more of a destructive man, Ensign.' He pointed to the rifle slung down his back. 'This is my pen and my paintbrush. It helps me keep hold of this wonderful land of mine.'

Seb suddenly remembered the Boer animosity towards the British, who had walked in and taken over under the noses of the incumbents. He quickly grasped the new subject.

'Yes, what is your rifle? It's not a Martini-Henry.'

Zeldenthuis glanced back over his own shoulder. 'This? This is a good German rifle, my friend. Bolt-action Mauser. Calibre's .43 – slightly smaller than your Martini-Henry. You can get locally made ammunition, but I use the regulation brass cartridges used by the German Imperial Army. That way you know you're getting the best. They roll the brass too thin on the local stuff and if you're carrying a pouchful they press against each other and bend. A bent bullet doesn't make great ammunition, believe me. Sometimes the heads fall off and they shed their powder.'

'IG Mod. 71,' said Seb, reading the Gothic-script stamp on the breech. 'What's the IG?'

'*Infanterie-Gewehr*. Infantry weapon.'

'And is that a leaf-sight at the back, like I've got on mine?'

'No, that's a safety lever – it's called a wing lever.'

'Where are they made? In Germany I mean.'

'Spandau. What else do you want to know? Its birthday?'

Seb felt embarrassment, knowing that Zeldenthuis had guessed he was simply changing the course of the conversation.

'All the same,' said Seb, 'it's an interesting subject.'

'And yours? Mark 2?'

It was Seb's turn to glance at the rifle on his own back.

'Yes. Fires a .45 Boxer cartridge – as you say, slightly larger than yours. But a British soldier is more concerned with the weight of his weapon, if he's got to stand holding it for several hours on guard duty. The Martini-Henry weighs nine pounds, which is heavy enough. At four feet long it's almost as tall as some of the miners that carry it. Good weapon in the field. It's got a fearsome kick though and after firing five or six rounds the barrel gets red-hot – you can't touch it with the naked hand. The ammunition's not great either. It's useless when it gets damp.'

They were now coming down to the south bank of the Buffalo. Zeldenthuis dismounted and swung his rifle quickly and easily off his back and into the crook of his left arm. A hippo trundled into the water as if it feared it was about to become a target. Seb now swung a leg over the back of his mount, but before he could slip to the ground he was covered by the Mauser. Seb stared into the muzzle of the German rifle.

'What's this?' he asked.

'You tell me, *rooinek*,' said the Boer, evenly. 'And don't give me any shit about painting bloody caracals. What do you want with me, eh? You sought me out, boy. I want to know why.'

Seb caught something out of the corner of his eye and both eyes widened. 'There's some Zulus out there – six men in a canoe.'

Zeldenthuis had his back to the river, but he nodded. 'I see them. You stay as you are, half-on and half-off. I'm talking to *you*, boy. I could cut you down now and toss you in the river. By the time they find you, the war will be in full swing and no one will care who shot you.'

'Why are you doing this?' asked Seb, desperately. 'I've done nothing to you.'

'Not yet. But you're a policeman. You going to arrest me, is that it? What for? Question me? What about? I want to know.'

'No, I'm not going to arrest you,' replied an exasperated Seb, as he watched the canoe of tribesmen getting closer. He saw no reason now not to tell Zeldenthuis the truth, since the Boer was heavily suspicious. 'I've – I've been told to watch you. Look, are they Zulus, or not?'

'Who told you to watch me?'

A shot came from the canoe, which now veered away parallel to the river bank. The ball clipped through the leaves of the tree under which the two white men were standing. Still Zeldenthuis did not turn around. He stared straight into Seb's eyes.

'I asked you a question, boy.'

Seb sighed. 'Lord Chelmsford himself.'

'Told you to spy on me?'

'Implied your loyalties might be in question.'

'So they are – I've got no love for the British. I hate the British. But I hate the Zulus more.'

'Why – I mean, why do you hate the Zulus?'

'You don't need to know that.'

The Zulus in the canoe had got into the central current and were swiftly being taken back to the far bank. They beached their canoe and strolled in a leisurely fashion up into some trees. Only one of them, the one with the musket resting on his right shoulder, looked back at the two white men. Seb was convinced he was grinning and felt a little heated by that thought.

'We could have done something about those men,' he said to Zeldenthuis. 'We did nothing.'

'Ag, they weren't serious,' replied the Boer. 'Listen, do you want to make the first kill in this war? Because I don't. It's going to be a bloody business, I can tell you. I don't trust that lord general of yours to know what he's about, see. You British, you come out here – you know nothing about this place. What do you know? Eh? Those impi warriors, they're not common savages. They've got brains like you and me. They can fight like bloody hell, I know. They're organized. They're disciplined. And they're fitter than any bloody soldier of the Queen, that's certain. They'll do fifty miles on the trot, while you lot are struggling to get a wagon out of the mud.'

He spat in the dust, before continuing. 'General Thesiger thinks this is going to be easy. He's got rocks in his head. All he's worried about is whether they'll fight. They'll fight, all right. There'll be a few soldiers dead before the end of this, you mark my words, Ensign – and if you want the responsibility of starting all that, by killing a canoe full of Zulus, be my guest. That will be historic, eh? You want your name in the history books as the man who fired the first shot in a war which destroyed the Zulu nation at the expense of hundreds of British soldiers and militia men? Not me, bru. Not me.'

The Boers, no doubt for reasons of their own, often referred to General Lord Chelmsford by his German family name of Thesiger. Frederick Thesiger had only recently become Lord Chelmsford on his father's death. No doubt the Dutch settlers felt they could inject more venom into a Teutonic word.

'The Martini-Henry . . .' began Seb, defensively.

'The Martini-Henry? After the first battle, the Zulus will have a few of those in their hands too. If they haven't got them already. You've got a shock coming, you lot. And me. I'm here too, but I know what to expect, you don't.'

'I've fought the Gaikas. We've been fighting Kaffirs for the past year,' snarled Seb, his pride aroused. 'We're not wet behind the ears. Chelmsford's had a lot of experience in warfare of this sort.'

'Not this sort. Bush fighting, against a few scattered tribes. This is the Zulu nation, boy. This is an empire you're challenging. Anyway, I'm not going to stand here and argue with you. Do you want to paint, or what? There's a kudu just along the bank – see him? It's not a caracal, but beggars can't be choosers, eh? Get out your watercolours, Ensign. I want to earn my two English pounds. I'm looking forward to my glass of squareface. Let's get to it. Let's get it over and done.'

Seb was astonished that the Boer expected him to calmly sit down and paint now. However, the kudu bull was indeed a beautiful beast. Seb was soon absorbed in the world of his art, which Zeldenthuis, watching, had to admit was impressive.

Seven

Riding back to camp with the Boer, Seb was curious to discover Zeldenthuis's feelings on the subject of being spied on.

'So what are we going to do about this situation?' asked Seb, having difficulty in controlling his piebald on the rocky ground.

'What situation would you be speaking about?'

Embarrassment returned. 'Well – the fact that I've been asked to watch you closely.'

'Oh that?' Pieter Zeldenthuis shrugged. 'Well, I guess you watch me, eh? Pretty damn closely, if you value your hide. I'm told Thesiger can be pretty hard on you boys, if he takes a dislike to you. You redcoats like to be promoted, don't you?'

'Of course,' replied Seb, thinking they had crossed a bridge here with Zeldenthuis referring to 'redcoats' rather than 'rednecks'.

'Then do as the man says.'

'You don't mind?'

'Mind, of course I bloody well mind – but the situation is set in stone, so let's give him what he wants. I like you, boy. I don't know why, because despite the fact that you've spent a year in my country I think you're still green. But human nature is a strange thing and in any case, you can tell me what's going on with the high command. Sort of act as a double agent, eh?'

'I can't do that,' said Seb, aghast. 'I couldn't, anyway – no one tells an ensign anything.'

'Well, we'll do what we can, eh? Now, let me have the nag back and I'll see you around camp. You owe me two pounds, by the way. I'll collect it later, when we have that glass of gin together. All right?'

Seb felt buoyed by his new acquaintance.

When he returned to his tent area Evans pounced on him.

'That officer, sir – he's been. Hopping mad, he was. Thought he was going to burst his liver. Red in the face, like. Veins popping on his forehead. They called him back . . .'

'Officer?' muttered Seb, then, 'Oh,' as he remembered Lord Chelmsford's promise, 'you mean Captain Stenhall-Chase.' Seb lifted his head to stare at Evans. 'Stenhall-Chase?' he repeated, mouthing the words.

'That's the one,' said the tall willowy Welshman, swaying like a reed in a strong breeze. 'That officer. Angry as a wasp. He's gone off now. Took Sam Weary with him.'

Seb raised his eyebrows. 'Took Sam? Whatever for?'

'Said he needed someone to groom his horse.'

'Did he now? All right. You stay here, Corporal – I'll go and find him.'

Seb left Evans and went on a tour. He discovered Stenhall-Chase in the officers' drinking tent. Seb suppressed the feelings in his fluttering stomach and marched up to the captain.

'Sir, could I have a word?'

The captain had been talking to his companion, another captain, and he turned to glare at Seb.

'Oh it's you. Went running to the general, eh? Little snitch. Nobody likes a tattle-tale, Ensign. I was halfway on my errand.'

'I'm sorry, sir, but you refused me an interview.'

'Damn right I did. Got nothing to say to you.'

The officer with him nodded sternly at Seb. 'Be told or be ware.'

Good Lord, two of them!

'Still, I have my duty to do, sir,' Seb insisted, then to the other officer, 'Forgive me for interrupting your conversation.'

Aware that they were attracting a little attention now, Stenhall-Chase muttered, 'You'll have to wait. I'll finish my drink.'

'I'll wait outside, sir.'

'Wait where you damn well want.'

Stenhall-Chase turned his back on Seb and continued his conversation with the other man. Seb left the tent and stood outside, watching some drilling. In another area a band was playing. Were they at war? It was like being on camp on the South Downs. There was a faint festive air to the whole thing. Perhaps Zeldenthuis was right. The British were not taking this war seriously enough.

'What the hell do you want?'

Stenhall-Chase was standing behind him.

Seb whirled. 'I need to interview you, sir, regarding the death of Captain Brewer. But not here. We're in the way.'

'You have a rifle slung over your shoulder.'

Seb glanced at the Martini-Henry. 'Yes, sir – I've just been out into the bush.'

The captain was obviously aware of other officers coming and going to the drinking tent and he nodded. Seb followed the captain as he strode off and after a short walk they came to a ridge tent. The captain's horse was tethered not far away. Sam Weary was unenthusiastically running a brush down its flanks. Seb nodded curtly to his servant and since Stenhall-Chase was lifting the flap of the tent, Seb ducked inside. Left to stand, while Stenhall-Chase sat on a stool, he took out his notepad and pencil. But it was awkward with the low ridge and he had to bend his neck.

'Is there another seat?' asked Seb, unslinging his weapon and propping it against a tent pole.

Stenhall-Chase sighed and found a bucket which Seb upturned to use as a stool. 'Let's get this over with,' said the captain, 'then I don't want to see your face again.'

'Fair enough, sir,' said the ensign. 'I understand you were the officer Captain Brewer relieved on the night he died?'

'Where did you hear that?'

'I read it. Strangely, the army keeps records.'

The captain's eyes narrowed. 'Don't you take a funny tone with me, Ensign. I may have been ordered to give you this interview, but if you make my life uncomfortable, yours will become twice so. Do we understand one another?'

'Understood, sir. Apologies. You are, however, a hostile witness and I find it difficult.'

'You're boring me. Proceed.'

'Sir, did you *like* Alan Brewer?'

'What kind of question is that? Hardly knew the chap.'

'But you did *know* him. Did you also know Elaine?'

Stenhall-Chase blinked. 'Elaine? Elaine who?'

'Elaine Brewer, Alan Brewer's widow.'

The blood rushed to the captain's face so fast Seb thought for a minute his head would explode.

'WHAT?'

'Sir, please control your temper. I have a right to ask these questions of any of my witnesses or suspects. If I were to worry about sensibilities I would never find an answer to the problem of the captain's death – and I am determined to find an answer, believe me. I asked you a plain and simple question. Just answer it yes or no.'

'No!'

'You never met her?'

'No – that is, yes, of course I've *met* her. I might even have danced with her once – or twice – at balls. However, *knowing* her implies we were intimate friends. I have met her casually, in public places, at public gatherings, but have never spoken to her in private. Does that satisfy your sordid little mind, Ensign?'

'The state of my mind has nothing to do with this interview,' Seb replied, calmly, 'while your relationship with Mrs Brewer has everything to do with it.'

Stenhall-Chase replied evenly, 'There was no relationship. There is none and never was any. Am I clear?'

Seb scribbled in his notebook. 'So you are not the man who persuaded Elaine Brewer to leave her husband?'

A jerk of the captain's head. 'There is such a man?'

'Oh yes. There's a letter we have in our possession. Mrs Brewer confesses she loves another. She told her husband, the captain, that she no longer had any fondness for him and that when he returned to England – which of course he will never do now – she would not be waiting for him. The lover is not named in the letter, which leads me to believe he is here in Lord Chelmsford's army. If he were not here, what harm would there be in naming him? Alan Brewer would have found out who he was when he returned home, so why keep it secret? I think it feasible that Mrs Brewer was concerned for her lover's safety. She might think that her husband would force a duel and kill her lover. Are you a good shot, sir?'

The captain seemed mesmerized by this tale and came out of his trance to answer the question.

'Good shot? Fair, I suppose.'

'Alan Brewer was a *brilliant* marksman. Any man who was foolish enough to duel with him would surely come off worst. I doubt you would want to face such a man in a duel.'

'Honour is worth more than life,' snapped the captain. 'If you don't know that, you shouldn't be wearing that uniform.'

'Thank you for being so honest with me, sir. I appreciate it. But – but you have to admit, you were in an excellent position if you wished to murder the captain. You let him take over the duty officer's position from you, staying to chinwag for a few minutes, shoot him twice in the chest as you sit opposite one another, then lock the door from the outside with a duplicate key you've had made . . .'

'What rubbish you talk,' the captain said, his voice suddenly devoid of anger or sarcasm. 'I could have locked that door from the outside, with a duplicate key supposing there was one, but I could not have bolted it before I left. When the colour sergeant's men kicked the door down the next morning the bolts were in place. Even had I another key, and there were no bolts, I would not have been able to get it in, because the original key was still in the lock, the other side.'

The wind went out of Seb's sails.

'The key was still there? I didn't know that.'

Stenhall-Chase snorted. 'And you call yourself a provost-marshal?'

'New – I'm very new,' muttered Seb.

Stenhall-Chase gave him a thin smile. 'You thought the key was missing, didn't you?'

'Yes. So I have learned something through this interview.' Seb tried to regain some of his former ground. 'And, sir, I would appreciate it if you would not order my servants about. The black grooming your horse is paid by me, not you. You have no right to take him away from his duties.' As he was speaking Seb picked up his Martini-Henry and slung it over his right shoulder again.

'Blacks are blacks – universal around the camp.'

'My man is not for universal use. I hire him privately.'

'Take the bloody idiot – doesn't know a grooming brush from a shoe brush, anyway.'

'Oh, and one more thing,' said Seb, something niggling at his brain. 'You said the key was in the lock of the door. Not on the floor of the room? One would have thought it would fall out when the door was knocked in.'

'I imagine,' replied the captain disdainfully, 'it remained in the lock because it had only been turned once.'

'Turned once?'

Stenhall-Chase sighed. 'The door to the duty officer's quarters at Ladysmith garrison has a double locking action. You give the key a full turn once, then a second full turn. The second turn is the most difficult on that kind of lock. There's a stiffness there, even when the lock has been oiled. However, if you have only performed one of the turns, you can't remove the key from the lock. It'll only come out once both actions have been performed. Hence when the door was knocked down I imagine the key had only been through the first unlocking turn and needed the second. Is that significant to your enquiries, Ensign?'

'I don't know,' Seb replied. 'It might be.'

The captain took one long last withering cold look at Seb, then stated, 'Listen, Ensign, Captain Brewer committed suicide – it's as simple as that. You're not doing yourself any favours by trying to turn it into a murder, simply to further your career. It's having the reverse effect. Take my advice. Drop it. The man died at his own hand. A painful way to go, but perhaps the fellow was miserable enough? He was in a rough way, I heard, and you confirmed it with this letter from his wife. Personally I wouldn't kill myself over *any* woman. Never met one that was worth taking one's life for. But then, that's me. Brewer may have been one of those soft fellows. Sounds like he was.'

With that the captain ducked under the flap and left.

Seb was thoughtful as he stepped out of the captain's tent. He wrote in his notebook:

4. Door to DOQ double-locked.

He had no idea if this was significant or not, but he felt it might possibly be. It did not follow of course that the key had remained in the lock because it had only been turned once. It might have been a tight fit.

He was now immediately pounced on by his deaf corporal.

'Sir, sir, you're to report to Colonel Glyn immediately.'

'I thought the colonel was away?'

'He's back then, isn't he! In his quarters.'

'All right. Look, you collect Sam Weary from the paddock over there – he's there grooming a horse, or trying to. I'll go and find out what the colonel wants.'

The two men parted. Seb had a return of his earlier butterflies. It could only be bad news if Colonel Glyn wanted him. He had probably heard about Seb visiting the general. He might think Seb was going behind his back – which he was – since the colonel had told him to drop the investigation into Captain Brewer's death.

No point in putting the meeting off, though.

Seb straightened his uniform, readjusted his helmet, retied his red sash, and then marched off to the colonel's quarters. A sergeant escorted him in, but was waved away. The colonel leaned back in his creaky chair and tapped his bottom lip with a pencil.

'Ensign Early.'

Here it comes, thought Seb!

'Sir.'

'Problem.'

'Sir?'

'The soldier who was stabbed by a bayonet in the abdomen – said his comrades did it?'

'Yes, sir – I haven't yet . . .'

'He's absconded.'

Seb faltered at this unexpected news. 'Ab – absconded, sir?'

'Deserted. Run away.'

'Do we know whether he's set out for the coast, sir? Or has he gone back to Ladysmith?'

'There's the problem. He's gone east.'

It took a few seconds for this to filter into Seb's brain.

'East?' he then repeated. 'Into Zululand?'

'If you're quick you can get him back again, before he's discovered by the Zulus.'

Seb felt uncomfortable. It was hot in the colonel's room.

'Get him *back*? You mean go into Zululand myself? Sir, the man has deserted. He'll – he'll be shot anyway.'

The colonel stared at Seb with a blank expression on his face.

'So why risk your life to save him from savages? Because I'm asking you to, Ensign. Deserters are your responsibility, as Provost-Marshal. Agreed this is an unusual case. The private's name is Craster. He's sixteen years of age. More to the point, he's the son of the vicar of St Mary's in a small Sussex village. It was I who persuaded the father that the boy should enlist. He's been gone only three hours. I doubt he's reached the border of Zululand yet. If you go after him on horseback you should overtake him fairly quickly.'

'But he's guilty of desertion, sir – would the father rather he face an execution squad?'

'It's not certain he will be found guilty,' replied the colonel. 'There may be mitigating circumstances. Perhaps he was again threatened by his comrades? In any case, I feel it my duty to do all I can, given that the boy is here because of my remark to his father.' Colonel Glyn ran a hand over his face. 'It was only in passing conversation – after all, what does one say to a priest? – but having said it, I was taken seriously and the boy was sent into the army. Looking at it in hindsight, it was a mistake. He's not the right sort. Mentally fragile.' The colonel pointed. 'I see you are armed. You can leave immediately.'

'I'm on my way, sir.'

'Good. Early, take some men with you.'

'No thank you, sir – too many of us will only attract attention. I have one man in mind. A Boer.'

'Sensible thinking. A tracker.'

Seb left the colonel's quarters and ran all the way to where he had left Zeldenthuis. He found the Boer fussing with his horse.

'Pieter,' cried Seb, 'can you saddle up again?'

Zeldenthuis frowned, but whether it was because of the request he had just received, or because Seb had used his first name, Seb had no idea.

'What the hell for?'

'I have to catch a deserter.'

'And?'

'And I need your help.'

'Why?'

'He's gone to the river, into Zululand.'

'Ag, shit. Looks like you'll be firing the first shot after all.'

'Will you help me?'

'For fifty pounds, I will.'

'*Fifty* . . .?'

'I'm joking. Get your mount. When did he start running, this fool?'

'Three hours ago.'

'Bloody hell. What made him go that way?'

While they talked they saddled their horses.

'Death wish, I think. It's my guess he tried to commit suicide earlier. Stuck a bayonet in his own belly. Now he's walking to his death, hoping the Zulus will do it for him.'

'Who told you you could call me Pieter?'

'Zeldenthuis is such a mouthful. Does it mean anything?'

'English translation? *Seldom at home.* It's literal. It doesn't mean I'm a simpleton, with nothing in my head.'

'I never thought it did.'

They rode out in a cloud of dust, through the lines of grey-coned tents, past the sentries, out into the bush. It took twenty

minutes for Pieter to pick up Private Craster's trail. The youth, he
said, had started out at a run but had soon slackened his pace to
a quick walk. The horses were not at their best, having already had
a hard day, but Seb and Pieter were able to cover the ten miles to
the border in good time. They crossed the Buffalo River at a place
called Rorke's Drift, following Craster's trail towards the Batshe
River. This area was controlled by a Zulu chief named Sihayo.
They descended into a rock-strewn valley, the mounts having to
pick their way amongst boulders. In the far distance was a horse-
shoe-shaped gorge of sandstone, which Pieter told Seb was Chieftain
Sihayo's stronghold.

'Hopefully most of Sihayo's warriors will be either on their way
or at Ulundi, with King Cetshwayo. Still, keep alert, Ensign. There'll
be some of them around.'

Seb's heart was now pounding, both with riding in the heat,
and with real fear. He had of course taken part in the Xhosa wars,
and been in enemy territory before. But this was different. The
regiment was a long way away. No rescue out here. He felt entirely
exposed and very much alone. Yes, he had a good local man with
him, in Zeldenthuis, but the two of them would not fare well if
they ran into an impi of Zulu warriors.

Pieter had his binoculars to his eyes and was scanning the ground
ahead.

'Can you see him?' asked Seb, anxiously. 'What's that movement
over there, on the rise?'

Pieter glanced at where he was pointing and looked again
through his glasses.

'Cattle. About fifty head. One or two young boys herding them.'

'Thank Christ for that,' said Seb, relieved. 'Well, what about
Craster?'

'Nothing.'

'His tracks are here, though?'

'I lost them about a mile back,' confessed Pieter. 'There were
other tracks. I think they've got him. I came on further because I
wanted to be sure.'

Seb allowed this to sink in for a moment, before he asked, 'Do
you think he's still alive?'

Pieter shrugged. 'Maybe. Do you want to go and ask?'

'Of course not.'

'Then I suggest we go home.'

Pieter began wrapping the leather strap around his glasses prior to stowing them in their case, when Seb said, 'Is that an impi over there?'

Pieter sighed. 'More like impala. Where?'

Seb pointed. Pieter's face drained of blood.

'Ag, man, there's about fifty of them.' He spun his horse. 'Let's ride, Ensign!'

Seb had time to see the sheen of hide shields caught in the sun, before he too whirled his mount and began to gallop. A glance over his shoulder told him the warriors were not as far away as he had first imagined. They were naked, except for loin cloths, and their gleaming bodies were moving at an alarming pace. They ran like black cheetahs across the valley floor and though the horses were flat out Seb knew he and Pieter were going to be caught by at least a dozen of the forerunners. While still at full gallop Seb swung his rifle off his shoulder and pointed it backwards, firing the single shot in the chamber. There was a vicious kick from the Martini-Henry and the butt recoiled and struck Seb in the kidneys. He let out a scream of pain, dropping his weapon.

'Are you hit, man?' cried Pieter, pulling back alongside him.

'No,' gasped Seb. 'It's nothing. I dropped my rifle.'

The leading Zulu, hard, lean and muscled, was almost upon them now. A revolver appeared in the Boer's hand. He shot the man full in the chest as a knobkerrie club swung at his leg. The Zulu yelled and fell forwards tumbling on the ground. Seb's horse went over the fellow, hooves cracking on bone. Seb grimaced, but at the same time felt a tug at his ankle and looked down to see another Zulu clutching at his stirrup. He kicked out sideways, catching the man on the jaw. The Zulu spun away and fell, rolling. Five more warriors were almost on them now as Seb's fingers, spider-like, searched for his own revolver.

'How can they run so fast? How can they keep up with horses?' he cried in frustration.

'They're fit as springboks, man,' replied Pieter, 'and the mounts are tiring.'

It was true, the horses were weakening. They had been out all day now.

Pieter added, 'All right, Ensign – got your pistol?'

'Yes.'

'When I give the word, rein in and then empty your revolver

into that lot – take out as many as you can. It'll slow the ones behind. These are the brave fellahs, the ones out in front. We need an example. Show those behind that courage is not everything it's made out to be.'

'All right.'

'NOW!'

Both men brought their horses to a halt, turned and fired into the five Zulus who were running up behind. Three went down. Seb had used all his ammunition. Pieter's revolver was also clicking on empty chambers. The weapon on a cord, Seb let it dangle and reached for his sword. Then he remembered he was not wearing it. There was nothing he could do to stop the warriors. They seemed determined to draw blood, one way or another. The horses were almost spent. They were not going to outrun these resolute men of the Zulu nation.

Now Pieter unslung his rifle from his shoulder. In a smooth easy action he took deliberate aim. The Mauser cracked. The leading Zulu took the shot square in the chest. With dramatic effect he flung his arms up and let out a terrible yell. Then he crumpled in front of his companion, who stumbled over his body. The last warrior was back on his feet in an instant, stabbing spear at the ready. Pieter rode at him, swinging his Mauser. The Zulu side-stepped the first blow and Pieter struck at air. The warrior stabbed with his iklwa at the Boer as Pieter wheeled his mount, driving the blade through his leather boot into his calf. Pieter yelled in pain then swung the Mauser in a circle, this time striking the warrior on the side of the head. The man fell still gripping his iklwa, drawing it from Pieter's leg. Seb saw the blood running down the blade, but there was no time for questions.

'Go,' cried Seb. 'Others are coming.'

They pressed their tired mounts again, happily finding that a steady canter was enough to stay ahead of the distant runners. They rode on and on, until Seb saw a streak of silver ahead. The Buffalo River. It was a blessed sight. Soon the buildings of Rorke's Drift were visible in the evening sun. Some of those behind had not quite given up, but flagging was evident in most. Pieter halted, reloaded in the saddle, aimed and fired. The shot fell short, but the lead Zulu stopped in his tracks. His companions caught up to him and halted with him. They stared at the white men for quite a while before turning and beginning to trot back the way they had come. They would probably be aware that a battle was coming anyway, tomorrow, or next week, or very soon. They would have another chance to wet their spears.

'Come on,' said Seb. 'We have to get that wound seen to.'

Pieter glanced down at his leg. 'You're right. It doesn't hurt now, but my boot's full of blood.' He grimaced. 'My sock is soaked. I can squish it with my toes.'

The two men rode towards the river.

Eight

The first thing Seb had to do was report the missing Martini-Henry. Colonel Glyn was not happy about its loss, but when he heard the story of the chase he understood. He was also not very happy that Private Craster was now in the hands of the Zulus. There was a possibility that they would use the youth as a hostage. His adjutant remarked, in Seb's hearing, that it would be to everyone's advantage if the boy had been killed on the spot. If he had not, there was a good chance he would die a slow death later.

Colonel Glyn listened to the story of Seb's encounter with the Zulus with interest.

'So,' he said at length, 'you and this . . . what's the Boer's name?'

'Zeldenthuis – it means—'

'I'm not really interested in what the name means. You both escaped by the thickness of a shadow, by the sound of it, which is the important thing. Thirty Zulus, eh?'

'More. There were many more behind them.'

'Well, we'll shake them up tomorrow,' said Colonel Glyn, 'we're on the march. Lord Chelmsford has at last given the order to begin. Are you coming with my column, or do you have to be elsewhere? Have you found the major's watch yet?'

'No, sir – that is, I haven't found the watch. As for where I plan to be. I thought I'd follow the Central Column, unless something else turns up.'

A lieutenant-colonel, who was standing by Colonel Glyn, nodded his head in approval.

'That's where the excitement will be, I'm certain.'

'Pulleine's right,' said Glyn. 'We hope to flush out the main Zulu army with the Central Column. Lord Chelmsford's set on it. He's worried they won't come out and meet us, but I'm confident that they'll take the field. Cetshwayo won't let us roam around his land forever. His pride won't let him. And his young warriors are dying to get at us too – they want to wash their spears in British blood.'

Pulleine muttered, 'Well, we won't let that happen – but you're right, Colonel – we need them to try.'

Seb went back to his tent, where he found Sam and Evans packing it up with their provisions. The pair seemed to be working amiably enough together. Evans looked up as Seb's shadow fell over him.

'We're on the move, sir,' shouted Evans.

'I know, Corporal. Well done.'

Not long afterwards, the Central Column was on the march, crossing the Buffalo River into Zululand. They camped the first night between the two rivers, the second one being the Batshe. Like many other hearts, Seb's was beating at drumroll pace. They were now committed to a war. They had invaded another country. The soil beneath his feet was foreign land, belonging to another nation, and he along with other British soldiers was there without invitation. There was no turning back now. Were this Warwickshire, and the feet trespassing it those of warriors from Africa, he knew he would feel incensed. So it followed that Zulus would be enraged at this incursion into their homeland by soldiers from a country across the wide ocean. They might be savages, but they still had the hearts of men.

That night Seb found out that Pieter Zeldenthuis's wound was not serious. The Boer had immediately bathed his spear cut in alcohol and so far there was no infection. Pieter was back with the Natal Carabineers, with whom he had chosen to ride. Seb also learned that the man he had been told to watch had the rank of captain, which made the situation as far as he was concerned that much more uncomfortable. That a mere ensign was spying on a captain, even if he was only an auxiliary, was rather distasteful. Seb wished he did not have to do it, but an order from a general – from *the* general – could not be ignored.

The following day Lord Chelmsford's army met the men who had chased Ensign Early and Captain Zeldenthuis. Chief Sihayo had a stronghold in a sandstone gorge with high cliffs that had a narrow entrance. The opening to the gorge was on the far side of the Batshe River and was further protected by massive boulders as big as buildings. Seb was not the only officer who was unpopular with his seniors. Lieutenant Harford, leading a section of the Natal Native Contingent, along with some of the 24th, was also in their bad books.

Seb had learned that Harford, a keen biologist, had misused the officers' mess gin to bottle one of his specimens. He had in fact shown it to Seb, who had viewed the creature with great disgust, it being a particularly large ugly scorpion. Seb could not understand the lieutenant's enthusiasm for such wildlife. Yes, the mammals and reptiles were worth studying and painting, but the creepy-crawlies found in Africa were, in Seb's opinion, frequently revolting.

Anyway, Harford had been chastised and, perhaps as a punishment, had been placed with his men in the vanguard of the attack. Sihayo's fort was defended only by a token force of Zulus, most of them having gone to join the main Zulu army at Cetshwayo's capital, Ulundi. The fight for Sihayo's stronghold was more of a skirmishing action than a full-blooded battle. Seb watched it all from a good vantage point. At one time during the clash, with bullets zipping into the cliff face, and bullets flying out of it, a shout went up that Lieutenant Harford had been hit. He had suddenly buckled and gone down. Reinforcements were sent in to rescue the young officer, only to find him scrambling around on the ground chasing a beetle. Once the creature was in a matchbox he was up again and fighting with his men.

'Got another telling off,' Harford confessed to Seb, later, when Seb went to see him. 'Can't seem to stay out of trouble.'

'I'm not surprised,' replied Seb. 'What on earth were you thinking? You were supposed to be leading your men. What if everyone started picking up frogs, or lizards, or bush mice? You'd have the whole army on the ground, messing around.'

Harford grinned sheepishly. 'If the enemy did it too, it wouldn't be such a bad thing, would it? Everyone more interested in collecting nature's bounty than killing each other?'

'It ain't realistic, though. After a while they'd be fighting over rare spiders or highly prized stick insects, killing each other anyway. It's in the nature of man, Harford.'

Harford sighed. 'You could be right – but it's a depressing thought. Anyway, we beat them today. Poor devils. Were you there when we set fire to the village? And you know we captured a lot of cattle. Half a thousand head, I'm told. Beef's on the menu tonight. If the general had given it a bit more consideration he might have decided that it would save fuel to roast the meat on the burning huts. Yes, that would have been a frugal thing to do, eh? Spit-roast whole sides of beef over the ashes of the homesteads we put to the torch.'

Harford stared back where they had come from, the glow from the village still visible in the darkening evening.

'That's by the by,' said Seb, wondering if Harford was being cynical or just musing, 'I came to see you about something else. I wondered if you knew who attended Captain Brewer the morning he died? I mean, I know he was dead, but a surgeon must surely have inspected the wounds? Any ideas?'

'As it happens, I know exactly who it was, because at the time we were discussing the best way to preserve the sheen on the iridescent shells of certain beetles. It was Reynolds. Do you know him?'

'Not personally, no.'

'Well, you'll find him in that tent over there – that's the camp temporary hospital, though I understand they're moving the more serious cases to the farmhouse of that Irishman. The name escapes me . . .'

'Rorke?'

'Yep, that's the chappie. That's where they're taking 'em.'

'Thanks. And I wouldn't worry about the incident on the field today. It'll all be forgotten by tomorrow.'

'I expect you're right,' Harford said. 'There's far more important things on people's minds than me and my insects.'

Seb then walked towards the large tent and fell in behind two medical orderlies who were carrying a stretcher case to the same destination. On the stretcher was one of the NNC blacks, whose left arm hung as loosely as a piece of thick rope, fingers trailing the rough rocky ground. Seb bent and picked up the arm, placing it in the stretcher with its owner. The man had winced at the pain then looked up with bleak eyes and managed a 'Thank you, sir.' The orderlies had either not noticed or were too busy to care about the raw knuckles of a limb that would soon be taken off. The arm had felt as if it was broken in several places.

Seb followed the stretcher into the tent and blinked in the strong light from several lamps. There were three doctors in the tent. One Seb recognized as Surgeon-Major Shepherd, who commanded the Army Medical Department staff attached to the Central Column. The other two, at work on a patient, he did not know. The smell in the tent seemed to consist of a mixture of chemicals and blood.

'Surgeon Reynolds?' queried Seb.

There was a curt 'Yes?' which preceded the thump of a large

thick leg hitting the floor. One of the surgeons stepped away as it threatened to roll on to his feet. He wiped the edge of a saw on his apron, before looking up. 'What is it?'

Seb's eyes were automatically drawn to the strapped patient stretched out on the operating table. His stomach heaved and flip-flopped. The raw end of a sawn leg glistened at him. He could see the severed white thigh bone and bits that looked like red and white worms squirming about in the bloody mess. Then the other surgeon moved in quickly to cauterize the wound with a red-hot metal plate. The stump sizzled, filling the air with the nauseous fumes of burning flesh. On the table, the owner of the leg groaned loudly, but Seb could see he was happily still in the thrall of chloroform, though the shock had clearly reached some alert corner of his brain.

'Come on, man, what do you want?' asked Reynolds, irritably. 'Can't you see I'm busy?'

Surgeon-Major Shepherd, from another corner of the tent, said, 'Leave my surgeons alone, laddie, unless ye've an important message to impart.'

'No, sorry, sir, no message. I'll call back later.'

Seb almost collided with another party coming into the tent with a large leather bucket, presumably to collect the severed limb. He felt sick. He had seen such things before, but not at close range. He wondered how the surgeons held on to their stomachs. He failed to hold on to his and vomited all over his boots. Afterwards he went for a wash and felt a little better.

He decided to leave Reynolds to his human carpentry, making a mental note to visit the man *before* a battle, rather than after one.

The following morning Seb woke with a raging headache. He stared at the ceiling of the tent, watching a spider knit a web between a pole and a hanging strip of canvas. Finally he managed to summon the energy to lift himself up and stumble outside into the sunlight. There he found Sam cutting strips of beef from a fresh joint. Sam looked up as Seb stood there swaying in front of his tent.

'*Biltong*,' said Sam, by way of explanation for his industry. 'We can lay it on the cart, sir, to dry. It will taste very good.'

'Where's Evans?' Seb asked, huskily.

'He is puttin' our tent on the cart. We take yours after.' Sam stood up from his task. 'You look very pale, sir. Are you sick?'

'Yes – but Evans will get me some powders from the surgeon.'
Seb turned to go back in his tent.

Sam called, 'I send him to you, sir.'

Seb remembered lying down again, falling into a painful, troubled doze, then suddenly the world seemed to explode in his head.

'SIR, SAM SAY'S YOU'RE SICK?'

'Evans,' murmured Seb, miserably, 'you're shouting fit to wake
the dead. Please, please talk in a whisper.'

Evans' lips moved but no sound came out.

Seb groaned.

Sam's head then appeared, popping up behind the corporal.

'What kind of sick is it, sir?' His voice was gentle and smooth,
like warm water trickling over pebbles. 'It is most certain that Sam
can help.'

'Head. A headache.'

Sam took Evans and whirled him round, propelling him from
the tent. Then turning back to the officer, he nodded. 'I find you
good cure from an old woman.'

Seb was up on his elbows. 'Sam, I don't want any witchcraft . . .'

'No, sir. No magic. Proper medicine.'

'And where are you going to find an old woman out here?'

'No, no, sir. I have already spoke with the old woman, who is
my dear grandmother, sir. When I was a small boy she gave me
medicines. I will find the plant and bring it to you. Have no
worries, sir, Sam will make your head better very swiftly.'

Sam left and Seb heard him arguing with Evans, who was doing
a lot of indignant snorting. A little while later a sergeant of the
24th came by and poked his head under the flap.

'Wakey, wakey, in there! Striking camp. This tent needs to come
down and go on a wagon.'

'Sergeant,' moaned Seb, 'I am a commissioned officer.'

'Oh, sorry, sir,' came the bright reply as the man came to attention, saluted, and then re-poked his head inside the dimness, 'din't
know it was an officer. Still and all, sir, got to get this lot down.
Do you have your man, sir? Or shall I send someone?'

'Just go away for a while. It'll be dealt with shortly.'

Indeed, Sam was back within a few more minutes. He came
into the tent with a steaming mug.

'Tea, sir.'

'Well, that's something,' said Seb, trying to sit up without his head falling off. 'Thank you, Sam.' He sipped at the hot liquid, then swallowed it in gulps as it became cooler. 'Ah, that tastes good. Now, Sam, are you sure about this plant you want to give me. There are plants with poisonous roots and leaves out there, you know. I don't want to break out in huge purple blotches and die clutching my stomach in agony. You are sure about your grandmother's remedy?'

'I am very, very sure about *umakhulu*'s remedy, sir. She is an *amagqirha*, sir, a very good healer-woman. Her powders would make the headache vanish like morning mist from the banks of the river. But unfortunately I cannot find the plant my grandmother showed me, it is so very dry in this part with just rocks and dust and no vegetables, so I ask one of Mr Colonel Durnford's soldiers, who give me the brown leaves and say it is a mighty good cure for the headache.'

'Soldiers? You mean, one of the NNC?'

'Yes, sir, a respectable black soldier.'

'Well, I'm not taking it. How do I know what it is? No, no, I'd rather keep my headache than risk it.'

Sam swayed on his feet. 'Sir, you already drink it – the medicine is in the tea.'

Seb stared into the mug. He had drunk half the contents. He fell back on his hard pillow, fashioned from a rolled-up coatee, and prepared himself for death. Certainly his head was now about to come apart at the seams. He lay there for a few minutes. Lights began flashing inside his brain. They were blinding bits of silver that zipped like bullets across the inner darkness. Streams of them. Then a line of bright colours: blue, purple, red. Seb wondered if this was his skull breaking up and the outside world entering through the gaps. Finally the lights and colours left him and his mind faded into a gentle greyness. It seemed he was in a place of emptiness, a void of vast proportions. Surely this was death?

Seb woke with a start, his head clear as a mountain stream.

'What?' he cried, sitting up. 'Where am I?'

'Here, sir,' said Sam. 'Officer Evans,' he turned to show Evans his mouth, 'the master is awake.'

'Thank the Lord for that,' came the corporal's voice, a deep well of urgency in his tone, 'we'll get caught out here, in the open, and be gutted like mackerel if we're not quick. Sir, we've bin left behind, like, so we need to crack on and catch up with the column. I seen some blacks up on the slope just a mile away. If they're Zulus, we'll catch it.'

'Bantu,' murmured Sam. 'Boys with cows.'

Seb rose feeling amazingly clear-headed and buoyant. He pulled on his own boots, dressed and then helped his two men get down the tent.

'They left us a donkey cart,' Evans shouted. 'Just went off and told me to look after you.'

'How long have they been gone?' asked Seb. He looked up at the sun. 'What time is it?'

'Noon,' said Sam. 'But we catch up very quick.'

They struck camp and were soon on the trail, following the main column, whose dust cloud they could see in the distance. The column was of course moving very, very slowly. There were over three hundred wagons and carts being hauled along by one and a half thousand oxen, any one of which might break a wheel or get stuck in mud or earthen cracks at any one time, holding up others. This was apart from the six 7-pounder field guns that trundled along. Nearly five thousand men on the march, along with all their supplies, ammunition and equipment, do not travel like a Zulu impi. Such a monster moves like a wounded dinosaur, dragging itself inch by inch over unhelpful rough ground.

Seb had been subject to fierce headaches ever since he had been about six years of age. 'That cure was miraculous,' he chirped to Sam. 'You must let me know what it was.'

'I will ask the soldier, sir.'

'Will you recognize him again?'

'Sir, I know my own people.'

This was a jibe at the inability of many white officers and indeed the soldiers themselves to tell black people apart. Seb was stung but let it pass. After all, Sam Weary had saved his life today.

'What was that word you used for a witch doctor? Umakhulu?'

'Umakhulu means grandmother, sir. It is isiXhosa language. Sam thinks you mean the word amagqirha, also isiXhosa. An amagqirha is an amaXhosa person who heals. Sam thinks that *witch doctor* is a silly thing to say.'

'Humm, you do, do you? Silly?' Seb let that pass too, simply because he was interested in the subject. 'So, is an amagqirha like your grandmamma born, or is she made?'

'Made, sir. It take five years.'

'Five years' training?' Seb was thinking of the doctors back in Britain, who hardly got any training at all, except in pulling teeth and setting broken bones. 'I suppose that's enough. You get the name of that plant, Sam, and I'll give you a golden coin.'

Sam grinned, broadly.

Evans, sitting on the ox-cart, said huffily, 'When do I get a golden coin?'

'When daffodils and leeks cure headaches, Corporal,' said Seb, and because the NCO had not turned round, Sam translated this as best he could with the sign language he was teaching Evans.

'Bugger off,' growled the corporal. 'It's not fair. My grandmother could cure headaches with a spider's web. Don't that count?'

Seb turned round and laughed. 'It only counts when it works, Corporal. Now come on, you two, let's catch up with that column.'

They caught up with Lord Chelmsford's column and became part of it again. The men on the march were jittery. At any moment they expected an attack from a main force of the Zulu army. Officers hoped for it, other ranks were less enthusiastic but as ever, they were prepared to take their obligations as they came to them. This devotion to duty earned them a shilling a day, though most of that shilling was taken away from them in stoppages, often leaving them little more than a penny. At home, factory workers earned a similar wage and farm workers somewhat less, but they did not have to risk losing their lives. Nor did workers at home get most of their pay taken from them in deductions.

So there they were, the rank and file, looking through narrowed eyes at the red and yellow ochre landscape around them, watching intently for signs of the enemy, conscious that they were about to die for a single copper coin, which out here in the wilderness had actually no value at all, unless you were fond of playing cards for money.

That evening Seb studied Peter's notes under a lamplight that was being attacked by a swarm of many different kinds of insect.

'Lieutenant Henry Wycliffe,' murmured Seb to himself. 'Perhaps I'd better have a word with him myself.'

Seb knew Wycliffe. Or rather knew of him. Everyone had heard of Mad Henry, as he was known to his comrades. Henry Wycliffe was actually a baron, a peer of the realm who had gambled away the estates of his ancestors and escaped to the army abroad leaving many creditors still without settled bills. Mad Henry was a bank-rupt, a lost cause, an officer every army should be without. Some said he was a great deal of fun, but most thought him utterly disruptive.

Seb had heard stories of Mad Henry's eccentric escapades. When the twenty-four-year-old officer was at his home in Stonham, Suffolk, he would dress up as a railway guard, wander down to the local station and there spend the day blowing a whistle and waving a flag, much to the amusement of local passengers and the annoyance of officials. Also, it was said that the passageways of his ancestral home were pitted with bullet holes where he had emptied the chamber of a pistol at random, sometimes in the middle of the night, scaring the living daylights out of his servants. He rode horses recklessly, at breakneck speed, forcing them over impossible jumps. He had been wounded seven times in various duels, though had fortunately killed no one himself. He often walked naked in the moonlight, telling others the beams were cleansing his soul. He interrupted church services, taking over the pulpit from the vicar and threatening the congregation with everlasting damnation. He drank too much, sang too much, swore too much, and had lived far too long considering the state of his mind.

Mad Henry had been a friend of Captain Brewer.

Seb found him playing cards with some artillery officers.

'Lieutenant Wycliffe? I wonder if I could have a word?'

'Who the hell are you, sir?' said Mad Henry over his shoulder as he sorted his hand. 'Do I know you, or what?'

'Ensign Early. I'm the provost-marshal. I need to talk to you about Captain Brewer.'

'Do you now? Poor old Alan, eh? Blew his brains out. Daft as a Suffolk hare. What did he want to do that for, eh?'

Mad Henry began to play his cards now, ignoring Seb for the moment. The lunatic baron was dressed in a red velvet smoking jacket and a fez with a long silk tassel and he was smoking the same sort of long-curved stemmed chibouque pipe that Seb's Uncle Jack had favoured all his life. Once the hand was finished, Mad Henry gave Seb his full attention, taking him by the arm to stand by a gun carriage out of earshot of the other players. Seb found the man's eyes very disturbing. They were a very washed-out blue in which Seb's own gaze quickly became a wandering soul.

'So,' said Mad Henry, 'poor old Alan.'

'He did not *blow his brains out*, Lieutenant . . .'

'Call me Mad Henry, everyone does.'

Seb was a little shocked. 'I can't do that – this is an official enquiry.'

'Henry, then. Just Henry, though it's not as colourful as *Mad* Henry, which I adore. I can't bear formality, you see. If you call me *lieutenant* once more, I shall hum the "Ashokan Farewell" until you desist in the practice. It's a heartbreaking lament. You won't be able to stop weeping for a week after hearing it. I cried for a whole month the first time I heard it. Admittedly I was only ten at the time.'

'Well, Henry, then . . .'

'What about you? What do I call you?'

'Oh . . .' Seb was about to say *Sebastian*, when he realized he would get more out of this character if he became more colourful himself. 'My friends call me South-East.'

'South-East?'

'My initials are S.E. – Sebastian Early.'

'Ah, I like that. Yes, the points of the compass, eh? What a lark. You can call me North-West.'

'Look, Henry, you already have a nickname. You don't need another one, it'd make you top-heavy. Listen, this is a serious business. Now, you're aware that your friend Alan Brewer had two wounds to his chest? He did not, as you believe, blow his brains out. What I wanted to ask you, was, is it likely that he committed suicide? You were one of his closest friends. Was his state of mind fragile?'

'Alan?' Henry sucked on an empty pipe for a moment. 'No. Of course, anyone can blow out their brains for fun. You know, spinning the chamber on the revolver with one round in there somewhere. Done it myself. Not blown my brains out, of course. Spun the chamber. Clicked the trigger. Do it for amusement when I'm bored. But Alan? No. He got his fun in other ways.'

Seb did not bother to correct the idea that it was Brewer's head which had received the wounds. 'What sort of fun? Chasing girls? Other men's wives?'

'How dare you impugn a respectable officer's character, sir,' cried Henry, pretending to fence with the long-stemmed pipe. 'Have at ye!'

'Henry, did he like the girls?'

'Of course he did. Don't we all? He wasn't after little drummer boys, if that's what you're thinking. Full-breasted maidens with milky thighs, or even dark ones with dusky thighs, but not the wives of other men. No, no. Alan's fun was the genie in the bottle. He liked his gin, his rum, his whisky and his porter. When he was in his cups he was the life and soul, South-East, he was indeed. Known him to render a wonderful "Battle Hymn of the Republic" with a blade of grass between his thumbs. Very musical that way. Miss him a lot.'

'He drank a great deal? Enough to make him morose?'

'Alan? Never maudlin. Always happy when unsober.'

Seb took these answers as sincere, since he could see no reason why Henry should lie. Had he been fervently maintaining that his friend had committed suicide, it would be a different matter.

'One last question. Do you know of anyone who might have wanted Captain Brewer dead? Any strong enemies?'

'Nary a one.'

'Well, I'm no further along in my investigations,' Seb admitted, 'but at least you've confirmed that the victim had no reason to take his own life.'

'Well, now that's over,' Mad Henry said, 'why don't we go hunting? I've a notion to stick something. There's few pigs out there, but we might find a warthog or two?'

'It's night-time,' Seb pointed out.

'Oh, well, if you're going to quibble about the hour, then stay behind,' said Henry, cheerfully.

'But what I mean to say is, it's dark.'

'The devil it is! Tomorrow, then? At dawn?'

'I expect we'll be striking camp to be on the march.'

'God, is there no jollity to be had around this place?' cried Mad Henry. 'I've a mind to creep up on the sentries, just to see if they're awake. A bit of boot polish and you won't be able to tell me from a Zulu warrior. Coming?'

Seb left the crazy officer and made his way back to his tent. A short time afterwards there were shots on the perimeter of the camp. The picquets later reported that they had seen the moonlight shining on the faces of Zulus in the bush. Seb went looking for Mad Henry again. He could not believe the man had actually carried out his plan to surprise the guards. Henry was found back at the card table with his fellow officers, seemingly oblivious of the fact that his face was covered in black boot polish.

'Hello, South-East, old chap!' Mad Henry cried, waving his cards. 'Fancy a hand?'

Seb left him with his grinning friends, who included Ensigns Carpenter and Swales, who to his embarrassment kept winking at Seb in full view of Mad Henry.

Nine

The following late afternoon a sergeant-major brought three prisoners to Seb's tent. Two were blacks, one was white. The blacks came from the Natal Native Pioneer Corps and the white man from the auxiliaries. The three were chained to the wheel of a wagon and left there in Seb's charge. They were all due to be flogged the next morning in front of the rest of the troops.

'So,' Seb asked, as he got Corporal Evans to serve each of the three a plate of beef stew, 'what have we done to deserve this?'

'Sir,' said the white soldier, 'I object to be chained between two Kaffirs. Put me at one end. In fact, put me right away from them, on one of the other wheels, if you please.'

The man had the underpinnings of an accent foreign to Seb.

'Are you French?'

'Half-Belgique,' came the reply. The man was tall, lean and had long lank hair. 'I was born in Bruges, but my father was a Scot.'

'You'll stay where you are. You're a criminal awaiting punishment, just like those two. What did you do?'

'I didn't kill anyone.'

'I guessed that, otherwise you'd be waiting for a firing squad, not for a flogging.'

'Insubordination.'

'To an officer?'

'Yes, I told him to stick his head up a cow's arse.'

Seb had a job refraining from laughing at the mental picture this produced. However, the crime was quite a serious one, due to the fact that they were at war. Also punishments were doubled while on active service. Probably the only punishment that remained as it was, was execution. You could not kill a man twice.

'What about you two?' he asked the pioneers. 'Who's your officer i/c?'

'Captain Allen, sir. We are from Number 3 Company,' answered one of the two men.

'Sir,' said the other, 'we stole a bottle of rum.'

'Did you get to drink it all before they caught you?'

Both men grinned. 'Yes, sir, every drop.'

'Well, I hope it was worth it. You're all down for twenty-five lashes tomorrow.'

The faces of the blacks dropped and they stared at the ground. It was doubtful they were scared, since their lives were often on the edge of violence. Something like this was ordinary. It was more likely they were feeling ashamed at the thought of being humiliated in front of their friends and fighting companions.

'I can do twenty-five standing on my head,' said the Belgique, with a sneer on his face. 'They would give you fifty lashes in the navy every morning before breakfast, just to start off the day.'

Seb could see the soldier was given to hyperboles. 'You're a navy man?'

'Was before this. Seven years.'

'You should have learned to keep your mouth shut.'

'Nah. If someone's a pig, I tell 'em.'

Seb was going to leave it at that, but his curiosity got the better of him. He asked, 'What did the officer do to deserve the insult?'

'Called that young boy Craster a coward. The boy was no coward. It's a wonder he stayed as long as he did, before running.'

'Craster?' Seb's mind was suddenly alight. 'You mean the deserter, Private Craster? The soldier who crossed into Zululand?'

'That's him. He's a good type, that boy, made to go wrong by bloody bad officers. Not that there's any other kind.'

'Watch your mouth, soldier. I can add as much as I like to those twenty-five, if I have further grounds.'

The man grinned. 'Sorry, sir. Didn't mean to be insolent to you personally. Should have said present company excepted.'

'Yes, you should have done that,' shouted Evans, collecting the tin plates to go off and wash them. 'There's good and bad.'

When he had gone, the white prisoner said, 'What's with him?'

'You mean the yelling?' said Seb. 'He's deaf. Artillery.'

'Oh.'

Seb reopened the previous subject. 'Listen, it was my understanding that Craster tried to commit suicide with a bayonet and blamed it on his fellow soldiers. That act, and then running away to Zululand, gave the impression the young man was unbalanced in some way. Too much sun, or some tropical disease which hadn't yet shown itself. I know blackwater fever can—'

'Listen, I don't know why he did that stuff with the bayonet.

Maybe to draw attention to himself? Maybe he wanted to be sent home? Who knows? I would say yes to your conclusions. The boy did become unbalanced. Anyone who'd been through what he'd had to put up with would've become deranged. The way he was treated made me sick. I was on sentry duty with him one night when that fuckpig officer of his came to us and made him stand on one leg for two hours. Craster told me all about the bastard – as much as he dared.'

'Which was?'

'He was victimized. The officer hounded him from morning till night, inventing the most god-awful punishments and duties for him. Humiliated him in front of the other soldiers, ordering him to piss into his own boots, making him fill a bucket with buffalo turds with his bare hands, making him stand to attention naked out by the flagpole all night. Christ man, I would have left camp months ago. Not that boy. He stuck it. Then just before we came over here, something snapped.'

Seb knew that there were rogue officers who would abuse their power, which was considerable. But he had never been able to understand this kind of bullying. There was nothing to gain by it, except the enmity of the troops. Probably even the NCOs would despise such an officer and they themselves were not above picking on inept soldiers. No one likes a private who does not pull his weight, but usually such men were absorbed into the system by giving them tasks suited to their strengths and avoiding their failings. The sort of punishments young Craster had been given were enough to disgust the most indifferent officer.

'You must have seen this sort of thing in the navy,' suggested Seb. 'How does it match up?'

'Oh, we had officers that would turn your stomach, and this one was as bad as any I've seen.'

'It was all hearsay, though – you never actually saw it happen. It all came from the mouth of Craster himself.'

'We were billeted next to his company. I saw it, I tell you.'

Seb nodded. 'Do you know the name of the officer? I might find some way of bringing charges.' Seb was pragmatist enough to know this probably would not happen, but he was scandalized by the treatment this young man seemed to have received from one of his own class. He added, more for his own benefit than his listener's, 'I am after all the Provost-Marshal.'

The auxiliary laughed. 'Not unless you go to Hell to do it. He's the bastard that topped himself.'

Seb was stunned for a moment. 'You – you mean Captain Brewer?'

'That's the one. I hope he burns. I hope he's roasting down there.'

Seb was both elated and appalled. He now had a motive for the killing of one Captain Alan Brewer, which gave him hope that he might solve what he believed to be a murder. But he was confounded by the troubling circumstances surrounding it. A man had been bullied beyond reason and had tried to kill or disfigure himself. Then that same man had run away, not to safety, but into the arms of the enemy. It was difficult to know what he would be charged with if he ever came back, since he was probably a murderer, undoubtedly a deserter, and would without question be accused of being a traitor. A sixteen-year-old man-boy, whose time in the army seemed to have been nothing but hell on earth, for it was a difficult enough life without being victimized.

Still and all, if he had killed another man in cold blood, he was a murderer, however driven to the act. And if he was to be tried for anything, Seb wanted it to be for that particular deed. He was going to hang or be shot anyway, so it might as well be for murder.

'I've given you something, haven't I, sir?' said the man chained to the wagon wheel, studying the ensign's expression closely. 'I can see by your eyes, I've given you something. Perhaps you could return the favour?'

'I can't stop the flogging, if that's your request.'

'No, no – I want a picture, for my mother, before I get disgraced.'

'You've already been disgraced – you're chained to a wheel with two other felons.'

'Yes, but the sentence hasn't yet been carried out. I'm still a man without an army blemish on my soul. You can't count the navy ones. They flog you for nothing in the navy, the fucking seacows.'

Seb could very easily have countered this fanciful argument, but instead said, 'You mean blemishes on your back. You want me to draw or paint you, then?'

'No, no – a photograph. Can you do that, sir?'

Seb said, 'Ah. That. I know Mr Spense charges quite a lot. His plates and chemicals are expensive items of equipment . . .'

The man's face creased into a smile.

'I've no money at this time. I was docked a month's pay as part of my sentence. You could pay for it, sir? Eh? Look, I'm going to be whipped tomorrow, by some bastard who probably enjoys his work. I'll be full of gall afterwards. I know my bitter side and it'll come out on my face. I don't want to wait until I look like some tyrant who's swallowed a lemon whole, glaring out at my poor mother fit to frighten her to death. My face is clear at the moment. You could do that for me, eh, sir? I'll pay you back sometime, I promise you that.'

Seb sighed. The man had given him something, it was true. What he could do with it was another thing, but certainly he could claim he was more knowledgeable than before.

'All right. I'll see if Mr Spense is available. I can't promise anything. He's a busy man.'

'Thank you, sir. The Good Lord bless you and keep you. I never liked policemen. I always considered them to be bloody mongrel curs in uniform. But you seem to be all right.'

'Well, that's a great comfort to me, soldier. Evans?'

Corporal Evans naturally failed to appear since he was unable to hear the call.

'Sam?' cried Seb, realizing the problem.

'Yes, sir?'

'Ask Corporal Evans to watch the prisoners, while I go and find someone.'

'Yes, sir.'

Seb began a walk through the hundreds of tents. All around him was the clash and clatter of troops at their tasks. Five thousand soldiers in one spot make a lot of noise. Kitchen utensils are struck against pans. Bridle bits and stirrups clank. Weapons are stripped and put back together again. Tent pegs are hammered into the earth. Ammunition is unpacked and repacked. Cattle are moaning and stamping their feet. Horses are snorting and whinnying. Dogs are barking. Officers are calling to NCOs, NCOs are shouting at soldiers, soldiers are chattering to other soldiers. Seb was thinking that they could hear this in the British parliament, let alone in the Zulu camps throughout the Drakensberg mountains.

He eventually found Jack Spense with a set piece of some two dozen men facing him, waiting in rigid suspense.

'Hold it! Hold it! *Now!*'

There was a bright flash and an acrid smell.

The tableau melted away and relaxed into a loose, animated, grinning group of soldiers. They were dressed all in black, from their boots to their pill-box caps. Seb had been around long enough to know this was the Buffalo Border Guard. They came from the area around a small South African hamlet named after the Scottish town of Dundee and this was their complete regiment. Now their place in history was assured, with a photograph proving their presence in the war against the Zulus.

'Thank you, Lieutenant Smith,' Jack said to the officer commanding. 'Got that one perfectly, I believe.'

'Jack,' Seb said, coming to the photographer's elbow. 'Still taking photos?'

Jack sighed. 'In the last few months I've photographed the Natal Hussars, the Isipingo Mounted Rifles, the Newcastle Mounted Rifles, the Natal Carabineers, Baker's Horse, Raaff's Horse, the Transvaal Rangers, Weatherley's Border Horse, Lonsdale's Horse and the Frontier Light Horse, and I'm only halfway through the regiments of the irregulars and auxiliaries, if that. They all want a picture to send back to mum. Some of these regiments have less than eight men in them. Would you want to serve in a battalion where every member could be named after the days in the week with no repeats? Where do they all come from?'

Seb laughed. 'When you get a war, the volunteers come out of the woodwork – at least in the beginning.'

'And I suppose you want one for your mum?' said Jack.

'Not me, a prisoner, back at my tent.'

'A prisoner? Is he due to be executed?'

'Just flogged, but he's been of assistance to me. I'll pay you for the service.'

'All right, but it's not the money. I just think it's a shame he's not going to hang at dawn. I'm particularly good at the macabre. If you set the shadows right on the faces of condemned men, you can make them look haunted by guilt and ready to go to their maker.'

'You have a gruesome imagination, Jack.'

'Nothing to do with imagination – art of the trade, old chum.'

In the event, the Belgique-Scot insisted on having the two other prisoners in the picture with him, he in the middle and his arms around each of their shoulders. This from a man who just a short while before had protested at being chained to the same wheel as black men. Seb had ceased to be astonished by the vagaries of men as he watched the three subjects grinning into the camera lens as if they had been chums the whole of their lives and never want to be separated for a moment. After the photograph they were chained back on the wagon wheel and they discussed the experience for the next two hours. The blacks were surprised it had not hurt in the least and the white man was full of praise for the fact that they had all stood still for long enough. All in all, it was probably worth the flogging they were going to get.

'I'll bring you the photograph in the morning,' Jack told Seb, 'and you can do what you like with it. Don't worry about paying me. I'll be able to sell that one as "Doomed Prisoners Awaiting Just But Terrible Punishment" to any newspaper you like to mention. The mix of skin colours will make it a collectors' item, you can be sure.'

Ten

Waking the following morning, Seb was aware that he had not been watching the scout, Pieter Zeldenthuis, as closely as he had been ordered to do. In fact he had completely lost contact with the Boer over the past few days. He set out to find him only to discover that Pieter was out on patrol with the Newcastle Mounted Rifles. It was while he was awaiting his return that Sam Weary came to him and breathlessly explained that there had been a murder.

'You must go and report to Major Casey,' cried Sam, 'straight away, he said.'

Seb did not know of a Major Casey, but through enquiries eventually found his tent.

'Ah, the policeman,' said the elderly major, rising from a canvas-topped stool. 'Follow me, young 'un.'

Seb was led to an area where the NNC were camped, most of them out in the open, and shown a body on the ground. It appeared that the man had been sleeping in that exact spot and position when someone unknown had hammered his face to a pulp with a blunt instrument, possibly a rock, but more like the butt of a rifle. The attack had been so vicious the skull was almost flattened against the ground. Nothing could be made of the features of the man and his hair and headdress were mashed into one single small mat. His shield and spear were still lying by his side. There was a flaccid water skin which had been placed on his stomach, either by himself or by the man who killed him.

The fatal wound was revolting and Seb's stomach turned over as he gingerly inspected the body. Already the mashed head was black with buzzing flies, the bane of all things living in the bush. The stump of the neck was also alive with them. The insects flowed in continuous wave-like movements over the red flesh and white bone, giving the flattened skull animation. It was almost as if the warrior were struggling to come back to life. At any second Seb expected the head to reinflate and the man to sit up and complain about his lot.

There was something redder than dried blood in amongst the mess and the flies. Seb took a pencil out of his pocket and stirred the spilt stew, fishing out the object. It was a red headband. Seb, aware that he was being watched, studied this item closely. He actually did not know what he was looking at, but he pretended it was significant, just to give himself time for his stomach to settle and to think properly.

'Well then,' said Seb, cautiously, surrounded as he was by NNC warriors with enquiring faces, 'this man is certainly dead.'

Major Casey snorted. 'A remarkable diagnosis.'

'Sorry, sir, but this is a bit of a shock, having this thrust on me out of the blue,' said Seb. 'I'm just voicing my thoughts. No one knows who's done this thing, I suppose,' he added, looking around the faces of the man's regiment. 'Have these men any ideas?'

Suddenly, Sam was at his elbow, speaking a Bantu language, but receiving shakes of many heads.

'No, sir,' said Sam. 'No one.'

Seb turned to the major and asked, 'Is this anything to do with me, sir? I mean, I don't have much to do with the native contingent.'

The major snorted again. 'Just because the man's black doesn't let you off the hook, young man. You're the Provost-Marshal and they're members of the army you're supposed to be policing. We don't want a mass exodus of auxiliary troops and irregulars simply because you can't see your way to solving the murder of someone different. These savages are easily spooked. They're superstitious to their back teeth. You find a culprit before they start believing in angry elephant-men from the spirit world, or whatever it is their minds conjure up for them.'

'Well, I didn't quite mean it that way,' Seb argued, knowing he had meant it exactly that way. 'I mean, couldn't it have been a Zulu? You know, sneaked in at night, did the deed, then sneaked back out again?'

'That's for you to find out, ain't it?'

'I suppose so.'

'No suppose about it, Ensign. Get on with it. Report to me tomorrow morning.'

He left Seb with the body and the man's company.

Seb, still with a queasy feeling in his gut, bent down and undid the belt holding the ammunition pouch. The soldier had an Enfield rifle in the grip of his right hand. Seb began to prise the man's

fingers from the stock, one by one. The fingers were as rigid and
cold as iron. It was as if the man wanted to take his weapon with
him to the Otherworld, in order to protect himself against whatever monsters lurked in wait there. Finally the Enfield was released.
Seb gave it to Evans and told him to take it to one of the white
NNC officers.

'Was this man an officer, or an NCO?' Seb asked, knowing that
privates in the native auxiliary regiments seldom carried firearms.

Sam was quick to yell out the question to the troops and receive
a reply from a dozen mouths.

'Corporal, sir,' said Sam. 'He'd just been promoted.'

'Ah.' Seb nodded. 'That might be significant.'

He was thinking that the man might have started persecuting
one or more of his company, now that he had rank. In the way
it seemed that Craster had been persecuted by his officer. Seb
decided to set up an enquiry room. He was not going to conduct
his business out here in the sun and with the flies for fellowship.
It would have to be his tent of course and it needed to look cold,
forbidding and very official in order to intimidate those he was
going to question.

There were no more clues to be got from the dead man's body
so he ordered it taken away and buried.

'. . . or whatever the rites are with this man's tribe.'

Corporal Evans returned and helped Seb set up the tent, with
the flap pulled back wide to open up the entrance. Seb borrowed
Major Casey's canvas-topped stool and put a packing crate
covered with a union flag in front of it to use as a table. It was
awkward for his knees against the box side, but was a shortish man
and could put up with the cramped position for quite a long time.
He then gathered some sheets of paper on the flag and placed
them under a paperweight consisting of a shell from a 7-pounder
gun. He added to this a set of coloured crayons, a *chop* from Hong
Kong (borrowed from a fellow officer) which looked like an official franking stamp along with its black ink pad, a frayed black
Bible with an embossed golden cross on the front (always intim-
idating, even to non-Christians), and a pair of spectacles in an open
velvet-lined case with the sun glinting on the lenses and metal
frames.

Next, he got into his dress uniform, and presented a very
imposing figure, especially with the boots polished to a gleaming

perfection by Sam Weary. He was just about to button the top of his tunic when, Mauser rifle in hand, Pieter Zeldenthuis appeared looking dusty and parched.

'Very impressive,' said Pieter, drily. 'You court-martialling some poor loskop?'

'Loskop?' enquired Seb, thinking the Boer was talking about some tribe or other.

'Loose head,' explained Pieter. 'Someone with space between their ears.'

'Oh, no. This is a court of enquiry. We've had another murder. One of the NNC.'

Pieter laughed. 'You have to be joking. You'll never get to the bottom of that, lightey. Are you dof, or what? They kill each other for the most obscure reasons. What did you want me for, anyway? They said you were looking for me.'

'Oh,' Seb suddenly felt uncomfortable. 'No real reason. Just a social chat.'

Pieter grinned. 'You wanted to see me, so you could say to the general, "I've been watching the beggar closely, sir – I'm sure he'll make his move soon."'

'No – well, yes, I suppose so, in a way. After all, I've been given an order and you never seem to be around. A fine set-down I'll get when I tell Lord Chelmsford that I haven't seen you in days.'

'Tell him you've been busy playing policeman.' Pieter nodded at the paraphernalia on Seb's makeshift desk. 'You think that will impress the blacks, all that stuff there?'

'I'm hoping so.'

'Ag, you could be right. Anyway, I'm going to the water wagon. My bottles are empty and I need to slake my thirst. That dust out there's thick enough to clog a man's windpipe. And a man can get real dwaal in the wilderness if he's not careful. I like open spaces but there's enough space out there to put some stars between. You get into this trance if you don't keep your mind sharp and clear. Come for a gin, later.'

'Yes, thanks,' said Seb. 'I will – when I get to the bottom of all this.'

'*If* you get to the bottom.' Pieter grinned and ambled off towards one of the water wagons.

Seb turned to Sam and Evans. 'Right, I'm ready. How do I look?'

'Magnificent, sir,' said Sam. 'Such as like Iskander the Great.'

'He means Alexander,' yelled Evans. 'I already had that out with him once.'

The first soldier of the NNC stood in front of Seb's splendid courtroom and fidgeted with his hair. Clearly he was unsettled now that he no longer had his comrades around him, and Seb's staging was having an effect on his confidence. Seb found out very quickly that he had a good command of English.

'So,' said Seb, severely, one hand on his sword hilt, staring directly into the soldier's eyes, 'are you a Christian?'

The man's eyes rolled in fright. 'Methodist, sah.'

'Ah, then I expect your minister told you that if you lie, especially to an official court like this one, you will of course go directly to Hell when you die – to fire and brimstone and all the Devil can conjure up in the way of eternal tortures. Horrible, ugly punishments, some we can't even imagine. Did he tell you that? That you will roast on a spit over the fires of the Underworld? I expect he did, for it's true. It's a terrible fate. Sometimes – sometimes, in my nightmares I believe I can smell the stink of roasting flesh . . .'

'Sah?' whispered the NNC soldier, with a look of horror on his face. 'I too.'

'Good,' replied Seb, in his officer's voice, 'so we are clear with one another. If you lie to me, the Lord will take revenge on you and punish you forever.'

'Oh, sir,' said Sam, shaking his head as if at a two-year-old, 'you are not the Lord's avenging angel.'

'Quiet, Sam,' hissed Seb. 'I'm doing something here.'

'Yes, but, sir, if you use such language, you too will go to . . .'

'Quiet, Sam.'

'Yes, sir.'

'Now,' said Seb, taking a swallow of water from his cup, 'what is your name?'

The man told him and Seb, after consulting with Sam Weary about the actual pronunciation, wrote an approximation of the name slowly and carefully on one of the sheets of paper before him in red crayon.

'There,' he said, stamping the piece of paper with the Chinese *chop*, 'we have your name, rank and your – your whereabouts.' Seb leaned forward, peering intently into the man's eyes, 'Now, put your hand on that Bible and tell me, honestly and truthfully, do you know the name of the killer of that poor corporal we found dead this morning?'

The soldier, his staring eyes a brilliant white in their sockets, placed a trembling hand on the Bible that Evans held out for him.

'Sah – yes, sah – I know who kill this man.'

Seb was elated, but he did not show it in his expression.

'And the name of the killer – or killers?'

The soldier murmured a word.

Seb sat back, losing all his reserve, completely astonished.

'Say that again.'

'It was me, sah. I give you my name, sah. I kill this corporal.'

'Evans,' said Seb faintly, turning to his corporal, 'get some men to take this soldier into custody.'

Seb took a long drink while the condemned soldier waited patiently for the escort to arrive. He was feeling both elated and lucky. The first man! The very first man. How fortunate was that for a new policeman? Why, he had solved the crime within an hour. Major Casey would surely be impressed at that? This policing business was easy, was it not? Nothing could have been simpler. Just get a few articles and objects together, put on your best uniform, sit and look as stern as possible, and threaten the witness with eternal damnation. All quite legitimate and above board, surely? Well, there it was, case solved, time to go for a drink with Pieter Zeldenthuis and brag about his success. Pieter had jibed at his abilities. Well then, up yours, Pieter.

Sam Weary said to his delighted employer, 'Sir, I think we ask some more men questions?'

'Quite right, Sam,' said Seb, realizing that one man's word might be questioned later. 'Get two or three more of this man's company here. We need some corroborative evidence.'

Sam did as he was told, while Seb sat swatting at flies with a whisk and his prisoner stood meekly awaiting his just deserts.

With three other black soldiers in front of the imposing desk, Seb went through a similar exercise, warning the men that they would suffer the torments of Hell, even if they were not Christians, if they told him any lies.

'Now,' said Seb to the first of the three men, the tallest one, who looked down on Seb as if he were a small boy, 'who do you think was responsible for the corporal's death?'

Sam repeated the question in Bantu and received an immediate reply from the tall soldier.

Sam now screwed up his mouth before translating.

'This man say that he also kill the corporal.'

Seb shook himself, then continued with, 'Perhaps he did not understand the question?'

This was translated.

'Yes, sir, he understand the question,' Sam insisted, 'and he still say he kill the corporal.'

This was becoming more complicated, more complex. Two men had now confessed to the crime. Obviously there was some kind of conspiracy. However, finding the killer with the first man to be questioned was a coincidence. Finding the first man's accomplice with the second man who had come up before him was an absolute miracle. Something was going on that Seb did not like. He quickly asked questions of the other two men, one with some tribal scars on his face, the other a boy of not more than sixteen years of age.

All three men confessed to assisting the prisoner in his criminal act of murdering the corporal.

Seb was thoroughly confused. He sent for several more of the company. Every man who was questioned admitted he took part in the killing. In the next two hours Seb questioned sixty-seven men of the company. Every single one confessed to the murder. Seb, sweating inside his dress uniform, was furious with himself and those he was questioning.

'Well, this is a tidy thing,' he addressed the company, now drawn up in threes on parade before his tent, 'you are all murderers.'

They stood impassive, staring at the middle distance.

'You realize you could all be executed?'

No answer, just the same blank faces.

Seb undid his tunic and threw off his helmet.

'Sam,' he said, 'get to the bottom of this. I want to know if it's true that they were all implicated in this murder. I need to know why the man was killed. I must sit and think about what to do about it.'

Sam, happy to be the centre of attention, sat down on the ground and invited the NNC company to gather and sit with him. They sat. The next half an hour was conducted in Bantu. There were lots of gestures and murmurings. Food was sent for. Drink was sent for. Finally Sam got up and reported to his master, the Provost-Marshal.

'Yes, they all kill the man. Each one smash his head with a rock or club.'

'And the reason?' asked Seb, wearily.

'He is Pedi, from Transvaal.'

'Pedi.'

'Yes, sir. Different tribe. All these men wait for big promotion. They are Gcaleka and Ngqika people. This man is only Pedi.'

'They killed him because he was from a different tribe?'

'And he get made corporal before they do.'

'Well, there's a tidy thing, I'm sure. You know, we wouldn't even *think* of killing a Yorkshireman who got promoted over someone from Warwickshire.'

'I know, sir. You are very good people.'

Seb did not feel at all comfortable with such praise.

'Well, I don't know about that, Sam, but is there any way we could find out who struck the first blow? I mean, surely the first man who caved in the victim's face is the actual murderer? If he was then dead, all the others can be let off the hook.'

'No, sir. No one knows.'

'I'll wager they do, but I don't suppose we'll ever get to find out. Now what am I to do? I can't arrest all sixty-seven of them. I haven't got anywhere to put them, for a start. And what would I do with them in the way of punishment? It's an impossible situation. No, no, you don't have to answer that, Sam. I'll go and see the major.'

Seb put on his helmet, buttoned his tunic, and marched off to find Major Casey.

He found him in the company of several other senior officers.

'Yes, Ensign,' said Casey. 'You've got your man?'

'Yes, sir, but,' Seb coughed into his fist, 'it's more like sixty-odd men.' He explained the results of his court of enquiry. 'You see, sir, I can't hang them all.'

The major was as confounded as Seb.

'We can't let them get away with it, Ensign. Discipline and all that. After all, a serious crime has been committed. A felony punishable by death.'

'I agree, sir. But I think it's out of my hands, personally. I suggest that their commanding officer punishes them in some way. I've done all I can. I repeat, I can't hang them all.'

The major eventually agreed and Seb was freed to go back and release the detained men.

'Return to your regiment,' he told them. 'You will be hearing from your officers.'

They trotted off, spears and shields in hands, not a trace of expression on their faces.

Seb was beginning to realize that policing an army was not as easy as it should be. He had believed that crimes would be committed, arrests would be made, punishments would be carried out. *Fin.* He had steeled himself for unpleasantness, for as well as the culprits of criminal action, everyone else in the world wants nothing to do with a policeman either. On top of everything else, he had received no training in the profession and did not look like getting any. The army expected its officers to be able to pick up any kind of work they were ordered to do, such officers being – as a consequence of the natural order of the chain of being – intelligent, well-bred men of honour and integrity. There was no allowance for wealthy aristocratic fools.

There were police already part of Lord Chelmsford's invading force: the Natal Mounted Police. They were, like other small cavalry units, a hard-riding bunch of men, tough as old leather. Not all were South Africans. Many of them had been recruited from Britain, not knowing what they were getting into. Their duties, however, were more of a military nature than normal policing. They did not go about solving crimes and arresting thieves. They were much like any other unit of horse, with much the same work to carry out.

Pieter was stripped to the waist and dousing himself with water when Seb found him again.

'Howzit, bru?' said Pieter, by way of greeting. 'You finished locking people up for the day?'

'You wouldn't believe.'

'Tell me.'

Seb sat down on a rock and regaled the Boer with the day's events. Pieter shook his head at the end of it all.

'You have to know their ways, and you can only do that by being one of them,' he said, after his wash, sitting down to clean his rifle. 'I was born here, lived here all my life, and I know very little about the way the blacks think. There's nothing wrong or right about it, it's simply a different train of thoughts, from a different culture.'

'There's always something wrong about murder,' argued Seb. 'You can't kill a man in cold blood and call it right.'

'We execute men in cold blood.'

Seb nodded. 'Yes, but that's because they've broken the law in some way and justice has to be served.'

'How do you know this wasn't a lawful execution in their eyes?'

That was something Seb had not thought of. Just because he had been told it was tribal jealousy did not mean it actually *was*.

'I get your point. But look, Pieter, you do believe in the death penalty, don't you? I mean, there has to be some deterrent to committing a serious crime.'

'It's the word *serious* I have problems with. They were hanging kids of eight not long ago, just for being *suspected* of stealing something small. Listen, it's very simple. If the state and the law say that killing a person is wrong, then how can they then go ahead and kill someone?'

'So you're against capital punishment.'

'I didn't say that. I'm pointing out the weaknesses of the law, the complete absence of logic. Look, I'm here killing Zulus, so are you, so we can't stand on a pedestal and claim to be pacifists. But we're here doing it because some bloody government official has told us to be here. It's the politicians who make laws and wars. It's those buggers who're the illogical bastards. Myself, so far as hanging goes, I think too many innocent men are executed. One is too many, but there are a great deal who're convicted on very little evidence. Until a man's face turns bright orange when he commits a crime, you can never be sure the perpetrator of the crime is hanging on the end of the rope.'

'So we let everyone go free?'

'No, just throw 'em in jail. At least if we find out they're innocent later, we can say sorry and let them go. But we can't bring them back to life again.'

Seb shook his head. 'I never thought you'd be against capital punishment.'

'I'm not. I'm on the fence, bru. Keep an open mind, that's my policy. Keep turning things over in your head, questioning the rights and wrongs. Then vote for the loskop who comes closest to how you feel at the time you put your cross on the paper.'

Eleven

There was yet another river to cross, the Manzimnyama, where wagons got stuck in the mud. Seb had long ago realized that the business of war was a dirty one. Fording these African rivers was not a difficult business unless you were an army of five thousand men carrying all your supplies and essential requirements with you. A man who joined as a soldier expected to march, fight and perhaps even die for his shilling a day, but few had expected to labour like Hercules, having to put their shoulders to loaded wagons and ending up covered in dirt and dung. Then at the end of an exhausting day, having to erect bell tents heavy with water from those same rivers, before any rest could be had. Latrines and defensive trenches had to be dug, kitchens assembled and cooking fires lit, ammunition boxes carried back and forth. Domestic livestock had to be fed along with the oxen and horses. This was apart from the normal sentry duties and any personal tasks a soldier might have to do around camp.

Men fell on the floor of their tents wrapped in a blanket asleep almost before they hit the ground. Often soldiers were soaked to the skin, but they spent the night fully clothed in their uniforms. None knew whether they would be called to defend the camp in the middle hours, or at dawn when many attacks are made. Reveille was normally at six: a rude awakening by a sleepy bugle boy.

They found themselves on a plateau above wide plains with a strange-looking sawn-off mountain in the distance.

'What's the name of this place?' asked Seb of another officer, as they made camp.

'Isandlwana,' replied the other. 'Godforsaken, ain't it?'

Indeed, it was a bleak and barren area.

'Are we staying here long?'

'Who knows? There's a rumour we'll be heading off again fairly soon, to a spot called Mangeni, to the south-east. Scouts have come back from there with reports of Zulus in the hills.'

'And what's at Mangeni?'

'A river, some falls, and hopefully the Zulu army. The sooner

we get this over with, the better. It'll be a long war if they won't
come out and fight, and I don't think they will. The Zulus know
what the Martini-Henry can do. It'd be suicide for them, even in
numbers. We'll cut them down by the score if they come at us.
Look at this place, for example. No real cover anywhere.'

Seb stared around him. 'No cover for us, either.'

'Ah, but they've got to get close to us to do us any harm. Some
of them have got muskets, but nothing as lethal as the Martini.
You need to be pretty close to use a stabbing spear, or even toss
a throwing spear. We won't let them get that close. They'll go down
in waves, believe me, and I'm pretty sure most of them are cowering
inside the Royal Kraal at Ulundi. Only madmen would attack an
army bristling with modern weapons.'

'Maybe they are mad?'

'Then God help them.'

Seb was inclined to agree with this viewpoint, which was
popular enough amongst both officers and men. That was until
a message from Major Dartnell, who commanded the Natal
Mounted Police, arrived in the camp. Even at that early hour,
not long after midnight, a rumour flew round that the main
Zulu army was after all in the field and was approaching from
the direction of Ulundi. The rumour further stated that Lord
Chelmsford was going to lead the column that way to meet the
threat and to try to draw the Zulus into a battle.

At two a messenger came to Seb, with an order to report to
General Lord Chelmsford.

Like many others, Seb had not been able to fall asleep. He rose
and left his tent. The starlight created an eerie atmosphere out here
on this empty landscape. And there was a stillness to the air which
was disturbing. Soldiers have imaginations like anyone else and Seb's
mind was full of the stories of his youth, of *Beowulf* and *The Odyssey*,
of strange forces that operated beyond the ken of ordinary mortals.
It was not difficult to conjure up groundless fears at this time in the
morning, out in the wilderness. A man could easily fall victim to
such terrors, isolated as they were from civilization. Dark thoughts,
some of natural evils, others less definable, swamped a man's brain
in the early hours far from home or any familiar surroundings.

*What am I doing in this Godforsaken place, in the land of an enemy
who are completely alien to me, thousands of miles from my homeland
and my own folk?*

It was not a question many could answer without wondering whether they were victims of their own foolishness.

Others who could not sleep were gathered in bunches, talking in soft voices. Further out, silent picquets were stacked back-to-back in fours like sheaves of corn, each man trying to peer out into the dark unknown regions of a region foreign to them. It was easy to imagine the most deadly dangers creeping towards them, and they were inclined to jump at the slightest sound: a lizard disturbing stones, a snake searching for a warm hole in which to spend the night. Premonitions were rife amongst those men out there in the darkness, on that barren landscape. Their minds were spiked with dread. It needed a father figure to walk amongst them, soothing them with calm talk, telling them in a soft quiet tone that all was well and they would live to see an old age.

Seb found Lord Chelmsford standing outside his tent smoking a cigar.

'Ah, young Ensign Early, our local policeman, yes?'

'Yes, sir, reporting as ordered.'

'So, what have you got to tell me?'

Seb was at a loss. 'Tell you, sir?'

'About the Boer – you remember our agreement . . .'

Seb remembered it not as an agreement but as a direct order from the officer commanding the whole army.

'I – I've not anything to report, sir. I've been in close contact with – with Zeldenthuis – but so far as I can see he's simply been carrying out his duties of scouting for the army.'

'You're sure about that?'

'Yes – yes I am, sir.'

'Good, well keep your eyes peeled and your ears open.'

Seb saluted, just as Colonel Pulleine approached. He turned to go, then thought of something.

'Sir, I've been looking for Surgeon Reynolds. You don't happen to know where he is, do you?'

Lord Chelmsford looked as if he was a headmaster and Seb was a silly pupil.

'Why would I . . . Pulleine, do you know a Surgeon Reynolds?'

The approaching colonel nodded. 'Yes – he's back at the field hospital. At Witt's mission. Why do you ask, sir?'

'The policeman here wants to know.'

'Thank you, sir,' said Seb. 'Sir, permission to ride back to Rorke's Drift, to interview the surgeon?'

Lord Chelmsford's eyebrows rose a fraction. 'Why, what's he done?'

'He hasn't done anything, sir. I just have a few questions to ask him about – about a crime I'm working on.' Seb did not want to go into the business of the murder again.

'You do your duty as you see your way, young man. That's what we appoint Provost-Marshals for, isn't it? If you don't have free rein, then I'm sure you wouldn't be able to do your job. By the by, that business with the NNC – there was little you could do once it was established that the whole company took part. Had it been a regiment of the line, of course, it would have been a different matter. But the blacks . . . well, short of hanging the lot of them, there's not much you could do. And we need all the men we've got at the moment.'

'Oh, you heard about that? Yes, sir. Thank you, sir.'

Inkhosi Ntshingwayo kaMahole Khoza was one of the two commanders of the Zulu army sent by King Cetshwayo to meet the threat of a foreign invader in his land. At the time that Seb was having a nightmare about a bull chasing him through a wide meadow with no gate in sight, the Zulu commander was walking amongst his impi offering words of comfort to his warriors. Tomorrow was the night of the new moon when those dark spiritual forces the *umnyama* would be abroad and he did not want his warriors concerned about ethereal matters when they should be concentrating on the destruction of the enemy.

The Zulus were lying in a shallow valley not far from the camp of the whites. They numbered twenty-five thousand of the bravest and the best. The uDududu were there, and the uNokhenke, the iMbube, the uDloko and several other companies. They were ready and eager to fight and though the commander knew that the firepower of the British was devastating, he also knew that his men outnumbered the opposing army by five to one. If two were killed, then the third, or the fourth, or even the fifth would get through and triumph. These people had violated the country of the amaZulu and they would not go away unpunished.

Ntshingwayo, like Seb, was having trouble sleeping. With all the things he had on his mind, it was no wonder that sleep would not come. The Zulu army did not even have the comfort of fires, since to light one would locate them for the enemy. The commander went back and lay on his shield and waited for dawn. They would not attack tomorrow, of course, for it was not an auspicious day in the Zulu calendar, but the day after perhaps, if the situation was right. Of course, if they were discovered before then, they would attack nonetheless.

Seb woke about six in the morning when Sam Weary shook him by the shoulder.

'Tea, boss.'

Seb sat up and rubbed his eyes. 'Thanks, Sam. Where's Corporal Evans?'

'He is still asleep, sir.'

'Wake him and tell him to take down the tents.'

'Yes, boss.'

After drinking his tea, Seb splashed water on his hands and face, and then went to look for Pieter Zeldenthuis. He found the whole camp buzzing with the latest news. He questioned a passing cornet to find that Lord Chelmsford was splitting the column yet again. He and Colonel Glyn were taking approximately three thousand men consisting of the 2/24th plus irregulars and auxiliaries. He was leaving behind in the camp Lieutenant-Colonel Pulleine of the 1/24th with two thousand men and two 7-pounder guns of N Battery. Those staying with Pulleine would be 1/24th as well as 2/24th, mounted troops, and the 1st Battalion of the 3rd NNC regiment.

Seb could not find Pieter, who had obviously left on one of his scouting missions, so he went to find a quartermaster.

'Sir,' he said, finding his man, 'I need at least two horses.'

The major, a corpulent seedy-looking individual, eyed him up and down.

'An ensign? Needing two horses? Have they lowered the field ranks to the bottom, then?'

'Sir, I'm not just any ensign – I'm the Provost-Marshal.' He flicked his red sash. 'I have to have two mounts to get me to Rorke's Drift, the mission house, where I have an appointment with Surgeon Reynolds.'

'Oh you do, do you?' came the caustic reply, as the major blew into his thick yellow moustache. 'Well, funnily enough there's a damn war going on and horses are at a premium.'

Seb had expected this sort of reaction. It would not have mattered if there were a thousand spare geldings and mares idly chewing hay, the major would have argued over it. The supply corps were like that. They followed the maxim of never giving up anything unless they absolutely had to. They would hand over nothing with great regularity and tell you to think yourself lucky. Even if they had been God's own quartermasters and their stores and provisions were overflowing to nuisance levels, they would have baulked at handing them over. They held on to every small item grimly, for as long as possible, and when they were forced to relinquish them they grumbled and groaned as if they were handing over their own personal property.

'Sir, this is an investigation at the highest level. It involves the murder of a British officer. I don't say there won't be questions asked in the House back in parliament if it isn't solved. Do you really want to stand in the way of justice and retribution? The murderer might even now be making his escape! Come, sir. You must give all the assistance possible to my investigation or reap the consequences later.'

He was getting used to arguing with senior officers.

'Who's the murdered officer – it ain't that captain, back at Ladysmith, I hope.'

'I'm not permitted to say, sir. There is a veil of secrecy over the whole affair until it's sorted out. I was speaking about it with General Lord Chelmsford just this morning . . .'

'The general? Do you take me for a fool?'

'You may ask him yourself, sir – or ask Colonel Pulleine, who was in attendance at our meeting.'

The major put one end of his moustache in his mouth and chewed it for a moment, while he eyed this whippersnapper of an ensign through narrowed lids.

Finally he said, 'All right, but if I find you're lying to me!'

Seb's voice took on a passionately indignant tone.

'Lying? Sir, you may be of a senior rank, but the affront to my good name and family . . .'

'All right, all right,' grumbled the major, 'don't ice the cake.'

The horses were finally obtained. They were not the best, but then Seb felt he was lucky to have anything on four legs.

Sam and Evans had dismantled the tents.

'Put them on one of the wagons,' Seb ordered. 'We're going for a ride.'

'Where are we going?' asked Evans, in an excited voice. 'With the general's lot?'

Clearly this would be more exciting than hanging around the camp that was staying in Isandlwana.

'No – in the opposite direction. We're going to Rorke's Drift, where they've set up a temporary hospital. I need to interview the surgeon there.'

'Sam stayin' here, is he?'

'No again – you'll have to share the second horse. Requesting *three* nags would have given the quartermaster apoplexy. You'll have to make do, the pair of you.'

'Why can't Sam stay here?' whined the corporal. "E's not regular army, anyway. What if we meet any Zulus. He's no fighter, this one. He'll probably swap sides soon as things go against us. You can't trust these savages, see, sir. They're not like us.'

'Sam is no savage,' said Sam. 'Sam Weary can read and write, which he learned at the Mission School. Sir,' the Xhosa man addressed Seb, 'if you wish Sam to stay here, he will, but he wishes come with you.'

'You're coming, Sam, don't worry,' replied Seb. 'No more arguments, Evans. Now help me saddle up.'

By the time the tents were on the wagons, breakfast had been eaten and the mounts were ready, it was mid-morning. Seb on his horse, and Sam up behind Evans on the second mount, set off over the rocky grasslands towards the Buffalo River. Evans had his Martini-Henry. As well as his sword, Seb carried his Beaumont revolver and a Swinburne-Henry carbine in a saddle holster. Nothing had been said, but all three men were aware that there was a large stretch of open ground, about ten miles, between Isandlwana and Rorke's Drift. It would not need a large party of Zulus to overpower three men. They were going to have to be extremely vigilant during the ride.

As they left camp another group were just coming in. Seb recognized the disabled Colonel Durnford at the head of his mounted detachment of Number 2 Column. Durnford was highly respected by most officers and men. Some of the senior ranks were not too keen on him, due to his political views on the inadvisability of the war, and rumours of an affair with a young colonial woman had caused a few cheeks to be sucked in. But for the most part, most knew him to be a highly capable commanding officer.

Certainly his men of the Zikhali's Horse, Hlubi's Troop and the NNC thought he was a god.

As they passed each other, Seb saluted the colonel, and it was returned with a nod and a smile.

Sam whispered, 'Sam admires very much the colonel's moustache – it is longer than anything he has seen anywhere.'

'It certainly is a magnificent specimen,' replied Seb, fingering his own barely adequate effort. 'You need to be a veteran to grow something like that.'

The three left the camp, their eyes watchful. Seb's mount was a reasonable one, but the big lumbering carthorse carrying the other two was old and slightly lame, so progress was slow. All kept their eyes on the horizon, hoping that any movement would be wild animals or cattle and not Zulus running towards them. Seb glanced behind, once or twice, but the danger would not come from that way he was sure. There were two thousand armed soldiers behind him and any threat would have to get through Colonel Pulleine's position to get to Seb and his men.

They were about four miles out when they heard the guns.

Seb turned in his saddle to look back and the hairs on the nape of his neck stood on end at the sight.

'By God, it's an attack.'

It seemed the very ground beyond the camp was moving like a black tidal wave flowing towards the rows of white tents.

'But they haven't struck camp, have they?' asked Corporal Evans. 'They should have struck camp.'

Seb took a small telescope out of his pocket and trained it on the skyline beyond the camp. His heart started beating rapidly. Zulus were pouring over the ground, a huge mass in the centre, with two flanking horns curling round on either side. It seemed the camp would be surrounded. Seb was confident though that despite the obvious fact the camp had been surprised, Pulleine's and Durnford's men would hold off the enemy. Yet the more he watched the more Zulus appeared from behind those swarming down on the camp. Thousands and thousands of them, streaming forward in massed ranks, hurtling on three sides towards the thin lines of soldiers firing like men possessed.

'Them rifles'll be as hot as the hinges on Hell's gates,' shouted Evans, excitedly. 'Where'd them savages all come from? Why didn't the general see 'em on his way out?'

'God knows, Evans,' said Seb, whose chest felt so tight he was hardly able to speak. He felt a strong urge to ride back to the camp. 'It's going to be a tough fight and we missed it by an hour, damn it.' He suddenly made a decision, giving in to his instincts. 'Look, you keep going. I'm heading back to camp.'

'Sir, is that wise?' asked Sam. 'Look what is happening.'

Seb replied grimly, 'If I don't take part in this, I'll regret it for the rest of my army days – and more. Go on, you two. I'll join you later, when the battle's over.'

Seb started cantering back towards the camp. He dare not gallop for the ground was rough and the last thing he wanted to do was injure his horse. After a mile he halted and put his telescope to his eye and surveyed the scene ahead. It was not good. Some parts of the line looked as if they were about to be swamped by the black wave of warriors. They seemed as numerous as ants, pouring out of some hole in the ground, threatening to flow over the camp in the distance.

Yet the camp was taking a massive toll on the advancing horde. Zulus were going down in dozens, scores. The Martini-Henry was a murderous weapon. Volley firing was cutting swathes in the Zulu advance. The heavy 0.45 calibre bullets would be ripping through bodies and hitting those following behind. Each soldier would be firing an average of ten rounds a minute, bar the jams that black-powder cartridges were inclined to cause. In response, the small number of rifles and muskets of the attackers would be much less effective.

Seb had no doubt of the eventual outcome of the battle. He knew the defenders' firepower was unbeatable. Surely the Zulu generals would come to the same conclusion and retreat very soon?

He found the distinctive one-armed Colonel Durnford in his glass. He was striding amongst his troops above dongas that separated the camp from the high ground. At that moment the sky began to darken and an eerie half-light fell over the whole scene. What was this? Was God drawing a veil over the battle? A chill wind suddenly sprang up in the dimness, rustling the grasses and lifting his mount's mane.

It felt to Seb as if he were witnessing Armageddon, with angels and demons about to enter the affray.

Durnford was soon seriously on the retreat, his line of men firing, then jumping up and going back ten or so paces, before dropping to one knee and firing another volley. Rifles were obviously jamming with overuse. He watched as Durnford walked amongst his black troops, taking jammed weapons between his knees and prising spent cartridges from blocked breaches with his good hand. There did not seem to be any panic. Durnford's mouth was moving and Seb guessed he was offering encouragement to his native soldiers. Durnford's men were seasoned fighters and they had good leadership in their colonel.

Elsewhere in the camp there seemed to be a certain controlled hysteria. Men were rushing hither and thither, probably carrying ammunition to those at the front. In places the lines were holding, but in the more forward areas hand-to-hand fighting was in progress. Seb watched in horror as he saw some of the NNC break from their line and begin running, leaving their mounted officers to fight alone.

He spurred his mount forward.

The twilight continued to grow dimmer and a strange gloaming took hold of the world. Seb now realized he was witnessing a partial eclipse of the sun. This was no supernatural phenomenon but a natural wonder. Had there been no battle he might have stood and admired what was occurring in the heavens.

The noise of the Zulu chants, and the crackle of constant fire, swept over the plain to where Seb was watching. Once again he pressed forward hard, wondering if he would be in time to take part in the fighting. The rough ground was making his horse slip and stumble every so often and both rider and mount saw the need to be cautious.

When next he put his glass to his eye, he saw a small figure running from the camp. The nerve of one of the young boys had obviously snapped and his little legs were going ten to the dozen, as he fled over the grassland in Seb's direction. He did not look like a drummer, who would have been in a red coat, but was dressed in a black tunic. The first thing that flashed through Seb's mind was the fact that the boy's army career was over. He might not be executed for desertion during the battle, due to his age, but he would certainly be court-martialled and receive some nasty punishment.

Then common sense took over Seb's thinking. All the air was expelled from his lungs as he tried to come to terms with the sight before him. Even with the naked eye he could now see the impossible was happening. Despite the awesome firepower of their modern weapons the camp was being overwhelmed by Zulu warriors. The Zulus had attacked in their feared buffalo formation. The centre or the head was the main striking force, but there were wide sweeping horns on each side made up of fast-running warriors, which curled round and closed in around the camp. Thousands upon thousands of Zulus, swarming in on the British position. The soldiers in the camp stood no chance once those buffalo horns of the impi had them trapped. Even without the glass to his eye now, Seb could see his comrades-in-arms were too strung out. The lines were breaking up fast. They were being overrun by a black tide of loud triumphant warriors.

'Oh, good God, no!' he whispered into the ear of his horse. 'Surely not? Surely not?'

Individual struggles were in progress. Soldiers were even fist-fighting with Zulus, only to be cut down from the side or from behind. Elsewhere lines were screwing up into small knots of soldiers who were desperately fighting for their lives. The tents, still erected, were hampering the defenders of the camp as the Zulus swept in, using the cover afforded by the canvas screens to come upon the hapless, despairing troops. Even as he watched he saw soldiers deserting the camp, mostly riders, but some on foot.

The young boy simply had a head start on others.

'Oh my God, my God, the day's lost!' cried Seb out loud.

He was appalled by the sight. 'Lost!' he repeated, in shock and disbelief. The enormity of what he could see before him was over-whelming. Two thousand men were being put to the spear. All his friends and acquaintances, his comrades in arms, soldiers who had served with him elsewhere, were falling, falling, never to rise again. Everywhere soldiers were being hacked to pieces. It was surely not credible. This disaster could not be happening.

But it was.

He could hear the screams of soldiers being disembowelled by warriors eager to wash their spears in enemy blood. The whole camp was alive with black bodies hacking down small numbers of other blacks and whites. A total massacre! Seb was still stunned. How could this happen? Two thousand trained soldiers, armed to the teeth with the latest weapons, and they had been summarily defeated by savages.

And the slaughter continued. Men were still dying. Zulus were going down under rifle butts and on the end of bayonets, but the defenders had been swamped by vastly superior numbers. Any soldier still on his feet was hidden by a thrashing mob of Zulu warriors intent on dealing the final blow. Even the already dead were being thrust in the belly with the stabbing spears of young Zulus anxious to smear their blades in the blood of the enemy.

Seb suddenly realized that he was now in a real and grave danger. The ground around the camp was covered in bodies. Thousands of Zulus lay lifeless in the grasses, but they had been joined in their last journey by hundreds of British soldiers and British auxiliaries. A black-and-white quilt of dead on the plain. Yet though many of the Zulus were occupied in looting the camp and killing the remaining soldiers, others were chasing escaping runaways. The boy in the dark tunic was now about a mile from camp, but was being pursued by a knot of Zulus, some of them not much older than the child they were chasing.

On the boy's face was a look of utter terror.

Without a second thought Seb spurred his horse forward.

The boy glanced up in alarm as Seb's horse thundered down on him. Tears streaked his creased cheeks. His hair was stiff with dirt and sweat, his eyes were wild, his mouth open and gasping for air. His black coat was unbuttoned and flapping, and the white vest beneath throbbed with every rapid breath he took. Yet still his legs flashed like those of a rabbit being chased by a fox. Those small legs were in survival mode. They would have kept pumping even if his heart had given out. When he realized it was a soldier on the horse he let out a sharp meaningless cry like a bird in pain.

Bullets began to whine around both of them.

Seb wheeled his horse around the behind the boy. He then charged forward, grabbed the child by his collar, and whipped him from the ground. Indeed, the boy's legs were still cycling in mid-air. Seb swung him up in front of himself and yelled at him, 'Grab hold!'

The boy's frantic fingers scrabbled to find purchase and managed to clutch the horse's mane. Seb urged his mount forward, slapping the flank with his right hand, shouting, 'On you devil, on, on,' for he knew that close behind were men with spears and clubs in their hands. There were running Zulus all over the plains, and some mounted ones, chasing those soldiers who were fleeing the battlefield. He knew that a running warrior could overtake a flagging horse. He had to hope that the battle had taken its toll on the Zulus. Physically they would be fatigued, but winning a battle lifts a man's spirit high, so they would be filled with triumphant energy.

One thing was in Seb's favour. He had not fought a battle. He was fresh and alert.

Looking behind him he saw that there were two men far ahead of the rest. They were gaining on him. Neither of the two warriors had a rifle. One had a club, the other a stabbing spear. Seb let them get a little closer, then he drew his sword. He wheeled his horse and charged down on them with a yell. The first man, the one with the club, he cut between shoulder and neck. The warrior went down spurting blood, clutching his wound. The second man stopped and tried to throw his iklwa. The short stabbing spear missed by a yard. Now the warrior turned and began to run back. Seb sheathed his sword, drew the carbine, and shot the warrior on the run. Hit in the thigh, the man fell screaming, squirming with agony in the dust, a smashed, splintered bone showing white through the red gaping wound.

The boy was suddenly sick all over the horse's neck.

'Are you all right?' Seb asked him, the stink of the vomit making him feel queasy too. The boy looked feverishly hot and was holding on with tight, white fingers to the horse's mane. 'You'll pull all his hair out, you know?'

The boy nodded his tear-stained face, but remained clinging to the mane with fierce determination.

Those fleeing the camp headed directly for the river. They were being chased down by warriors eager for the last drop of blood. Seb turned the head of his mount, heading much further south, away from the mass of pursuers intent on last kills. He found a place to ford the Buffalo where it was wide and shallow as it met the Blood River. The pair managed to get across before several warriors came up on the far bank. The carbine had not been reloaded, so he drew his pistol and fired several shots amongst the Zulus. None of them was hit, but the action delayed their crossing long enough for Seb to get well ahead of them.

'Where are we going?' asked the youngster, coherent at last. 'They'll catch us.'

Seb replied, calmly, 'We're in Natal now. We're heading for Witt's mission. What's your name, boy?'

'Thomas Tranter, sir.'

'How old are you?'

'Eleven, sir.'

'Well, Master Tranter, I am Ensign Early. I see by your uniform you belong to the Natal Volunteers.'

He knew that boys of his age were fired with eagerness to wear a uniform and to join with a column going into battle. It was true also that they found war was not the wild and glorious activity they expected it to be. Wild it was, glorious it was not. This one had probably set out glowing with pride in his new uniform and had now found out that wearing it only entitled him to be slaughtered along with his friends and comrades if ever the tide of battle turned against his fellows.

'Yes, sir, I helped my older brother drive his wagon.'

'Well, you're safe now.'

Thomas choked out, 'Them other boys – them drummers . . .'

'I know.'

Seb had seen disembowelled drummer boys hanging from tent poles by their drum harnesses.

The soldier in Seb had to bite his tongue. Technically young Thomas had deserted. It was possible that Seb might later be ordered to arrest the boy. His presence in Pulleine's camp would have made no difference to the outcome of the battle and a general rout had begun not long after the boy's legs had decided to take the initiative but the army might want to court-martial him. Seb had been in long enough to know their generic eyes only saw things in black and white.

Thomas asked, 'Will my brother be all right?'

'We'll see. Some men escaped the Zulus.'

'And are the Zulus going to get us?'

'Don't worry, there are more soldiers at Rorke's Drift.'

He did not give numbers, knowing there was actually only company strength at the drift. Probably around a hundred men in all. If the Zulu army continued to follow on in any strength, Rorke's Drift too would fall under their spears. It seemed to Seb that the whole war was being settled in one day. What about Lord Chelmsford's column? Had that been ambushed? Were they all dead too? This was a disaster beyond Seb's imagining. Savages had managed to wipe out two thousand men of one of the world's greatest armies. A Pyrrhic victory, surely, with so many Zulu dead left on the battlefield? But a victory for the Zulu nation none the less. The British army had been shattered, torn apart, put to the spear, slaughtered, annihilated. He could not bear to think of it. The soldier's pride in him was screaming in pain.

And there were friends that had gone down, were lost forever. Ensigns Carpenter and Swale. Jack and Henry.

Gutted like fish, their bowels strewn over the ground.

That eclipse? Did it herald the end of the world? Was it a coincidence or a sign from God?

Seb's mind swam with a dozen thoughts at once, most of them dark, ugly visions of a terrible defeat.

Twelve

The boy and the man on the horse approached the red-roofed buildings of Rorke's Drift skirting the Oskarsberg hill. As they entered the compound they could see a great deal of activity. For some reason men were building walls of what looked like boxes of stores. On enquiry Seb was informed by a soldier that they contained biscuits. Seb might have made a joke about the biscuits to the boy, if he had not been devastated by the massacre. He felt shocked and bewildered by what he had seen at Isandlwana. This kind of defeat did not happen to the British army. This was what the redcoats inflicted on others.

A young colour sergeant containing some repressed excitement came to Seb's horse and said, 'Sir, it is possible we shall be attacked by the Zulus very soon – a Lieutenant Adendorff has ridden in from the battle at Isandlwana – he tells us that the Zulus overran the camp and that it's possible Lord Chelmsford has been defeated also.'

'I know about the camp,' said Seb. 'I saw what happened.'

A lieutenant of engineers came striding over to Seb.

'Chard.' He snapped out his name. 'You were at the battle?'

'No – I left the camp before the battle began. I set out here to see Surgeon Reynolds. The battle began when we were about halfway here. Is the doctor still in the camp?'

'Yes, Reynolds is here. And myself and Lieutenant Bromhead, the officer i/c B Company, 2/24th. I came to build a damn bridge . . .' Chard did not finish the sentence but clearly he was distracted and no doubt emotional, probably in a similar way to Seb. There had been a terrible British defeat. It was difficult for any officer not to feel appalled by that news. 'You're staying, of course?' Chard said. 'Possibly you have no orders to do so? But we could use any man.'

'Did my men arrive? There's a corporal and a black.'

The colour sergeant, still standing by, said, 'Yes – they're here, sir.'

'Corporal Evans and I will remain, but I want to send my black servant to Helpmekaar with this boy. He's a survivor of the massacre.'

Chard stared at Thomas, then nodded, after which his attention was taken by a messenger, who handed him a note. He read it and then strode off in the direction of the hospital. Seb heard him shout something about mealie bags and then led his tired horse to the water cart. He left Thomas in charge of the watering and went to find Evans and Sam. When he found them, Sam came running towards him.

'Boss, they have killed everyone . . .'

'I know, Sam, I saw it. I went back, but was not in time to take part. However, I did find a boy called Thomas Tranter. I want you to take him to Helpmekaar. Can you do that? Use Evans' horse.'

Evans was standing by, studying their lips.

Sam replied, 'Yes, sir. Sam can do that. But Sam should stay with you.'

'No, you must go. Evans will stay here.'

'Oh, that's good,' the corporal said, sarcastically. 'I was just this minute hopin' you'd order me to stay and be murdered by savages.'

'Evans!'

'All right, all right, sir – just havin' a grumble.'

The colour sergeant, a man in his mid-twenties, was still nearby and saw this exchange. He came over. He was used to young officers who did not know how to deal directly with difficult individual men. They often called on their senior non-commissioned officers to crack the whip and knock some sense into belligerent soldiers.

'I can handle the corporal, sir, if you want me to?'

The sergeant had a soft, Southern English dialect. Seb thought he was from Hampshire, or Surrey, one of those lower-down counties. Yet there was a toughness about him, short as he was in height.

'It's all right, Colour – I'll deal with him. He's deaf, you know – deaf as a post. It makes him think he can get away with insolence occasionally.' Seb made sure Evans could see his lips. 'But I'm just a short stick away from having him flogged. What's your name, Colour?'

'Bourne, sir.'

'Thank you, Colour Bourne, I'll remember to call you, if I need you.'

'I'll sort 'im, sir, if required.'

The sergeant marched away, while the much taller Evans mouthed a repeat of his words unseen, over his head and made a quick obscene gesture with his hand.

'Evans!' growled Seb. 'I swear!'

'Sir, we're not even on the strength,' the corporal continued with argument. 'Your name and mine, they aren't on the roll. I'm a gunner and I've got no gun to fire. You seen the number of Zulus out there, sir. They'll run over this place in two ticks. What's the point in stayin' here to be cut to bits?'

'You're an Assistant Provost-Marshal, that's what you are – and primarily a soldier.'

'I'm not a coward, sir, I hope you realize that.'

'I'm sure you're not, Evans.'

'It's just they take me away from my gun, when nothin' much else can happen to me in the way of deafness, see, an' so I feel the army's not kept their side of the bargain. I should be with my gun. I don't mind dyin' by my gun, defending my gun. But it's not here, you see.'

'I sympathize, but we're still soldiers, both of us. These people need us. We have to stay.'

Evans nodded, morosely. 'Oh, I know that – I just wish I had my gun.'

The argument, such as it was, was over.

Men were running ox-wagons into a space between the hospital and another building. Evans went to help them. Seb joined a party that was climbing a hill. Amongst them were the chaplain and the surgeon and a civilian minister whom Seb heard addressed as Witt. On reaching the top a telescope was produced and Witt looked through it and proclaimed he could see mounted blacks leading others.

'Are they NNC?' asked the surgeon. 'Our men?'

Witt kept the glass to his eye and finally shook his head.

'No, I'm afraid not. They look like Zulus to me.' He turned and started down the slope back to the camp. 'I must get my family away.'

Seb ran down the escarpment and ordered Sam to leave immediately, saying the Zulus would be there within minutes.

'Yes, boss, I will see you in Helpmekaar, boss.'

Sam and the boy Tranter left sharing Evans' horse.

Seb looked around him. Most of the soldiers were like himself from the 2/24th Warwickshire, a few from 1/24th, and some odds and sods from the Buffs, 90th, NNC, the Army Service Corps, the RE, RA, Natal Mounted Police, the surgeon, the chaplain – one or two others. You are all going to die, thought Seb, his heart racing – and me too! None of these men had witnessed the recent slaughter, except the lieutenant of the NNC, what was his name, Androff or something? He would know as well as Seb what they were in for in the very near future.

Indeed, within the next hour the company was facing over three thousand warriors, perhaps four thousand, though no one at the mission spent time counting the enemy. They were led by two fat chiefs on horseback. To Seb the warriors looked ordered and unbothered, and he guessed they had not taken part in the big battle. They were probably the reserves from the impi, tired from running vast distances, but relatively fresh for fighting. If they were the reserves they were not easily going to be discouraged, for they would want to wash their spears in British blood. Other regiments had sated themselves and these men would not want to go back looking foolish and to be humiliated by brother regiments.

Chard and Bromhead had done a good job of fortifying their position, in a very short time. The soldiers were quiet and thoughtful in the lull before the battle. There were only around a hundred and fifty men within the compound. Three to four thousand without. The arithmetic was not good. Isandlwana had been a little more than ten to one. Now the odds were more than twenty to one. Was this going to be a repeat of what had happened at midday? It did seem that the defenders stood little chance of living to see the sun go down.

Chard came to Seb.

'Where do you want to be?'

'Just ignore me. I'm not even supposed to be here. I'll use my carbine along with the men at the barricades.'

With two lieutenants around, there was enough leadership within such a small area of command.

'Fair enough.'

A deep hollow cry of '*uSuthu!*' from the mouths of several thousand Zulus was carried to their ears on the back of the wind.

'Well, here they come,' said Chard. 'Good luck.'

'No – good luck, to you, Lieutenant.'

The 24th's picquets raced into the compound.

Zulu skirmishers began their zigzag runs towards the barricades around Rorke's Drift, and the soldiers opened fire. Behind the skirmishers came the first wave of warriors, towards the back of the buildings, with the store on one corner and the wagon-and-mealiebag wall connecting to the hospital. Seb was behind the wall and fired his first shot when the enemy were at about four hundred and fifty yards. He did not believe he hit anything. The next shot was into a mass of men at about three hundred and fifty yards and this time he saw a Zulu jump in the air and fall flat.

'Got one,' he murmured, his shaking hands beginning to steady themselves.

'Good on yer, sir,' said a soldier, close to his shoulder. 'Now get another, if you please.'

Then the soldier raised his own weapon and took a leading Zulu at two hundred yards. The target warrior when hit spun like a top and rolled when he struck the ground, bowling over two of his own men.

After that it was just load and fire, load and fire, load and fire, until Seb's carbine was like a red-hot poker in his hands. The carnage was terrible, but those inflicting it had no time to reflect. They were fighting for their lives and all they saw were warriors running at them, gunsmoke drifting like mist across the bodies, and throwing spears flashing as they flew through the air as javelins.

There were also shots coming from a ridge, but the soldiers had to simply ignore this as an irritation for the moment. The warriors who were firing muskets or rifles were poor shots in any case, though every so often a soldier would turn and fire one back in their direction. Neither side hit very much in this tit-for-tat arrangement.

The second attack came round the south-west corner, where the hospital stood. Here the attackers had some cover in the bush and scrub. The vegetation came almost up to the hospital walls and the warriors were able to get quite close to the defenders. Now there was some fierce fighting, almost hand to hand. Lieutenant Bromhead was in charge of this corner of the compound and he and his men were battling with sword and bayonet. Seb joined some soldiers on a porch where the barricade was weak.

He saw one big-chested warrior grab the muzzle of a private's rifle and pull the soldier towards him to stab him. The soldier kept a determined hold on his rifle and in desperation snatched at the trigger, realizing he had forgotten to reload. Then the Zulu dropped

his iklwa and gripped muzzle and bayonet with both hands, trying
to wrench the private off his feet and over the barricade. The
soldier had strength. He maintained his hold on the stock with his
left hand and with his right reached for one of his cartridges piled
on a mealie bag. Loading the rifle now he squeezed the trigger.
The force of the thumb-sized round at such close quarters blew
the attacker off his feet and sent him flying five yards backwards
into the bush.

A young private near Seb suddenly let out a sigh. Seb glanced
at him to see that a spear had gone through the man's right side.
The youth fell, his eyes wide with surprise. The fighting was at
that moment so intense Seb could do nothing for the fellow. Once
a lull came, he bent down and took the youth's head on his knee,
but the private had passed on to a world where hopefully there
was no more fighting.

'Get some cover, sir,' yelled Evans, who had now joined his
officer. 'They're up on the terraces.'

Indeed, the fire from above had increased. Still the marksman-
ship was not good from the Zulus, but there was a swarm of lead
coming down on some of the more exposed defenders now. Soldiers
were being hit at last. A corporal staggered by Seb and Evans, his
arm pouring blood. Surgeon Reynolds came and ushered the
corporal into the hospital, to treat him out of the deadly rain of
fire from above.

Chard was calling for B Company marksmen to try to keep up
their own rate of fire, to suppress that of the enemy on the terraces.

The ferocious fighting continued for some time, with some
lucky escapes. Surgeon Reynolds was hit on his helmet, but suffered
no wound. Other men had close escapes from injury and death.
Some died. An NNC man was hit in the back and when an assistant storekeeper bent down to get him a drink, the storekeeper was
shot through the head. The compound yard was becoming a highly
dangerous place to be and finally Lieutenant Chard ordered the
men to fall back to the inner barricades near the storehouse, which
offered a tighter defence.

Unfortunately, as Seb could see, this left the hospital isolated
and the men inside were subject to intense pressure. One rushed
outside during the next attack and was killed on the spot. Shortly
after that the Zulus swarmed over the hospital, killing every man
they could find in the warren of passages and rooms. The fighting

went on for over an hour but eventually the hospital was taken. Some defenders and patients escaped the attack by hacking through the hospital walls.

At one point in the battle, Seb was being harassed by someone firing from the terraces. He felt he was being deliberately picked on by a sharpshooter, probably because they recognized him as an officer. Bullets pinged round him. In the end he stretched himself over the mealie bags and tried to get a shot at his tormentor. Unknown to Seb, though, there was a Zulu crouched down under the barricade, ready for just such a careless moment in a British soldier.

The Zulu grabbed Seb by the collar and tried to drag him over to his side of the barrier. Seb, choking with the pressure on his collar, let go of his carbine and struggled to tear the hands away. The Zulu was determined and pulled and yanked hard in his attempts to get Seb down beside him, at the same time trying to keep a low profile. Seb's legs left the ground as he was bent double over the barricade. They flailed in the air as the warrior began to twist his collar to strangle him.

Then suddenly Corporal Evans was there, having leapt the mealie bags. The Welshman lunged at the warrior with his bayonet, piercing him through the stomach. The point of the bayonet came out alongside the man's spine. Then Evans threw his rifle back over the barrier, picked up the coughing ensign as if he was a child and threw him over too.

An armed Zulu now rushed forward to engage Evans. Evans turned and punched the warrior with a straight right. The man went down like a felled tree. Evans snatched the warrior's iklwa and drove it through his throat, pinning him to the earth. Then the tall Welshman scrambled back over the mealie bags to recover his rifle.

Seb sat up, still coughing, but he managed to say, 'Thank you, Evans – appreciated.'

'Ah, think nothing of it, sir. S'my job to look after the likes of you, isn't it, eh? Now I haven't got a gun to look after, eh?'

Once Seb could breathe properly, he thanked Evans again, saying, 'Apart from everything else, that was an impressive show of strength, Corporal. I'm no lightweight.'

'You're about the same size as a ewe and I've picked up and tossed around a good few of them in my time, sir.'

'Technique, I suppose?'

'And bloody big muscles, if you like.'

Seb would have been better pleased to be compared to a ram, rather than a ewe, but said nothing more.

There was another soldier that night who impressed Seb a great deal. He heard another man call him 'Hookey', which was no doubt a nickname. He then heard Hookey tell that soldier that their comrade-in-arms 'Old King Cole' had been killed in the attack '. . . and damn, I had to leave a sick NNC black in one of the rooms. Couldn't take him with me. They were comin' in from everywhere at that minute. I think they killed him quickly.' Others had had remarkable escapes from the hospital, but Seb only caught snatches of excited conversations from these men as they continued to fight side by side in the gathering gloom of an evening which might prove their last on Earth.

With the fighting still in progress a warm African blanket of darkness began folding itself over the drift. The Zulus still seemed totally intent on overrunning the mission. Their dead were humped upon the ground around the compound now, as more and more of them were killed in the attacks. The hospital building had been set on fire by the attackers and this actually worked against them, for they were visible to the defenders behind the barricade of biscuit boxes, who continued to shoot at any dark shape or shadow that moved in the glare.

However, the thick smoke and bits of flying charcoal when added to the gunsmoke made the air difficult to breathe. It was a distraction to some who had to constantly move upwind for a few moments to fill their lungs with clean oxygen. The sound of cracking timbers and burning mud-bricks also had the defenders afraid that this noise might mask the approach of a sneak attack. They strained their ears against the night, jumping when a beam broke, or a stone split in two like a gunshot in the intense heat. One soldier even felt himself around the chest when a door lintel suddenly parted, wondering if he had been hit.

Seb felt that Chard had made the right decision to reduce the area which they were defending. Their position now was much more secure than it had been when they had the whole yard to cover. Seb's carbine was beginning to jam consistently and he finally abandoned it and obtained a Martini-Henry rifle from one of the dead soldiers. Evans was constantly by his officer's side throughout the whole of the next few hours.

A cheer suddenly went up amongst the men, but Seb never did find out what that was all about. It seemed to him there was nothing to be hopeful for, since the onset of darkness did not appear to be deterring the attackers. The night out there was still full of spikes and bits of metal flying through the air like swarms of bees. It was still possible to die on the end of a point, or to be stung to death. Seb was kicking himself for coming to the mission in the first place. He knew he should have gone with Lord Chelmsford's column, as the general had expected him to do. After all, that was where Pieter Zeldenthuis was, the man he was supposed to be watching. When the shadow of death falls on a man, he has such regrets, and Seb was as human as any other. Having witnessed the slaughter at Isandlwana, he knew what his fate would be, once the Zulus finally swarmed over the barricades, as surely they must. The defenders could not hold their position forever. If no re-inforcements came – and why should they? – the mission would fall.

'Penny for 'em, sir?' shouted Evans, close to his head.

Seb screwed a finger in his ear. 'Do you have to, Corporal? You'll make me as deaf as you are.'

Evans stared at Seb's face in the firelight.

'You'll be in good company, sir – they say that officer over there is as deaf as brick too.'

The corporal pointed at Lieutenant Bromhead, who was moving about his men, encouraging them, lifting their spirits.

'You dunno what it's like in our world, sir. It's not half so terri-fyin' when you can't hear the screams of the dyin' and the yelling of them black savages out there. Sort of peaceful, like. You should try it sometime. Quite useful, actually, in the circumstances.'

'I'm sure it is, man – but thank you, no.'

Evans said with some insight, 'You was gettin' maudlin there, wasn't you, sir? Thinking you wouldn't be seeing your family again? We'll get through this, don't you worry. That there officer, Lieutenant Chard – he's engineered this all right. Clever bugger. He's got us nice and tight in here. It'll take a winkle-picker to get us out.'

'Evans, you can't go around calling officers "buggers" even if it is in praise of their soldiery.'

'Sorry, sir.' Evans grinned. 'But most of you are, you know. And if we're all going to die tonight, as you think we're like to do, you might as well go to Heaven knowin' the truth, eh?'

'I've never met such an insubordinate soldier as you, Corporal, and if we live through this I'm not sure I shan't be calling you "private".'

Evans aimed and fired his rifle, out into the darkness, just as '*uSuthu!*' came out of the night, heralding yet another charge by the determined Zulus, which made Seb wonder whether Evans was actually as deaf as he made out to be.

'Oh, you won't do that, sir. You haven't the heart.'

No, thought Seb, I haven't, which is all very aggravating.

The Zulus were now all around the mission, completely surrounding it. They forced the defenders into an even smaller space with repeated attacks on the shadowed side of the post. The enemy then tried to set fire to the storeroom, where men were firing through loopholes, but each attempt failed. Zulus were now being shot at every approach. Some fell without a sound. Some died with a scream on their lips. And strangely, some leapt in the air like scalded cats and then dropped to the ground to crumple and lay quiet and still.

Seb wondered if these last deaths were theatrical tricks, to try and fool the defenders into thinking they had hit their man. Maybe these leaping men were lying unharmed in wait amongst the bodies of their comrades ready to rise up in an attack. How gruesome that would be, dead men coming back to life! Would it put superstitious fear into the hearts and minds of the defenders? It might do another tribe, but the Welshmen, Englishmen and Irish that were defending this post would probably regard it as an affront to their common sense. They might even think it rather unsporting of their enemy to pretend to be dead.

By midnight the Zulus had fallen quiet. Seb and Evans waited, tensely, for some time for another attack to come, but it never did. After two hours it seemed apparent that there would be no more fighting, at least until dawn crawled up over the horizon. Seb decided to use the lull to speak with Surgeon Reynolds. After all, that was what he came to the mission to do. Reynolds was walking through the exhausted men in the post, having done as much as he could for the wounded and injured. Seb asked him if he could have a word.

'Yes?' said Reynolds. 'What is it?'

'You may or may not know, but I'm Lord Chelmsford's Provost-Marshal—'

'Congratulations,' interrupted Reynolds, wearily.

'No, please listen to me. I'm investigating the murder of Captain Brewer and I need one or two questions answered.'

'By me? I understand it was suicide.'

'I have it on good authority that three shots were fired. Now if it was suicide either the lieutenant missed with his first shot at short range, or he fired a shot after he was dead. One seems highly improbable, the other impossible, wouldn't you agree?'

'I suppose so.'

Seb got down to his enquiry.

'You examined the body, did you not?'

'I did.'

'And what did you find – precisely?'

'Two bullet wounds to the chest.'

'Made by the same weapon?'

Reynolds raised his eyebrows.

'I hadn't thought – well, I found one round still in the chest cavity, the other had gone right through the body.'

'Wouldn't you say that was unusual?'

Reynolds shrugged. 'One might have hit bone, the other not. Anyway, the round that I did dig out was obviously from a revolver and I assume it was from Brewer's own handgun, the Beaumont that he carried. I can tell you that the holes the wounds made were approximately the same size.'

'That,' said Seb, 'tells me nothing. A Beaumont fires a .442 calibre cartridge. The Martini rifle fires a .45. Not a lot of difference there. However, the round of a rifle fired into a man's chest at short range would without a doubt go through the body, which would not necessarily be the case with a round from a revolver. I understand there were no powder marks on shirt or chest, so it was not point blank.'

'Ah,' Reynolds said, 'hence your puzzle with the three shots? No, no powder marks, but there were two cartridge cases from the revolver on the ground beneath the table over which the body was slumped. And two shots had been fired from the Beaumont . . .'

Seb said, 'I think one of those shots went out of the window.'

'A wasted shot.'

'Precisely.'

Reynolds sat down under cover of the side of the storeroom and stared thoughtfully into Seb's face.

'Is that all you've got?'

'So far, yes. But it's enough to make the idea of suicide less probable. My predecessor always maintained that a man would have great difficulty in shooting himself twice in the chest. The pain from the first shot would deter him. I'm inclined to agree with that assessment. Have you any ideas on the subject?'

'Now that you say it, I remember being staggered by the thought of Brewer turning a pistol on himself and firing twice. But at the time I was rushed. I had to be elsewhere and didn't give it any further thought. Now? Now I'm inclined to think you're right – we're dealing with a murder.'

Seb heaved a sigh and took Surgeon Reynolds' hand.

'Thank you,' he said, quietly. 'I'll leave you in peace now.'

During the night, ghostly figures moved between one darkness and another. Sounds were heard, of the mortally wounded, of men looking for friends, of warriors already mourning. The fire was a backlight to the scene of the slaughter that had taken place earlier. The earth was richer for it, soaked in the blood of those who were the most courageous. The bushes were draped in lifeless flesh and dead bones. They had come here hopeful of victory over those who had invaded their land, had in turn invaded the land of the invaders, and had paid the final dues of a warrior.

In the mission post, emotions were still coursing through the defenders. Some felt hollow and drained. In others strong feelings were still simmering. There was still anxiousness and fear that things were not yet over. They slept a soldier's sleep that night, in snatches of a few minutes. Or not at all. There were many false alarms and many small panics. There was a sense of hopelessness, that men could spend the wealth that is life itself so easily. Pride too, came bubbling up. Pride in the regiment, pride in the company, pride in the individual. They looked out into the eerie darkness wondering at what still lay out there. Even now the Zulus that had crossed the river might be joined by thousands of others from the battle-field of Isandlwana. When morning came would they be as numerous as ants out there, waiting for sunrise and the final assault on these few soldiers who had held them at bay?

Thirteen

When the sun came up not long after five a.m., the dead were still there, but living Zulus were nowhere to be seen. The impi had gone, had slipped away during the dark hours, probably just as sick of the violence as the men they had been hoping to kill. There is only so much bloodletting a man can stomach, no matter how resolute.

It was an ugly sight, that carnage. Bodies were twisted and bent in horrible shapes amongst the paraphernalia of war: the shields, spears, headdresses and clubs of the Zulus. Some were sitting upright as if attentive and alert, propped by the bodies of others. Most lay broken like discarded toys. A few were curled in the foetus position as if trying to return to their birth at the point of death.

It was like a rubbish heap of human detritus. There were brave men out there, looking like discarded logs. Zulus who had charged into the muzzles of rifles and pistols without showing a flicker of fear. Their commanders were no doubt proud of them, though they had not achieved their final goal of overrunning the mission post.

As an exhausted Seb and Evans stood looking out over this waste of human life, a body stood up and fired a shot. Then the Zulu ran off, without having hit his target. Soldiers fired after him, as they would after a running hare, but failed to hit the audacious fellow.

Then, astonishingly, a second figure stood up from amongst the bodies and Seb was inclined to believe his earlier assessment: that there were a lot of Zulus pretending to be dead out there.

'Another Zulu!' cried a bleary-eyed 24th, and raised his rifle to shoot the figure.

'No, no!' yelled the man in English, holding up his arms as he staggered forwards. 'It's me, Private Waters.' He ran a finger down his face. 'It's just soot. I've been here all night . . .' the last words came out on the back of a sort of relieved sobbing note '. . . all night. Hiding in the – in among the dead blacks.'

'Incredible,' murmured Seb, stunned. 'Absolutely incredible.'

Then a man in a gunner's blue uniform crawled out from a pile of dead horses on the far side of the barricade.

'Me too,' he said, 'all bloody night.'

Seb learned that both men had escaped from the hospital at the height of the fighting in that building and had somehow survived. Waters told his astonished comrades that Zulus ran over him in their attacks during the night and he showed them bruises to prove it.

'Horny feet, they had. Hard as brick.'

He went off to be treated by the surgeon.

One further story emerged that impressed Seb a great deal. Private Waters had been with another man, Beckett, and they had hidden in a large wardrobe when the Zulus came into the hospital room. Beckett had tried unsuccessfully to flee, but the undetected Waters remained in the wardrobe until the Zulus had left the room. Beckett was now unfortunately one of the dead, while Waters, though wounded twice, was amongst the living.

Some time later Seb heard that Lord Chelmsford's column had been sighted.

'. . . yes, yes, it's not the Zulus comin' back,' cried a relieved but excited voice, 'it's the 3rd NNC!'

Seb did not want to wait for the general to arrive. There might be some awkward questions regarding his presence at the mission when he was supposed to be spying on Boers. He and Evans led Seb's horse quietly away from Rorke's Drift, then they mounted and rode towards Helpmekaar. It was with some perverse satisfaction that Seb realized he had not given his name or his post to Lieutenant Chard and he doubted Bromhead had even noticed him. Rorke's Drift was in such a state of anxiety when he had arrived that the officers in charge had more on their mind than odd ensigns. Even if Evans had given his name, so what? – the Welsh name was common enough amongst the ranks. No doubt they would remember having seen an ensign there, but who he was, or what he was doing there Seb believed would stay a mystery.

When they arrived at Helpmekaar, Seb told Evans to go and get bathed.

'You stink, Corporal.'

'So do you, sir.'

'Yes, but I'm allowed to say it, you're not. And don't think I've forgotten you saved my life, because I haven't.'

'Yes, sir,' grinned Evans.

'By rights, I should put you in for a medal – you certainly deserve it – but the circumstances . . .'

'Yes, sir. We were never there, were we?'

'I'll make it up to you.'

'No need, sir.'

'Well – I'll see what I can do about a third stripe.'

'That would be nice – the pay and all.'

Seb then went and found Sam Weary, and the boy Thomas Tranter. They were sitting outside a bell tent chatting. The eleven-year-old looked animated now, his face clean of tear-streaks and his eyes free of terror. When he saw Seb coming he stood up and buttoned his dark blue tunic. Then seemed to search for a cap which was not there. Finally he stood to attention and without the lost cap he saluted smartly.

'Well, Thomas, are you feeling a little better now?'

'Yes, sir – thank you, sir. Have you heard from Jack, sir?'

'Jack, I take it, is your brother? He's older than you, of course.'

'Yes, sir, he's a man, seventeen full-grown.'

Seb shook his head. 'No, I'm sorry, Thomas, there's no news from Isandlwana yet.'

Sam now addressed him as the boy turned away glumly.

'Aita, boss,' said Sam, by way of greeting. 'It is good to see you alive. You fought with the Zulu?'

'Yes, Sam, I fought against the Zulu – they were almost as fierce as the Xhosa, when I fought against them last year.'

Sam, being a Xhosa, smiled at this compliment, his face creasing like crumpled paper.

'I thought to see you dead, sir. Did the redcoats beat the Zulu?'

'I wouldn't say we beat them, but we defended the post and kept them out. They gave up and went home in the end. I expect they'll be in for a tongue-lashing at least, when King Cetshwayo gets hold of them.'

'Not for failing, boss. The impi will do that. But the king will be angry with them for crossing the Buffalo. King Cetshwayo ordered his men not to invade Natal, sir, and now they have done.'

'Ah, I see what you mean. They've lost the moral high ground?'

'If that's what you mean there, yes, boss.'

'Now,' said Seb, sitting in a wicker chair and addressing himself to the boy again, 'what are we going to do about *you*? You did a wrong thing, you know. Deserting the field of battle is a bad offence, even for a wagon boy.'

Thomas looked very frightened at these words. 'Will – will I be shot, sir?'

Seb said, 'No, I think not – you are very young. But it is a very serious charge against you.'

Sam said, 'You didn't join the battle, boss.'

Seb reflected on this, then remarked, 'That's true, but by that time the camp had been overrun and the battle was lost.'

'But, sir, if Tom here had waited until then to start running away, he would have been caught and killed.'

'Yes, I'm aware of that too. It's a difficult problem.'

He was the Provost-Marshal. If anyone was going to arrest the boy, it would be him. One thing was in Thomas's favour: he was a non-combatant. Though strictly speaking all those in the camp at the time of the attack were supposed to remain to assist those who were fighting. Take the drummer boys for instance. A drummer was there to communicate, usually by bugle on the field. If all the drummer boys and buglers ran as soon as any fighting occurred, there would be no one to help the commander communicate an advance, or retreat, or any one of a dozen or so general actions to be carried out by the troops.

It all depended on at what point it was acceptable for someone to take to his heels and run for his life. Certainly a few grown men, officers and other ranks alike, had fled Isandlwana once the camp was lost to the enemy. This boy had left only shortly before them. But was his exit at a pivotal time? It was on the cusp, prob-ably, just as victory had begun to swing in favour of the attackers. Yet certain defeats had been turned into victories before now, when all had remained at their posts.

'It's a sticky problem,' he said. 'We shall see.'

Later, after he had bathed, drunk and eaten, and had some sleep, he was told that drummer boys at Isandlwana 'had been hung up on butchers' hooks, which had been jabbed under their chins, and then they had been disembowelled . . . opened up like sheep while still alive.'

Seb's family motto was 'Love Well, Hate Well, Serve God, Fear No Man'. The Earlys were good at both love and hate, though serving God was done with tongue in cheek and they were sensible enough to fear certain men who were more powerful than themselves.

Seb was now quite sure the boy would not be called forward to answer for desertion in the face of the enemy. Some sixty-odd men had survived the battlefield by fleeing. Seb would swear to any court-martial that the tide had turned before Thomas had started to run. But actually, in truth no one seemed interested in blaming the rank and file at the moment. The pursed lips were reserved for colonels and generals, and governors who began this war without first consulting the government or the Queen, who were as yet ignorant of the war with the Zulu nation and who its king was.

However, there was still the problem of what to do with Thomas Tranter. Seb felt the best answer was to send him home. There was no word of his brother, and it seemed virtually certain that he was lying on the battlefield at Isandlwana. He thought the Tranter family would want Thomas home when they heard of the death of their eldest son. They would want him safe, surely?

'Thomas,' said Seb, with the boy in his tent, 'I'm going to send you home to your mother and father.'

Tom's eyes glistened. 'I haven't got 'em.'

'Haven't got what?' asked Seb, not quite understanding.

'Me mum and dad died of yeller fever.'

Sam Weary, also present at the time, turned his head away and stared out of the tent opening.

'When – when did they die?'

'Last year. There's only me an' Jack.'

Seb's heart sank and Sam shuffled his hard, bare, horny feet on the canvas groundsheet making rasping noises in the silence.

'Well, what about aunts or uncles? Cousins?'

Tom said, 'Nobody. We come out here two years back without nobody else, only us.'

'Ah – right.' Seb swallowed hard. 'Now, Tom, I want you to be very brave when I tell you something . . .'

'Jack's dead, in't he?'

Seb stared into the boy's brown eyes, which were now brimming with liquid.

Tom added, 'I know he's dead – I saw it. The spear went into his belly. He told me to run, so I did. I din't want to leave him, sir, but he yelled at me.' Tom now burst into tears. 'He said, "Run, Tom, run!" an' I was scared, sir, desperate scared I was. I wanted to stay with Jack, but I couldn't . . .' His body began shaking with the sobs. 'Now Jack's dead an' I left him there.'

Sam suddenly reached down and did what Seb should have done. He took the boy in his arms and held him tightly for a moment, saying, 'Not your fault, little soldier. Not your fault.'

Seb said quickly, 'You did the right thing, Tom. Don't worry. I'm sorry for Jack. I'm sorry you had to see your brother killed. It's war, you know. Bad things happen in war. And Jack did the right thing by telling you to run. I know what I said before, but I didn't know the circumstances. You'll stay with us for a while, until I can think of something. Sam, you'll look after him, won't you?'

'Like one of my own sons, boss.'

'Good. Good. All right, now, Tom, you go with Sam and help him with his chores. Will you do that?'

'Yes, sir.'

'Good. Good.'

Seb sat for a long time on an upturned barrel in his tent, simply staring into middle space. Something had happened to him since he had become a policeman. All that carefree feeling had gone. He was aware of responsibility coming at him from all directions. Had he still been an ordinary ensign of the line he would have handed the boy over to someone in authority and believed his duty done. Now he felt concerned for his welfare. It was a strange feeling, and not a particularly pleasant one. There was no Peter to talk things over with, either. Peter had always been more serious about life than Seb ever had been and he would have given a good opinion. But Peter was dead too. Seb felt his soul had suddenly grown a lot older than his body.

At the moment, though, there were more important matters to attend to than musing on his spiritual state. A court of enquiry had been convened and the business of raking through the reasons for the massive failure was in progress. Pieter Zeldenthuis had turned up. Seb had seen him at a distance, and he started out after him once he had gathered his feelings together again and boxed them up inside.

He found Pieter sitting with some friends, smoking a cigar and drinking squareface.

'Zeldenthuis? Can I speak to you?'

Several eyes turned on Seb. They were the eyes of older men, colonials and Boers, who had seen everything the world could possibly have to show them. As scouts they were dressed in a variety of civilian clothes and unmatched bits of uniforms. There was a lack of discipline about scouts which Seb decided offended his sense of military order. He disapproved of their casual attitude, the dry humour they applied to serious situations, the lack of respect they showed Her Majesty's commissioned officers. In general they were a rough lot: shaggy-bearded, leather-faced, dusty, lazy-eyed. In character they were mostly ill-mannered, coarse and brutal in a fight. In short, they were men whose finer feelings had sunk to the bottom of their souls and were now regarded as the dregs of life. Yes, Seb thought them the scum of the army – and yet, oh and yet, how he envied them!

Pieter climbed to his feet. 'Eish, what a mess, eh? Could you have made a bigger hash of it?'

'Me?' replied Seb, hotly. 'I'm not the general.'

'No, but he's *your* general.'

'And yours. You take his pay. That makes you one of us, whether you like it or not.'

Pieter gave him a weak grin. 'Point taken, young ensign. Now, what was it?'

Seb was aware they were still in earshot of the other scouts and he pulled on Pieter's sleeve.

'Let's go over there, in the shade of that thorn tree.'

Once they were standing out of the sun, Seb said, 'Now, Zeldenthuis, no prevaricating. I want to know what you joined us for in this bloody war. You don't believe in it, now do you?'

'The war itself, no. I don't like the bloody Zulus, but I'd rather we dealt with them ourselves, in our own way.'

'By *we* you mean the Boers.'

'I mean the Boers. We've had the Zulus as neighbours for longer than you. You don't go marching in there with armies. You handle them piecemeal, when they infringe on your territory.'

Seb said, 'I'm not going to get into arguments about the legitimacy of the war. I'm probably more in tune with you on that than you think. What I want to know is why you're part of it all.'

Pieter's eyes narrowed. 'You're not entitled to demand information like that until you've done your share of fighting them. You weren't at Isandlwana, otherwise you wouldn't be here, unless you ran before the fighting started . . .'

'I saw it. I left an hour or so before the Zulus attacked, but I was witness to the slaughter from a distance.'

The Boer's upper lip curled. 'You didn't go back to assist your regiment?'

'I wasn't in time. It was too far. I started back, but by the time I was halfway there, it was all over.'

'So you tell me.'

'Zeldenthuis,' said an exasperated Seb, 'if you insist on trying to impugn my character, I'll tell you – I was at Rorke's Drift.'

Pieter stared down at the smaller man, his eyes searching those of the soldier.

'You were there?'

'From the first attack to the last.'

'I've heard the talk, seen the lists – you're not on them.'

'I was there.'

After a while, Pieter nodded, thoughtfully. 'I believe you.'

'I hope so, because I don't want to call Corporal Evans to verify the fact – he was there too. He saved my life.'

'Stopped you from running, did he?'

'Zeldenthuis,' cried Seb, 'I swear—'

'It was a joke, boy, a joke,' said Pieter, smiling. 'I'm proud of you, eh? That was some fight. I wish I'd been there too. Would give my right arm to have been there. You're not such a Van der Merwe after all, eh?'

Seb was lost. 'Who the hell is Van der Merwe?'

'He's fictitious. A *plaas japie*. A farm boy. The butt of Boer jokes, my friend. Anything goes wrong, it's always Van der Merwe. All right,' his eyes narrowed again, 'you want to know what I'm all about, eh? I'll tell you. You've heard the story about Piet Retief?'

Seb nodded. 'Everyone has. He was the Boer trekker who along with his family and friends was clubbed and impaled by the Zulus in 1838.'

'The whole lot of them, impaled through their arses on stakes. My people.' Pieter's face looked hot. 'The Zulu king Dingane invited the trekkers to a native dance then treacherously had them all killed in that ugly way of theirs.'

'It was a long time ago, Pieter,' said Seb, gently.

'Not for me. They did the same to my father.'

Seb went quiet. He did not know what to say. Pieter Zeldenthuis was blinking hard, not with tears, but as if his eyes were filled with acid and he was having trouble seeing. His breath was coming out in short, sharp grunts. His shoulders had slumped alarmingly. One of the other scouts called out, 'Hey, Pieter – you all right?'

'Yes, I'm fine,' replied Pieter, his voice a little choked. 'Just a bit of dust in the throat.'

Seb said after a while, 'You saw it, didn't you?'

Pieter nodded. 'I watched my father being rammed on that stake. They let me go. I was only thirteen at the time. They laughed – they laughed at me.'

'Rogue Zulus, surely? Not something ordered by their commanders?'

'I don't know. They were part of the impi. They were members of an *ibutho*, a guild or regiment. It was their chief, their *inkhosi*, who ordered the death of my father.'

Seb sighed. 'I'm sorry. No child should have to witness something like that.'

Pieter said, 'No – but I know them, you see. The regiments each have distinctive headdresses. I know them. And when I come up against that regiment, when I find that *inkhosi*, I'm going to tear his fucking throat out. That's why I joined your bloody army, so that I can roam around Zululand looking for my father's killer.'

Seb said, 'But good God, man – you surely won't recognize him after all this time?'

'I'll know him. I know his shield. Every warrior in an *ibutho* has a shield made from the same herd of cattle. I know the markings on the shield of my father's killer. All shield markings are unique. I'll find him, one day.'

'You will recognize the markings? One cow hide looks like another, surely?'

Pieter laughed grimly. 'We're farmers, Ensign. The markings on cow hides are like the faces of people to me. I'll know him. And when I find him . . . but now you know what it's about. You can tell your master, Lord Chelmsford, he has nothing to fear from this Boer. I'm not going to assassinate anyone in his army. I'm after a prey far more elusive and stealthy than a plodding bloody British soldier.'

Fourteen

1. Thatch: possible escape route for a murderer?
2. Three shots fired, the first from a different weapon.
3. (From Peter's notes): No powder marks on victim's chest.
4. Door to DOQ double-locked.

To this list Seb had recently added:

5. Martini-Henry used to kill victim.
6. The bullying of Private Craster.

He showed these notes to Pieter Zeldenthuis.

'What I want to do now is get hold of Private Craster. He's got the strongest of motives for wanting to kill his officer.'

'He's the one we were after before, eh? The one who went off into Zululand. You think he's still alive?'

'I've been thinking about it. If you remember, Craster set out north-east. Unless he's gone completely mad he would come to his senses once he realized what he was doing, and then head towards the nearest army post.'

'That would be the force at Khambula.'

'Yes, Colonel Wood's column. How far's Khambula?'

'It's only about twenty miles east of Utrecht. About sixty miles from here.'

'Would you come with me?'

'What? To Khambula?'

'You've got nothing else to do at the minute. Lord Chelmsford's waiting for reinforcements from Britain. We'll be kicking our heels around here for weeks yet. How about it?'

Pieter was quiet for a moment, then he spoke.

'Why not, I might see that bloody shield on the way.'

Seb grinned. 'Thank you, Pieter.'

'Oh, first names now, is it? Now we're camp brus, eh?'

'How do we get there? To Khambula? Any ideas?'

'Any ideas? Of course I've got bloody ideas. You follow the Blood River until you come to it.'

'That's the one that joins with the Buffalo a little north of here.'

'The locals call it the Ncome. A very famous river, scene of a very famous battle with the Zulus – much more famous than that piddling little fight you had at Jim Rorke's place. A small party of Boers laagered their wagons – something your Colonel Pulleine should have done – and fought off tens of thousands of Zulus with barrel-loading muskets. Not a single Boer was lost.'

'I know the story.'

'Good. Now, are you bringing the corporal and the black?'

'No, I want Evans here, investigating another crime. And Sam has a young boy to look after.'

'Just me and you then, policeman. Though why you've set your heart on this I don't know. It could kill you. It could kill both of us. It's a dangerous time to travel. Good God, man, two thousand men are lying dead. Yet you're still worried about one single officer? Do you need to ask permission to leave?'

'I've already done so.' Seb did not add that his interview with Colonel Glyn had been a little disturbing. The colonel had seemed remote and remose. Clearly the defeat at Isandlwana had affected him deeply, as well it might, for it was his regiment that had been slaughtered. 'Those soldiers at Isandlwana. They were killed in warfare, not murdered. There's still a great difference between the two. It wouldn't matter if the whole army was cut down. If one of them had been shot in the back by his own side, then it would be my job to find the killer and bring him to justice. You surely understand that?'

'I understand it all right, but I don't necessarily go along with it.'

'You don't believe in justice?'

'I believe in revenge.'

Seb left the Boer, who promised to get them two fast horses and pack animals. Seb walked back to his tent to collect what he needed for the trip. He had purchased some field glasses from another officer and he also wanted to take a carbine with him. Outside his tent, however, stood a tall, lean man with grey hair and scars on his otherwise chiselled handsome face. A middle-aged major. The major, by the facings on his uniform, was one of the 88th Connaught Rangers. One of his hands, the left one, was missing. He had obviously seen action in more than one war and bore the marks.

'Uncle Alex!' he cried. 'What are you doing here?'

'Ah, young Sebastian,' growled the major. 'Good to see you.'

They shook firm hands with enthusiasm.

'Major Crossman to you, Ensign, and I'm not your blasted uncle, I'm your cousin's husband, but if you have to presume on our relationship make it Uncle *Jack.*'

The words were more severe than the tone. There was genuine affection between these two men. Alexander Kirk had joined the army under the assumed name of Jack Crossman and had kept the pseudonym long after it had served its use, which was to prevent his aristocratic father from finding his whereabouts. After serving in the whole of the Crimean War he had married Jane Mulinder, Seb's older cousin on his mother's side. The two soldiers had met at funerals and weddings, and one or two other occasions, and Jack had taken a keen interest in Seb's career, hoping to further it where he could. Seb on the other hand admired and was fond of his 'uncle', a title which seemed appropriate given the distance in age between the two. They were both quite comfortable with it and it seemed to suit the relationship.

'Oh, I forgot. Your army nom-de-plume. What are you doing here, sir? Still gathering intelligence for General Lovelace?'

'Something of the sort. Your cousin Jane, my dear wife, sends her fondest thoughts, by the way.'

Seb laughed. 'Please convey my own to her.' He stared into his uncle's face. 'Horrible business, eh? Doesn't seem real.'

Jack's face suddenly turned long and grey. 'No, it doesn't, does it?' They were of course referring to Isandlwana. 'Bloody politicians and generals jumping in with both feet. As if we haven't enough wars without creating more out of nothing. Egos.' His tone turned more cheerful. 'Now, what's this I hear about you being promoted?'

Seb laughed again. 'Hardly promotion, Uncle.'

'Provost-Marshal? Sounds very grand to me.'

'I'm just a common army policeman. Nothing very exciting, I'm afraid. It came on Peter's death.'

Jack nodded, looking him up and down. 'Ah yes, young Peter Williams. I heard about it. I'm sorry. Very sad. I've seen too many good men . . . Anyway, you look very fit, young fellow. Very fit. I wish I felt the same. Lots of twinges in the old frame these days . . .'

'Uncle, you're only fifty.'

'Only fifty. I went to the funeral of a forty-six-year-old before leaving Britain.'

'Oh – friend of yours?'

Major Jack Crossman stared into the middle distance. 'Not likely. He was the worst soldier that ever served under me – probably the worst soldier who had ever joined the British army. His name was Harry Wynter. I loathed the man – yet, I suppose in other ways, I admired him. I never could break him, no matter what I threw at him. He had a character that would make Ghengis Khan look like the Archangel Michael, and in the end features to match, with his one glaring eye and scar. Worse than this facade, I can tell you . . . but his spirit was as durable as granite . . . well, he's gone. The Devil will have his work cut out with that one. Wynter won't knuckle under to anyone, Satan or not.'

'How did he go? What took him?'

'Drink. He was so soaked in brandy when they put him in his coffin they had to wear soft-soled shoes in case they made sparks with their studs. He would have gone up like methane. That's the danger of becoming wealthy while you're still young enough to enjoy it, Sebastian. You over-enjoy it. I think the opium had something to do with it too. And also I understand he was riddled with venereal diseases.'

'This Wynter really did have a jolly time, didn't he?'

'I'm amazed he lived as long as he did, but life will hang on to a shredded body in some cases, whereas in others it gets snuffed out as quickly and easily as fingers pinching out a candle flame. I've seen drummer boys lying dead on a battlefield, pale but in perfect form, the life simply wafted from their bodies without leaving a mark. No visible reason why they should have gone. Then there are men like Wynter – physically shredded, half-blind, bitter of soul, mentally unstable, internal organs damaged beyond repair by alcohol and other poisons, and various ugly diseases – and they seem to live on and on, gripping to life tenaciously, refusing to let go.'

The pair of them talked for quite a while, then Seb realized that Zeldenthuis would be waiting for him.

'I'm sorry, Uncle, I have to go. Will I see you again?'

'I'd like to think so. Good luck, young Sebastian. I hope you find your man.'

'I think I've already got him, sir. I just need to put him behind bars.'

Corporal Evans approached Seb, just as they were shaking hands to part. He saluted both officers then bellowed, 'Sir, I hear you're looking for me.'

Jack Crossman's eyes widened at this thunderous greeting from an NCO and he looked to Seb for an explanation.

'Deaf,' said Seb. 'Artillery. Good man, though. He's no Harry Wynter.'

Jack nodded and walked away with a parting flick of his hand.

Seb turned to Evans and, using the hand-and-finger sign language Sam Weary had taught them, told the corporal to continue investigating the theft of the major's pocket watch, saying he must solve the business of the different-sized footprints.

How do I do that? signed Evans.

By turning it over in your mind, thinking hard about it, using your powers of observation.

'Right!' yelled Evans. 'Will do, sir.'

And he marched away with an expression that left no one in any doubt that he was thinking very hard.

At noon Seb and Pieter crossed the Buffalo into Zululand and rode north-east along its eastern bank. The day was clear, with a brisk wind that caused the surface of the river to frown. Along with foliage there was always wildlife near any water's edge and Seb's fingers itched to be at his charcoal sticks and brushes. He would have given half the world to have a day free to do his sketching and painting. He saw a beautiful leopard that he knew he could have captured on canvas to delight his parents. However, that would all have to wait for a while yet. Once Craster was under arrest, then he could think about relaxing for a bit.

They passed through Sihayo's kraal, blackened and wasted now after the battle. Seb smiled to himself when he thought about the Harford incident, when the lieutenant had gone down on his knees to pick up an insect right in the heat of the action. He wondered at the man. All in all, though, it made for a good story to tell over dining tables at home. 'There was this fellow called Harford, who pickled a scorpion in the colonel's gin and at the height of the battle they cried out, "Harford is down! Harford is down! . . ."' How amused his folks back home would be and how the story would change, become embellished and embroidered with time and retelling, until even Harford would not recognize it. Seb had a little collection of stories like that. He hoped he would live long enough to be able to amuse people with them.

'There's Jim Rorke's place,' said Seb, peering through his new field glasses. 'I can see his grave marker. There's some of the 24th still there . . .'

'Your blooding-place, eh?'

'Not so, Pieter. I fought the Xhosa and others too.'

'There's no people like the Zulus,' replied Pieter. 'A Zulu can run fifty miles in a day and still fight a battle.'

Seb lowered his field glasses and winced. 'You know, some chap came back from the Americas and told me the same thing about the Red Indians there. It's funny how it's always "fifty miles" as if there's some secret code locked into that figure.'

'It's a remarkable feat,' replied Pieter, defensively. 'Name me a white race who can do the same.'

'The Anglo-Saxons.'

Pieter laughed out loud. 'What, you lot?'

'Us lot, as you put it, are not all Anglo-Saxons. There are Celts among us – the Irish, Welsh and Scots – who would argue very hotly about that fact. And we're a great mix. We've all got Scandinavian blood in us from the Vikings, German and Spanish from the Roman auxiliaries, French immigrants, and even some of your lot. Dutch engineers have worked on our east-coast sea walls and settled there with their families over the last three centuries. In any case, the Anglo-Saxons and Celts have intermarried, even with the Normans, though we don't like to talk about that in polite company.'

'You haven't answered my question, bru – you've avoided it.'

'The Anglo-Saxons? They ran fifty miles a day for four days in 1066, then fought a Viking army and beat them.'

Pieter screwed up his face. 'Ag, wait a minute, wait a minute, aren't you getting mixed up with the Battle of Hastings? Weren't the English soundly whipped by a Norman called William in 1066?'

'Like most farmers, your history is a little ragged, Pieter. The Battle of Stamford Bridge was fought three weeks before the Battle of Hastings. King Harold's army were waiting for William on the beaches of the south coast, but then heard of the Viking landing in Yorkshire. His army took four days to cover two hundred miles – correct me if I'm wrong, but that appears to be *fifty miles a day* – and then he trounced the said Vikings, sending them home with only twenty-three ships out of the three hundred they came in. Yes, I'm sure my calculations are right. Two hundred miles in four days is fifty miles a day.'

'Less of the sarcasm, boyo.'

Seb gave his companion a smug look.

Pieter said, '*Then* Master William whipped their arses.'

'This is unfortunately true, but that was the third battle the Anglo-Saxons had fought in as many months and even so William had to rely on a random arrow taking out the eye of our unfortunate monarch, the last English king we ever had. Since then, we've had Frenchmen, Welshmen, Scotsmen, Germans and God bless 'em, Dutchmen. Probably one or two I've forgot, but definitely no true Englishmen. So all those wars they blame us for, started by our kings, were not the fault of Englishmen at all, but all those foreign monarchs.'

At the fork with Blood River they had to wait for a herd of elephants who were drinking and bathing. Not far from the elephants were some bush pigs, probably using the big fellows as a screen should any of the big cats come down looking for a pork lunch. Then Seb and Pieter were on their way again, working sometimes through thick vegetation and at others along clear paths. Seb marvelled at this wide open landscape above which even the clouds were longer and thicker than any he had ever seen in his own country.

The whole time, though, they kept their eyes alert for any signs of parties of Zulus. All Natal was in a state of high apprehension and fear, expecting a Zulu attack on the towns or villages. In Dundee and Newcastle, especially, wives and children were quaking in terror at the thought that they might be overrun by thousands of bloodthirsty black savages. The Greytown burghers were on the edges of their seats. Stanger businessmen were drawing on their funds for tickets to faraway places. In Escourt they were wondering why they had not settled in the Transvaal instead of Natal. It was all very worrying for the British authorities, especially Bartle Frere, who had started the war without first asking permission from the British parliament.

The pair camped for the night without lighting a fire. Seb felt they were beginning to like each other. Yes, they argued a lot, their national pride ever bubbling near to the surface, but they were even beginning to enjoy that side of their relationship. It was a distraction from the relentless attacks from insects and the thought of snakes getting in their bedrolls at night. Pieter was used to reptiles and big spiders and thought very little of them. Seb, though, was a typical Englishman from a temperate land that had only one poisonous snake, and that one not very venomous. The sight of anything slithering around in the bush alarmed him, especially if it was brightly patterned. He tried not to show his revulsion for such creatures in front of Pieter, though.

Eating their cold fare of biltong and bread, they talked of the battle, which Seb thought of as a British defeat and Pieter spoke of as a Zulu victory.

'You've got to give it to the blacks,' Pieter said, 'they can fight as well as any nation I know.'

'Better. Many of us have said we have not seen braver men,' agreed Seb. 'A spear and a shield, and nothing else? I've yet to see a British regiment bayonet-charge a fortified position that was unleashing the firepower we had at Isandlwana and Rorke's Drift. A bayonet charge through a hail of small-arms fire and shells from guns? Not since the Light Brigade rode at the Russian cannons by mistake. When we do, we get our best poets to immortalize the event. No, you can't fault the courage of the men and boys in that impi. I am stung to the heart by the defeat and puffed with pride at the small victory at the drift, but I will never again underestimate the fighting prowess and bravery of the Zulu warrior. He is indeed one of the best soldiers I have come across.'

'The "buffalo head" charge – that's some tactic.'

'Indeed. A brilliant manoeuvre. It reminds me of the Anglo-Saxon "boar's snout" – a packed body of warriors in a wedge shape, which they used to break up the Viking line.'

'Or the Roman "turtle".'

'Oh, you have had an education?'

'You and your bloody Anglo-Saxons.'

Seb smiled at this, then asked, 'Do you think you'll ever find your rogue chieftain? The man who killed your father?'

'Probably not, but I'm going to keep looking. Every man needs a purpose in this army. That's mine.'

They slept in the open that night, their weapons near to hand. Seb lay there on the blanket and stared at the stars overhead. Some of the constellations were new to him. Southern stars. Others on the edge of the sky were familiar friends. He thought about the times as a boy he had slept in haystacks after helping to gather in the harvest. How black the nights had seemed in England. That was because England was small and tight, and closed around a man. Here, in the African veldt, everything was wide and open. The sense of space was quite frightening to an Englishman. And the land was teeming with wildlife, from bats to wild buffalo. It was some while before he could get to sleep, what with the noise of the animals out there, and the feeling of insecurity. Who knew whether he would not wake in the morning with his throat cut?

Seb woke at dawn, with the mist and wet air hanging heavy on his clothes. His throat was still intact, but even as he opened one eye and stared around him, he saw they were not alone. He did not move.

'Pieter?' he whispered.

'I know,' came the reply, 'I've seen them.'

Some three hundred yards away was a party of Zulus: about a dozen or more. They were armed for war and they were approaching cautiously. Seb could see their feathered headdresses bobbing in the light breeze funnelled down by the river. Silent as stone they crept closer and closer, until they were suddenly but fifty yards away.

'Now,' cried Pieter, leaping to his feet.

The Boer had loosed two shots from his Mauser before Seb's finger was even on the trigger of his carbine. One Zulu fell like a log. His companions scattered, darting off into the bush. By the time Seb was ready to squeeze the trigger, a split second later, there was nothing to shoot at. The enemy had evaporated.

Seb and Pieter went to look at the man who had been hit. He was indeed very dead. Pieter's bullet had gone through his chest and had torn a large exit hole in his back just under the left scapula. He was lying face down and they turned him over. Broad-shouldered, narrow-waisted, he could have been carved from jet by Michelangelo. A black David. His finely muscled body was that of a young god. So very young. He looked at complete peace with the world. A handsome youth, there was not a line on his face, just something of a wry half-smile, as if he was taking an amusing secret with him to the afterlife. He had crushed his headdress on falling, so Seb took it off and laid it on his breast.

Seb could not help thinking that a mother was going to collapse in grief tonight.

Then Seb picked up the hide shield and showed it to Pieter. 'Any good?'

'Nothing like.'

'Pity, it would have been good to lay something else to rest, along with this poor fellow. What shall we do with him?'

'Leave him. His friends will be back for him.'

'Before the vultures and the hyenas?'

'Yes, yes, I'm sure. Now let's get out of here. They may come back in large numbers. These were scouts, but who knows whether their regiment might not be close at hand.'

The pair broke camp and continued along the bank of the river, alert to the fact that they were being followed at a distance.

Corporal Evans was a beer drinker. He was not fond of gin or rum, or any of those hard liquors. He liked to get drunk slowly and carefully with nice long draughts of ale. A lot of thought went into his drinking. That night he was in a makeshift tavern with one of his artillery friends, a gunner by the name of Billy Scraws. Billy was one of those patient young men who did not mind repeating his sentences in a loud voice several times over for the benefit of the hard of hearing. Others were not quite so tolerant and moved away, exasperated by the repetitions. Even Jock McNiece, the only other gunner in the hut, who was fond of 'deef auld bastards like Evans', joined the infantrymen at the other end of the plank between two barrels that served as a counter for the bar.

'So,' cried Billy, supping at the tin tankard he had carried with him on every campaign so far, 'what's it like being a bobby, mate?'

'I'm no bobby, see,' replied Evans, indignantly. 'I'm what you call an Assistant Provost-Marshal.'

'Well, there's posh for you,' said Billy in a mock Welsh accent, for he was from the West Country of England himself. 'An Assistant Provost-Marshal? Sounds very grand, eh? But you still do the same job as the rusty guns, eh? You got to arrest criminals and such. What about if you get drunk yourself, eh? Does Evans arrest Evans?'

'I don't bother with drunks or petty thieves,' replied the corporal. 'That's for the regiment. I only deal with serious stuff, like. Really bad stuff, like murder and theft from an officer. You pinch from an officer and then you'll find me on your tail, that's what it's about.'

He quaffed his drink with great satisfaction, noting that even those at the end of the bar were pricking up their ears.

'Cases,' said Evans. 'That's what me and the officer works on – serious cases.'

'Like what?' asked Billy. 'What cases?'

'Theft of a pocket watch from a major, that's what,' came the smug reply. 'Gold watch worth a fortune, I'm told. I've got one or two ideas already. He'd better watch out, that thief, because I'll be on to 'im pretty quick, once I get my brain around the case.'

'Well,' said Billy, who was only four feet eight inches tall in his army boots, but as thick-skinned and bulky as a rhinoceros, 'if I was you I'd go about recovery, rather'n arresting the dip that did it. You might get one of your pals in deep muck, simply because he'd had a skinful and did somethin' he wouldn't normally do. What if it's Joe Howdyago or Harry Norbut? You know what tarts they are when they're drunk as a fiddler's monkeys. They won't thank you for gettin' 'em a flogging, now will they?'

This was true. Why, Evans himself had done some pretty bad things in the past, when overcome by the blind staggers. Perhaps Billy was right? Maybe it would be wise to try to recover the stolen goods without prosecuting the thief. A thief who no more wanted to be such than men wanted to be here shooting savages before breakfast. But how did one go about recovering property taken by a drunk?

'You got any ideas?' he asked Billy. 'About getting the watch back, I mean?'

'Yes,' said Billy, 'as a matter o' fact, I have.'

Fifteen

Seb could not help feeling regret regarding the young man who had been killed back on the trail. Yes, he told himself, Ensign Sebastian Early was a soldier, but though that involved killing an enemy, there was not often time for reflection afterwards. It had been quite unnerving looking down on that youthful Zulu warrior, lying in apparent tranquillity among the grasses. It was as if the fellow was saying, 'I'm out of it. It's up to everyone else now.' Seb was beginning to wish he was out of it too. A defeat like Isandlwana knocks all the confidence out of a professional soldier. He begins to doubt the invincibility of his army. Yet, he told himself, this was not the first major setback the British army had experienced in the last hundred or so years. They had lost the Americas to the colonialists who had settled there. They had been slaughtered by tribesmen on their way back to the Punjab from Kabul (actually, that was not strictly the British army, but the army of the Honourable East India Company). And they had been given several bloody noses by the Sepoys during the Indian mutiny.

'You think they've picked up that dead warrior now?' he asked Pieter, who snorted.

'Stop worrying about things you can't change. He won't come back to life again, and we've got to preserve our own. There could be any number of Zulus hiding in the dongas hereabouts. Worry about the live ones, if you must, not the dead fellows.'

They were riding side by side through undulating veldt, with a reluctant pack-mule behind. The mule kept imagining it could smell lions, and would let out a wheezing yell and dig in its hooves, eyes white and rolling. It would take both riders to shift the animal from its moorings, pulling on two ropes. They would go another two miles and then the mule would anchor itself again, with the same dramatic performance.

'Ag, I swear I'm going to kebab and eat this loskop tonight,' snarled Pieter. 'He's more trouble than he's worth.'

'Maybe he really can smell danger?' said Seb. 'You know, animals have a much better sense of smell than humans.'

'Not this human. I've lived in the bush far longer than this chickenshit beast. He's a bloody townie, you can see it in his stride. Been used to drawing a milk cart, most probably. Never seen anything wilder than a dog without a collar. I'll chop him up tonight, you just wait. Yes, you,' he said to the mule, 'I'm going to roast you, boysie.'

Strangely enough the mule either sensed he had pushed his luck far enough or had got tired of his dramatics, for he trotted forward now and looked as though he was ready to carry angels on his back.

That night they again camped without a fire.

'How about you?' asked Pieter. 'What's your life story.'

'Totally uninteresting,' answered Seb. 'Uninteresting, that is, until I came to Africa. I was born in a village called Much Wenlock, in Shropshire. My father is the headmaster of a school there. My mother came from gentry who no longer speak to her, or any of us on our side of the family, but she had her own money so we don't need them. When I was a youngster my mother promised to purchase a commission for me, when I was old enough to join. Fortunately it became unnecessary. I was able to join the army without the need for expense.'

Pieter shook his head. 'That's something that's totally alien to me and my brothers – to buy an officer rank in an army! Crazy. How are you going to get the best men for the job that way? What makes you think that money can produce the best strategists, the best generals, eh? Ghengis Khan was no gentleman.'

'The purchase of commissions ceased, oh, eight years ago, but it worked all right when we had it. We have an empire that stretches around the globe, Pieter. The idea is that men who buy into the army have the nation's best interest at heart, because they own land. Landed gentry would have everything to lose and nothing to gain by a military dictatorship, such as has happened in other countries, other armies. Thus we kept ourselves safe from such horrors by having aristocrats lead our army. Of course there were some idiots amongst them, but a lot of good ones too.'

'So how much would your mother have had to pay?'

'For my ensigncy? Four hundred pounds.'

Pieter whistled softly. 'That's a lot of money, bru.'

Seb sighed. 'Well, that was just for an ordinary regiment of infantry. I actually wanted to go in the dragoons, but it would have been too expensive at seven hundred and thirty-five pounds. Even the Guards would have cost six hundred. I did try for both of those of course – and failed.'

'What a dof system. Couldn't you become an officer in any other way in those days?'

Seb thought about that and said, 'Yes, you could get promotion from the ranks, if you were extremely lucky. My Uncle Jack did that, despite being able to afford a commission in any regiment he chose to join. Jack had his reasons, which were to do with family. But there needed to be a space that had to be filled with some urgency if you wanted to walk into a commission without paying for it. War was helpful in that respect. An officer killed on the field abroad might have had his place taken by a man waiting in the wings. Or you could have joined the Ordnance Corps for nothing and have gone to Woolwich Academy to be trained as an engineer or in the artillery.'

'I like the sound of your Uncle Jack, but you – you rather sniff at those commissions?'

'No – well, yes – no . . .'

'You're a bloody snob, boy, let's face it.'

'I suppose I am, concerning my regiment. That's the whole point. Within the cavalry the Light Brigade know they are much more dashing than the Heavy Brigade, lancer regiments coming from much more aristocratic backgrounds than the dragoons. Naturally the cavalry looks down on the infantry. Within the infantry the Guards of course consider themselves to be a higher form of life than the fusiliers. The fusiliers in their turn regard themselves superior to ordinary regiments of foot. And the cavalry and all the infantry and everyone else in the army look down their long noses at the Ordnance Corps – and the poor Ordnance Corps of engineers and artillery just bless the Lord every night that they are allowed to enter the officers' mess, even though they have to huddle together with the surgeons because no real gentleman will talk to either of them.'

Both men laughed at this ludicrous picture Seb had painted of his brother officers.

'I'm glad I'm only one of your scouts,' said Pieter. 'I wouldn't know where my place was amongst that lot.'

'Oh, and there is one other way you can get a commission in the army, if you're shabby genteel.'

'What's that? Shabby genteel.'

'An aristocrat with very little money. One needs enough to keep oneself, day-by-day of course, but if one can't raise the whole purchase price one can join as a gentleman volunteer. That means you wear a uniform of a similar cut to an officer, but without any braid or finery. You can socialize with the officers, but you carry a rifle and march with the ranks. You become a sort of officer-in-waiting. You get no pay and have to support yourself on whatever meagre allowance you receive from your family, but once a vacancy appears in the officers' quarters, you may get a chance to fill it. You know Mad Henry?'

'Everyone knows Mad Henry.'

'Well, he was a gentleman volunteer, until they gave him his lieutenancy. It all sounds ludicrous, but the system actually serves us well and works. It has done so for nine hundred years, with only one or two hiccups.'

'Kabul.'

'And now Isandlwana.'

The pair rode into the camp at Khambula, which sat on a grassy hill. Rows of bell tents stood in front of a hexagonal laager where the horses were corralled. To the east of this laager of wagons was a similar area containing cattle with a palisade that looped out like a lasso to a redoubt. The fence was six feet high and made of thornwood. There were four guns on the ridge which were lined up between the two laagered areas. There were also trenches dug in front of the wagons, to slow down any attack. Isandlwana has taught someone a lesson, thought Seb, as he hailed the sentries on approach. Seb sought out Colonel Wood but found only his aide. He explained to a bored-looking major that he was there to investigate a murder, but that his presence need not concern Colonel Wood.

'I'm sure it won't,' replied the major. 'The colonel is rarely concerned by any kind of ensign, let alone one on policeman's duties.'

'I expect the colonel is rather busy at the present.'

'Hairless, is the word. Lieutenant-Colonel Buller is coming back with reports every day, of skirmishes with the enemy. We have to be on our toes here, every minute of the hour. The families of Natal depend on us to keep the Zulu out of their back gardens.'

It was true there was a certain air of urgency around the camp. Men moved quickly, their eyes everywhere. Even before Seb left reports had reached Helpmekaar of Buller's campaigns against the Zulu. The lieutenant-colonel had been harassing them with quick raids and swift retreats since Isandlwana, and was having a great deal of success with these hit-and-run tactics.

'I don't suppose you know of any soldiers who came into the camp from Zululand during the past week or so?'

The major was startled out of his boredom for a moment.

'What? Why would they do that? I mean, what would they be doing alone in Zululand?'

'Perhaps fugitives from Isandlwana?'

'Not that I know of.'

Seb left the major, collected Pieter from where he had tended to the needs of their horses and mule, and found a lieutenant willing to talk to him.

'Yes, we had a fellow came in the other day,' said the lieutenant, whose name had a West Country feel to it. 'Called himself Benson. Had a twinge of a Midlands accent. Benson? Not particularly Midlands, is it? Anyway, he was in a bad way. Sunstroke and other complaints. We sent him on to Newcastle by wagon. Shouldn't think he made it. Not wounded in any way, but burnt and dehydrated. Horrible, actually. Red as a boiled crab. Fellow's skin was coming off in layers. Blisters the size of blankets on his back. Ugly injuries. Would have been in a worse state if he'd not had the foresight to cover himself in fire ash.'

'When did he come in?' asked Seb. 'Before or after Isandlwana?'

No one spoke of a battle. They simply used the place name.

'Oh, after. Said he'd escaped during the final slaughter. Luckily he ran north-west and not towards the river.'

'How long afterwards?'

'Couple of days, I think.'

Seb looked at Pieter and asked, 'How far is it from here to Isandlwana?'

Pieter shrugged. 'Sixty, seventy miles.'

Seb frowned. 'I suppose it *is* possible to cover such a distance in two days – but . . .'

'But not probable,' said Pieter, 'considering he couldn't have known where he was going or what to avoid in the way of rough ground and rivers.'

Seb turned back to the lieutenant. 'Thanks for the information.'

'Welcome,' said the lieutenant, then added, 'I say, awfully good news about the Queen's Colour.'

'Oh, you heard?'

'Yes, absolutely. Just today, in fact.'

After the lieutenant had gone, Pieter said, 'Is he talking about your regimental flags?'

'Yes – we call them the colours. All infantry regiments carry them, except the Rifles. The Rifles carry standards.'

The Boer shook his head. 'Astonishing.'

'What is?'

'You British think more of a bit of cloth than you do of men. Two thousand dead at Isandlwana and you're ecstatic that a bloody flag has been found. Neither of you cried out blessings that this Benson crawled here alive. You'd rather a rag survived than a soldier.'

'Only partially true,' agreed Seb, thoughtfully. 'Thing is, old chap, we can't hang Benson from a pole and use him to rally the troops. The colours are the most important symbol of a regiment. At least two men died to save the Queen's Colour of the 1/24th. Lieutenants Melville and Coghill. It's a good thing it was only the Queen's Colour that was in the camp. The Regimental Colour, with its history of awards and victories of the battalion, was back at Helpmekaar, I believe. Otherwise there would have been universal mourning.'

'You're all mad.'

'Yes,' agreed the ensign mildly, 'I expect it does look that way to an outsider.'

During the last throes of Isandlwana, Lieutenant Teignmouth Melville had tried to escape with the Queen's Colour draped over his saddle. He and another lieutenant, Coghill, managed to reach the river but Melville and the colour got swept away. Coghill went to help and also became a victim of the river. The colour was taken away by the swift current and the men managed to crawl exhausted on to the river bank, only to be shot by the Zulus. A party was sent to the river just over a week after the battle and they found the Queen's Colour in the waters and mud, further down the river. They bore it back to the regiment to the great relief of the whole battalion to whom it belonged.

'Mad as warthogs,' said Pieter.

Seb was only half listening. 'Actually,' he said, 'we probably will be hanging this man who calls himself Benson from some sort of pole.'

That night they camped amongst the other tents. It would have been stupid to set themselves apart in a place which was targeted by the Zulus. Picquets called to each other all night: a sure sign that everyone was on edge. They needed the comfort of hearing another voice close by, even though they had been embedded in pairs. The enemy was now taken much more seriously. They were not just a bunch of savages. They fought with military intelligence. They were an army, with a structure and a hierarchy that matched any European army.

The last foe Seb had fought against, the Gaikas, had been fierce and courageous but also undisciplined and wild. They had simply thrown forays at the British in motley groups without any kind of organization. The Zulus were clearly different. The Zulus were well regulated and formidable. The only basic difference between them and the British were the latter's superior weapons and a confident belief they were the God's chosen army. When Armageddon arrived the angel hosts would surely recruit the souls of dead British soldiers and would without any doubt appoint Wellington as field marshal.

There was mutton, biscuits and coffee for breakfast. Seb and Pieter ate their fill and then prepared to ride to Newcastle. It had rained heavily during the night and Pieter was worried about the river: whether it might be swollen at the crossing. So they set out with a certain trepidation on the fifty-odd mile ride. This time they went without the mule, who was more trouble than he was worth.

Despite the fact that Seb had purchased a new uniform before the war had begun, the serge had now taken on a campaign look. It was faded and ragged at the hem, with stains and blemishes everywhere. This was not surprising, since like most officers he hardly took his uniform off. The soldiers in the ranks never did. Some commanders would only let their men unlace their boots and go no further. The human stink was unbearable in the tents. Redcoats had marched out of their training grounds in Britain looking like princes and were now reduced to paupers, which, considering their pay, was probably more appropriate.

In contrast, Pieter Zeldenthuis in his wideawake hat, with its broad brim and leopardskin band, looked casually smart. His dark-grey shirt and pants, made of hard-wearing cloth, were loose and cool-looking. He was a tall man, with an upright carriage, and in truth Seb envied the Boer his bearing. Pieter's manners might be coarse, and his speech rough and ready, but he fitted into Southern Africa like a springbok. Seb was more like a russet fox in a foreign land. He could get by, with his native cunning, but always needing to be learning new ways.

They crossed the Buffalo without difficulty and continued their journey on the Natal side.

'Your mother proud of you?' asked Pieter, breaking a long silence as they rode. 'I mean, you being an army man?'

Seb was caught surprised. 'Yes, of course – why?'

'Father?'

'Father even more so.'

'Hmm.'

Seb thought to let this enquiry pass, but found he could not.

'You had a reason for asking that.'

'Well, if you ask one of your common soldiers the same question, they go all shy and shake their heads.'

Seb now knew what Pieter was talking about.

'Officers are different,' he said. 'Their families are very proud when they join the army. Ordinary soldiers? Well, the soldier in my country has a poor reputation as a drunkard and a waster. It's thought that they join the army to get out of prison sentences or to escape some act of debauchery. Evans' mother I know is thoroughly ashamed that he has gone for a soldier and keeps it a secret from her neighbours. He told me so only the other day. The respectable working man believes soldiers to be the scum of the earth. Be he field worker or factory hand, a father would rather his son starved than join the British army.'

'And are they drunkards and wasters? I've seen some brave men amongst them. Dedicated men. I wouldn't call them scum.'

'Of course they're not. It's a myth. There are those amongst them who're poor specimens of humankind, but you get that anywhere. And they do drink and smoke a lot, but that's mostly to relieve the peacetime boredom. You see less of that when the fighting starts. I'd like some of those so-called "respectable" parents see their son spend a night freezing in his boots on picquet duty, or even just on campaign. They're made of iron, most of these men. They march and die with very little pleasure between, save the camaraderie of their fellows. The regiment becomes their family, their commander their father-figure.'

'That's what I've observed,' replied Pieter, generously, for the Boer was not fond of the redcoat. 'They're hard little bastards, for the most part, even if they are rooineks.'

When they reached Newcastle, Seb went straight to the hospital to find Private Benson. He was fortunate to find him still alive, but only just. One of the surgeons, a very eminent physician from California, USA, who was travelling through but spending a little time assisting in the hospital, told Seb that Benson would be dead within twenty-four hours. 'Kidneys,' said the doctor, tapping the spot on his own body. 'Renal failure is expected. Result of the heat.'

Seb looked at Benson in the third bed down the ward.

'But he looks reasonably alive now. Surely a lot of water . . .?'

'Doesn't work like that,' said the doctor. 'Once the damage has been done, it can't be reversed. I've seen men who've crawled out of the Nevada desert. It's a foregone conclusion.'

'All right, thanks.'

Seb approached the soldier's bedside with a different attitude to the one with which he had entered the ward. Benson, who still owned a schoolboy's face, was an alarming sight. His skin was raw. In fact he did not seem to have a great deal of skin at all. It was just sore flesh covered in a pink ointment which hardly hid the damage beneath. Benson's eyes rolled in his head as Seb approached. Frightened, staring, misery-filled eyes. Seb took a chair and sat next to the boy, looking into those dreadful orbs constantly rimmed with white.

'Have they given you laudanum? For the pain?'

A croaked, 'Yes,' was the reply.

'But why haven't they put bandages on . . .' Seb turned, to call a nurse, but Benson touched his arm.

'No – sir – please no – it – hurts too much.'

'Ah, the cloth touching your wounds?'

'Yes.'

'Now, Private Craster.'

Seb saw a flicker of the eyelids.

'Yes, I know who you are.'

'Pri-vate-Ben-son.'

'No, Private Craster. You deserted and ran off into Zululand. You forget, I've met you before. I know your face.'

The eyelids closed slowly.

'Will – will they – hang me?'

Seb remembered what the doctor had told him.

'No – they won't hang you.'

The boy opened his eyes again and looked into Seb's face.

'You – you promise?'

'I'm certain of it. Now, what happened to you, after you ran into Zululand? Can you tell me?'

'They caught me.'

'But they didn't kill you, obviously.'

'I – I said I'd fight with – with them.'

Seb raised his eyebrows. This was certainly a twist.

'And they let you? You joined the impi that attacked at Isandlwana?'

'No – ran away again.' He tried to smile, but it obviously hurt too much, for the smile collapsed. 'Good at running – away. They – they made me into a black man. Took my clothes. Put fire ash on me to make me black like them. Slipped away – in – in the night. Went north. Cavalry found me. Took – took me to Khambula camp.'

Seb then helped the boy to a sip of water, before he asked the crucial question in a firm voice.

'Private Craster – why did you shoot Captain Brewer?'

The boy shook his head. 'No.'

'Yes, yes you did, because he was cruel to you – he bullied you, didn't he? And you retaliated by killing him. I understand why.'

'No – never – not me.'

Seb bit his own lip. He hated himself for what he was about to do, but he felt it was the only way to get at the truth.

'Craster . . . what's your Christian name?'

'Matthew. Matt.'

'Listen, Matt, I'm sorry to be the one to tell you this – I'm afraid you're going to die.'

Tears brimmed the white-rimmed eyes.

'Your injuries – well, they are such that you can't possibly come through. The doctor – well, there's no chance, I'm afraid. We'll get a priest in for you. Are you Protestant or Catholic?'

'Catholic.'

'I'll see to it. I am very sorry to be the one to tell you this news, but I think it better you know.'

'Yes, sir – thank you, sir.'

The distress in the boy's face was awful to witness and Seb knew he had not told the young soldier out of kindness or even because he thought it was the right thing to do, but because he wanted answers to his questions. He now felt like the dregs of his profession and wished he had not done it. He could have let the boy die in his sleep without the added torment of perhaps hours of waiting for that death. What an ugly, disgusting job this policing was, where you had to do such things to get at the truth. The only saving grace in it was the possibility of preventing someone else of being accused of the crime: the saving of an innocent man going to the gallows.

Seb cleared his throat of the vile taste that lingered there.

'Now, Matthew, you know you can't be further punished. There's nothing more that I or anyone else can do to you. I have to know the truth of the matter of the captain's death. Tell me you did it and tell me how you did it. It – it might save your soul if nothing else. Go to your God with a clean spirit. Confess your crime, Matt.'

The boy suddenly tried to raise himself up on his elbows, his eyes burning now with some strong feeling.

'I – I did *not* murder the captain,' he hissed, indignantly. 'Not me, sir. Not me. No.'

Seb was stunned. He had been sure that the boy's motive had driven him to the murder. Not done it? Then who?

'Do you know, Matt, who killed the captain?'

'No. Not me. Don't know. Hated him. *Hated* him, yes. But not me. Someone else. I laughed when they told me, but I didn't do it.'

'You had a right to hate Captain Brewer – he is responsible for – for what has happened to you. But you're sure you don't know anything about his death? Anything?'

Matthew Craster closed his eyes and rocked his head slowly.

'Am I really going?'

Oh God, thought Seb, shall I lie now, and tell him it was just to get him to confess, and leave the boy a more peaceful end? Before he could answer, however, Craster said, 'I am, I know – the doctor and the nurses – I can tell by the way they treat me – yes, I know. My mother. You'll tell her I had the last rites? Please, sir?'

'I'll write to her.'

'Thousands of men dead, sir. Thousands of mothers, grieving.

Letters floating back to Britain – a snowstorm of letters, carrying tears and broken hearts. Oh, it's all so sad, sir. All so sad.'

'Yes. You'll go with good company. Brave company, Matt.'

Seb left the bedside feeling wretched. Not only had he managed to be part of a boy's tragic last hours, but he was now no nearer to finding his murderer. The whole exercise had been in vain. Not only in vain, but it had left a horrible stain on his soul. The boy had to know sometime, though, did he not? Once he saw the priest he would know that he was leaving this world. Yet Seb was not mentally equipped to the task of comforting a dying man. Dash, elan, yes, he had those. But not the slow gentle patience of a listening man whose courage is in the way he consoles those who need spiritual help. That sort of service did not come naturally to him. He felt despicable for what he had done and had gained nothing for himself in the way of offering succour.

'Damn this work!' he shouted in the passage. 'I just want to do soldiering!'

A nurse came out and stared along the passage. Seb hurried off, embarrassed by his outburst. He found Pieter and the pair began the ride back to Helpmekaar. When they arrived they found there had been yet another British defeat, at the Ntombe River, where almost one hundred soldiers and auxiliaries had been killed. Captain Moriarty of the 80th Regiment was one of the dead. Another officer had ridden off at the height of the battle, he said to get help, but he was now under investigation for allegedly deserting his men in the heat of the fighting and leaving them to their fate. A sergeant had taken over, a man named Booth, and had rallied the men – some of them stark naked – who had kept the Zulus at bay until help indeed arrived. Afterwards they found twenty-five Zulu bodies in the river, but twenty British soldiers were missing presumed drowned in the retreat across the flood.

Sixteen

1. *Thatch: possible escape route for a murderer?*
2. *Three shots fired, the first from a different weapon.*
3. *(From Peter's notes): No powder marks on victim's chest.*
4. *Door to DOQ double-locked.*
5. *Martini-Henry used to kill victim.*
6. ~~*The bullying of Private Craster.*~~

Seb had struck a line through the sixth clue on his list, now that he knew Craster to be innocent of the crime of murder.

'Instead of becoming clearer,' he complained to Pieter, 'the whole thing is slipping away from me.'

'What are you going to do next?' asked the Boer.

'I honestly don't know.' They had just dismounted, having arrived at Helpmekaar. Seb was feeling very despondent. He had thought he was doing so well and had the case almost solved. Now he had lost his main suspect he was just as much in the mist as he ever had been. 'Thanks for guiding me, Pieter. I'm going to see how Corporal Evans got on with the other thing – the gold half-hunter watch.'

Evans was waiting for him. He must have seen his officer ride into camp. He looked nervous as the ensign strode towards him.

'No luck, then?' asked Seb, reading the corporal's expression.

'Well, sir, yes and no,' shouted Evans. 'Depends how you look at it.'

That was fair enough. Perhaps Evans had some very cryptic information which needed a keen brain to dissect? Seb did not at that moment feel quite up to mental gymnastics, but he reckoned that a few hours' sleep and a bath would remedy that. By the evening he decided he could be as sharp as a tack, should Evans want him to analyse any material evidence he had uncovered.

'Show me what you've got, then,' he ordered. 'I can't promise to review it now, but I will do later.'

Evans led him across the hard-packed earth parade ground, past the flagpole, with its flag at half mast, to what looked like an old

wooden storeroom that was coming apart at the joints.The corporal
unlocked the padlocked door and invited his officer to step inside.
Seb did so, wondering what all this was about. If the man had
some written notes he would be just as well delivering them outside
where the light was better. Indeed it was quite gloomy within the
shed!

Seb stared around him, trying to peer into the dimness within.
He caught glimpses of glinting glass and gleaming brass. Here and
there a squarish shape, but mostly disks and circles of light. And
what was that noise? How strange. How very strange. Ticking
sounds all over the interior. One or two rather deeper noises: the
tocking of bigger devices. It sounded as if the hut were full of
timepieces!

Evans struck a match and lit a candle.

Clocks and watches sprang into view, everywhere.

Mostly they were small brass carriage clocks or metal pocket
watches dangling from their chains. But there were some larger
mantel clocks and in the centre of the hut a big square cuckoo
clock.

'What's this?' cried Seb. 'Corporal?'

'I expect you're asking what it's all about,' said Evans, unable to
see his officer's lips. 'Well, sir, it's what they call an amnesty.'

Seb turned to face Evans, who was holding up the candle as if
leading someone to his bedroom.

'An amnesty?'

'Yes, sir, I had one declared unofficial like, amongst the rank and
file, on my own responsibility. It was said that if anyone had stole
a timepiece at any time, and was to hand it in, then no action
would be took against the thief. This is what we got, sir, though
I don't see any gold watch amongst 'em, which is a great shame.'

Seb was aghast.

'What are we going to do with them all?'

'Ah, that didn't come to mind, sir, when I was doing the amnesty
– it was Billy Scraws what got the idea, and I didn't think to ask
him.'

Seb stepped forward and hooked a little finger around a small
loop of leather with a tiny watch attached. He held it up in front
of his corporal's face and mouthed a question.

'And this?'

'A wristlet watch, sir. A lady's one, but you can get them for a gentleman, I'm told. Latest fashion in Paris or Vienna. Bit fancy, if you ask me. Can't see a real man wearin' one of those, eh? Look a bit of a girl's pinny with one of them on your wrist.'

'An amnesty.'

'Yes, sir, Billy Scraws suggested it, to save all the detecting. It sort of worked.'

'It didn't work at all,' Seb pointed out in an exasperated tone. 'You failed to get the gold half-hunter belonging to Major Parkinson.'

'Ah, that bit is true, sir. But then again, we've got all these stolen ones, without doin' any detecting.'

The sound of the tick-tocking was already getting on Seb's nerves when suddenly various chimes and tinkles filled the air inside the shed and the bird in the cuckoo clock sprang into view with its droll '*Cuckoo, cuckoo, cuckoo, cuckoo*,' making Seb jump.

'Four o'clock,' said Evans in a loud, satisfied voice.

Seb put his face directly in front of his corporal's.

'Who the hell wound these up?'

'I did, sir.'

'What in God's name for?'

'Well, it seemed a shame like, to leave 'em dead to the world, sir. Doesn't do a timepiece good to leave it not wound up. The mechanical parts need to keep movin' or they might seize.'

'Is that a fact?'

'So I've heard, sir.'

Seb sighed. 'And how are we going to find out who they belong to? Did Billy Scraws tell you that?'

Evans shook his head slowly. 'No, he didn't tell me that. But we could tell people they're here and they can come and sort through them themselves, eh sir? Pick out their own property.'

'And how will we know they genuinely own the timepiece they choose to pick out?'

Evans screwed up his face. 'Good point, sir. Then we could keep 'em hid, and ask them to describe their particular clock or watch before they go into the shed, eh?'

Seb stepped outside, thinking such an exercise would take them weeks.

'Who does this shed belong to?' he asked Evans.

'Dunno, sir. I found it and asked the quartermaster for a lock. He give me this one.'

'Lock the door again, Corporal.'

'Yes, sir.'

Evans padlocked the door as ordered.

'Now give me the key.'

'Yes, sir.'

The corporal gave his officer the key.

Seb flung it as far away as he could, into the shrubs beyond the parade ground.

'Sir, sir, what was that, eh?' cried Evans, bewildered.

'Never mention this shed to me again, Corporal,' Seb said, marching away. 'So far as I'm concerned, it doesn't exist.'

'It doesn't?'

'What doesn't?' asked Seb, arching one eyebrow.

Evans nodded. 'Nothin' sir.'

'That's the ticket, Corporal. Now we understand one another. What's happened to Sam and the boy Tom?'

'They're back at our tent.'

Seb followed his corporal back to the area where he had erected their two bell tents. There were buildings at Helpmekaar, but not enough to house all the troops. The Provost-Marshal, a man who was here, there and everywhere, needed no permanent structure, unless he was going to lock someone up. So far he had not needed a jail, so he had not requested one. Seb believed in thinking positively. There were of course plenty of crimes being committed, from drunkenness to insubordination to brawling to deserting picquet posts during the night hours. Floggings, fines and other punishments were being meted out on a regular basis, as with any army in the field. But none so far had been serious enough to warrant his attention. The regiments were well able to castigate malefactors without the assistance of a policeman.

Of the minor crimes, probably the most serious was a sentry leaving his post, but up in the highlands nights were cold and some sentries became so miserable they abandoned their watch for a warmer tent. This was so common it was being dealt with almost daily and if all post-deserters were to be flung into prison there would be very few soldiers left to carry out the picquet duty.

Thomas Tranter came out to meet him. The boy's face was shining, seemingly with pleasure at seeing Seb, and this concerned the ensign. He did not want to become a surrogate older brother,

or a replacement father. He need not have worried. It was simply
that the boy wanted to show him an elephant he had carved.

'Sam's teaching me how to do this,' he told Seb. 'He's really
good at it, but I'm getting better.'

'Very good, young Thomas. Yes, an excellent example of a pachy-
derm in belligerent mood.'

'Sir?'

'A wild elephant.'

'Yes, sir, a wild elephant, 'cos there ain't no tame ones, is there?'

'I meant wild as in angry – in a rage – never mind. Look, I
need a bath, or an all-over wash. Can you get me a big bucket of
water, Tom, and put it in my tent?'

The boy scuttled away.

'Sam,' he asked the Xhosa man, 'how's he been?'

'Boss, he has bad dreams . . .'

Seb muttered, 'Who the hell doesn't?'

'. . . and he wets his blanket some time. If he weeps, sir, I let
him do so for a while, then I have comfort for him. I tell him he
is not alone in the world, for Sam is here, and Corporal Evans,
and also the good and generous officer, Ensign Early.'

'Well, we can't keep him forever, Sam. I'm a soldier. When this
war is over I'll probably be posted somewhere else. Another country.'

Seb's trunk had been delivered from Ladysmith. It contained a
fresh, previously unworn uniform. He had his all-over wash, got
Evans to trim his hair and beard, changed into his clean clothes,
and finally ordered a meal from a local peddler of cooked food.
He suspected the meat was not in fact the advertised eland, but
rather baboon or monkey. However he was so hungry for hot food
he would have eaten warthog brains. Evans was suffering with a
bad tooth and had asked Sam Weary to extract the offending tusk,
so while he ate he had to put up with screams coming from outside
the neighbouring tent. When he left his own tent to complain, he
was presented with the vision of Evans lying flat on his back and
Sam tugging on his bad tooth with a pair of pincers, his dusty
black foot on the Welshman's shoulder for leverage.

The tooth came out suddenly and Sam was flung backwards,
yelling in triumph. Blood began pouring from Evans' mouth and
running down his chin on to his coat. Since the coat had over the
last year turned from red to faded purple the bloodstains actually
stood out on the fabric. Evans dashed over to a canvas bucket and

lifted it to take a mouthful of water to swill around his sore gums. Seb shouted a warning but of course Evans heard nothing in his silent world. The corporal then filled his mouth with cool water, swilled, spat it out, and then to Seb's horror took a long gulping draught of the bucket's contents.

Tom came out of the other tent and gave the game away. He stuck his face into that of Evans and told him with glee in his voice, 'That's the hossifer's dirty wash-water, that!'

Evans, his mouth full again, stared first at Seb, then turned and deliberately sprayed the boy with bloody wash-water.

'You rotten bugger!' cried Tom, laughing, and picked up a handful of dust to throw over Evans.

'Rotten bugger, is it?' cried Evans, the words distorted by the floppiness of his mouth. 'I'll give you rotten bugger.'

There was more of this horseplay, with Sam joining in too. Before long the three of them were knotted in a black-and-white ball on the ground, wrestling. There was still enough youth in Seb for him to ache to be part of this harmless rowdy behaviour, but as an officer he had to stand by and simply witness the fun. It ended with Seb sending the lot of them off to clean up at the water point.

While they were away, Seb had a visitor.

'Uncle,' cried Seb, as Major Jack Crossman approached. 'Still here?'

'Still here,' replied the older man, resplendent in a clean neat uniform of the 88th. 'I've got a job for you, young Sebastian.'

Seb was a little worried by this. 'Are you permitted to give me jobs, Uncle? My official position . . .'

'Don't worry, Seb, I wouldn't presume on family connections. I've already spoken to your colonel and he's given me the authority to second you for an intelligence duty. I need you to ride to Fort Tenedos to collect a prisoner.'

Seb was a little surprised to hear this, not because of the nature of the work, which might possibly come under a Provost-Marshal's duties, but because there were problems on the coast.

On the day that Colonel Pulleine's camp at Isandlwana was destroyed some three thousand five hundred warriors were detached from the main impi and sent down to attack Colonel Pearson's Coastal Column of around four thousand men. This smaller impi managed to gather other Zulus on the way down and by the time it reached Pearson it had swelled to six thousand warriors. The coastal force was attacked while crossing the Nyezane River but the soldiers beat off the Zulus. Colonel Pearson buried his dead and then continued northwards. The column marched over some very rough bush country in extremely hot weather and managed to make the mission station at Eshowe. Here they fortified their position and dug in for a protracted siege.

Behind him, at the mouth of the Tugela, Colonel Pearson had left a garrison manned by two companies of the 99th, some sailors, and a number of NNC. This was Fort Tenedos. Jack Crossman explained to Seb that the fort had captured a party of Zulus, a dozen or so, and amongst them was a minor chieftain. The chieftain had expressed his desire to assist the British in exchange for his freedom. Jack wished to interrogate him and get what information he could regarding King Cetshwayo's plans. It was possible that the chieftain knew very little, if there was anything to know, because the Zulus were mostly reacting to the movements of the British. However, information of any kind, regarding the enemy's numbers, positions, plans and even their general state of mind, was important to the staff.

'How will I do this?' asked Seb. 'Do I need to take an escort with me?'

Jack replied, 'I've got a troop of a dozen Natal Mounted Police for you with a corporal in charge. They'll be waiting for you at the fork in the road, by the coffee stall.'

'Right – good. You want me to start out straight away, I suppose?'

'I'm afraid so.'

Seb went back to his tent and found Corporal Evans.

'I've got to leave for the coast,' he told him. 'You keep things in shape here. *Don't* offer any more amnesties to clock-stealers. *Do* work on the problem of the gold half-hunter.'

'Yes, sir,' shouted Evans. 'Don't you worry, sir – I'll put my best brain to it.'

Seb left with some misgivings about his assistant. Evans had shown he was not without intelligence. In fact he had a considerable amount of it. But it was not well directed. There was something erratic about the corporal's methods which was difficult to contain. Instead of approaching problems from the front, Evans seemed to come at them sideways on. It was probably something to do with his years as a shepherd in the Welsh hills. Shepherds have a great deal too much time in which to think. In consequence they overthink beyond a simple approach and then have to come in from another direction.

The 'amnesty' idea was one such. Evans had jumped over the idea of finding the culprit of the crime and had tried to recover the stolen goods anonymously. Seb, on the other hand, wanted the perpetrator, because that was who the victim wanted. Seb imagined Major Parkinson wanted his watch back, but probably he wanted the thief more. Much, much more. Almost certainly the major was enraged that a soldier should have the temerity to steal from him, a commissioned officer of field rank. *How dare he! An unthinkable insult! It was beyond comprehension.* The major's sense of his own importance had been severely wounded and he wanted the man who had done this to him. The watch was secondary.

Seb could not go to Zeldenthuis for a horse this time so he walked to the crossroads where he found the NMP troopers drinking coffee. They had pack animals but no horse for him, probably because they expected him to provide his own. He asked the corporal to obtain two mounts, one for his own use and the other for the prisoner. The corporal and a private went off and duly returned with a brace of nags. They then set off south-east, following the river, down towards the coast. Seb tried talking to the corporal, a young man of around twenty years of age, but the youth was one of those frontiersmen who commune silently with nature. He might swear at a wild beast or a bird of prey occasionally, but apart from barking orders at his men he had very little else to say. Seb's questions were met with monosyllabic answers, mostly of the yes and no variety.

It was not an easy journey to the group of forts at the mouth of the Thukela – Forts Pearson, Williamson and Tenedos – but it was inside Natal and therefore relatively safe. Apart from attacking Rorke's Drift, the Zulus had not seriously crossed into Natal. King Cetshwayo obviously wanted to remain the victim and did not wish to give his enemies any of the moral high ground. The British had invaded Zululand and the Zulu had not retaliated by invading Natal. However, even a lowly ensign knew that the British government would never allow a defeat such as Isandlwana to go unpunished. Even if, when the news reached the British parliament, there was sympathy for the Zulu cause because of the machinations of politicians and generals in South Africa, no humiliated government was going to accept without retaliation the massacre of its soldiers, its officers, its young boys. No one saw this as poor soldiering. It was viewed as a terrible affront.

The Zulu nation would have to pay dearly for having the audacity to defend their country against an invader who blatantly ignored the findings of an independent enquiry into land rights.

The party reached Fort Buckingham at midday on the second day. Fort Buckingham was about thirty miles from Fort Pearson, which was on the western bank of the Thukela River. Fort Tenedos was just a short hop over the waters of the Thukela from Fort Pearson, within the borders of Zululand, the river being the Natal boundary. Seb had a restful night in Fort Buckingham and he and his party set out again the next day.

They finally reached Fort Tenedos after crossing the river on a flat-bottomed boat on the fourth day. The fort was typical of the design of many of the forts in Zululand, roughly hexagonal with earth ramparts behind which were raised firing platforms for the troops. There were also platforms for the guns which pointed out menacingly into Zululand. In front of the ramparts, on the outside of the fort, were six-foot-deep ditches and a barrier of 'wolf-pits', holes in the earth containing sharpened stakes.

Seb reported to the O.C. on arrival and was told he could take his prisoner in the morning.

'The sooner the better. I don't like having the fellow in the fort,' said the officer. 'Who knows that his presence might not precipitate an attack?'

Seb went straight to the prisoner himself. The man was in a small corral guarded by four soldiers posted on the corners. He was still in his battle dress. A headdress of bright birds' feathers and a loin covering of strips of fur. He had been given an army blanket and this he had draped over his shoulders and chest. Beside him was his shield, but his iklwa, his stabbing spear, had been taken from him.

When he stood up, Seb saw that he was a tall lean man with sharp eyes and an intense expression was cut into his features.

'Sah, you come for me?'

'Yes, I have,' replied Seb. 'I'm to take—'

The man interrupted him with, 'I tell you everything you want to know, sah. I have very secret informations. You must listen to me very, very close while I tell you these words.'

His accent was so thick Seb hardly understood what was being said to him.

'No, no. You do not need to tell *me* anything. We are going to Helpmekaar, where you will meet another officer, someone more important than me. You must tell him what you know, not me. If you have some secret it must be for his ears only and no one else's.'

Seb did not want to be saddled with carrying complex information in his head. He had enough to deal with in there regarding his murder case. His mind was not exactly buzzing with theories but there were one or two vague ideas that he needed to mull over without interruption from other puzzles. It was Jack's job to decipher intelligence. Seb was merely the reliable but dull policeman delivering the parcel that contained that intelligence.

'Yes. And when you do meet him, *then* you must tell all you know.'

The chieftain suddenly straightened his back and stared down imperiously into Seb's face.

'Then I will wait. When we leave?'

'Tomorrow. May I know your name?'

'My name is Thandiwe.'

'Mine is Ensign Early. I am merely your escort to Helpmekaar. You must do as I say at all times. If you try to escape I shall shoot you, do you understand?'

'Why would I try to escape?'

There was no 'sir' tagged on to the Zulu's sentences now that he knew he was dealing with a very junior officer.

'You seem an intelligent man. Why would you not devise this meeting simply to give yourself an opportunity to escape? Perhaps you thought to give yourself some time and get yourself back out into the open countryside? For all I know you have a regiment of Zulus out there, waiting for you to leave the fort. Let me assure you, Thandiwe, that if we are attacked you will be the first to die.'

Thandiwe smiled as if he found this highly amusing.

Seb asked, 'What are you laughing at?'

'You – you are small man with big noise.'

Seb drew in a deep breath before replying.

'Am I? Perhaps my stature, which is not great I must admit, has given you the wrong impression? Barrel chests and thick muscles do not make a man, Thandiwe, not in our society. My strength comes from this,' Seb pointed to his uniform, 'and this,' to his revolver. 'I will shoot you down like a dog, sir, if you try to run. At the first sign of any deceit, any attack by your fellow Zulus, and I shall cut off your head with this,' he drew his sharp sword with an impressive ring of steel, 'which I can use with great skill and efficiency.' He suddenly made a cut at the Zulu's head, slicing away one of the outer feathers of his headdress.

Thandiwe stepped backwards quickly in alarm as the feather floated to the ground. He reached up and felt the quill stump. There was an angry look in the Zulu's eyes and Seb knew that for a pinch of salt, had it not been for the guards, the chieftain would have tried to kill him.

'You insult me!' hissed the Zulu.

Seb sheathed his sword. 'As you insulted me,' he replied, calmly. 'Now listen to me – you are the prisoner and I am the jailer. You are not special to me and I expect respect from you. I am at this moment your superior and I won't stand for any more impertinent behaviour. I hope I'm understood?'

He received a sullen glare for an answer.

'I asked you a question,' snapped Seb. 'Reply.'

'Yes. Understand.'

'Very well. We leave just after dawn tomorrow.'

Seb spent an unsettled night wondering if indeed the chieftain had some idea of signalling an ambush on his escort. True, it was doubtful that Thandiwe had got himself captured on purpose. That would not have made a great deal of sense. But there might be some sort of preconceived plan that had been prepared in the event of capture. It could very well be that a horde of warriors were waiting for Seb to leave the fort behind before charging down on him like a pride of lions. He knew he would have to keep very alert on the way back, perhaps even making a wider sweep out into Natal, before curving back in to the road to Helpmekaar. The Zulus would surely not follow them too far into Natal, even if Thandiwe was an important man.

Seb woke on the edge of a dream. He lay there, staring through an open tent flap at the rash of stars on the sky's dark back. What had been in his head, tantalizingly almost within reach, yet agonizingly evasive? It appeared to him now to be both a revelation and a mystery. He seemed to know, yet could not quite grasp its meaning.

Irritatingly close to his memory. So close. So close. Yet he could not recall it with any clarity. It was something to do with the battle at Rorke's Drift. His dream was definitely about that night at the drift, with the firing going on all around him, the Zulu war cries, the death rattles of young men, the flames of the hospital roof, smoke, dust, darkness. What? Something – something in that dream had answered his question of how Captain Brewer's murderer had escaped from that room. He had the wisp of an answer, but it had flown from him like a moth into a lamp flame and vanished.

He sat up, to find an arm coming through the flapping doorway with a mug of tea in its hand.

'Thought you might like a cuppa, sir,' said a voice just outside the tent. 'Can you take it, sir, it's 'ot.'

Seb took the tin mug and cursed his lively mind.

'Thank you, soldier.'

He sipped the hot tea.

What was the clue that evaded him? Surely he could remember if he put his mind to it? Zulus attacking in great numbers? Men dying at his feet? Biscuit boxes! No, not them. Mealie bags? No, nothing there. Escape from a building. Yes, that meant something. Evacuation of the hospital? Yes, yes, something to do with the hospital and its occupants. What had happened there? Private Hook and others had knocked holes in the walls to escape, hadn't they? Yet there were no holes in the duty officer's quarters. What else then? Perhaps it was something the Zulus did themselves. What did they do? Of course, they set fire to the roof of the hospital. Surely that was it? The roof of the DOQ was thatch. Hadn't he already written on his list in his notebook: investigate those soldiers who were thatchers in the civilian life? That *must* be what was nagging at the corner of his brain. The roof thatch. He made himself a promise to further his investigations once he got back to Helpmekaar.

Seventeen

'All right, Corporal, file out.'

They left the fort. The prisoner was closely contained in the middle of four troopers, riding an elderly slow horse. Seb wanted to be able to catch him if he tried to flee. Other troopers rode fore and aft, while Seb took up the rear. Normally he would have ridden in front, but he wanted to keep an eye on all the personnel under his command, especially Thandiwe. Thandiwe sat very low in the saddle, his balance wrong, his hands held too close to his body. He appeared unused to being on a horse, though he had told Seb he had ridden before. If he had, thought Seb, it must have been a very brief experience.

From the moment they left Fort Tenedos, Seb's eyes were constantly on any high ground, watching for the least sign of an attack designed to free their prisoner.

They started out west, for Thring's Post, a trading station which unsurprisingly had been established by a family named Thring. Thring's Post was close to the last bend on the river before Fort Buckingham. The Thrings were British immigrants and naturally quite fearful in the present climate, being as they were within spear-throwing distance of Zululand. Watchful eyes were at windows as the troopers approached and they grew rounder when they saw a Zulu amongst them. The Thrings were relieved to see the Zulu was unarmed except for his cow-hide shield, slung over the left rump of that doddering old nag.

'Swing out for Greytown, Corporal,' ordered Seb, once they had passed the post.

'Sir?'

'We're not heading for Fort Buckingham. We're going via Greytown.'

'Yes, sir,' replied the confused corporal.

Seb rode up and nudged his horse into the square containing the prisoner.

'Thandiwe,' he said, 'if you had any thoughts of escaping, please put them right out of your head.'

Brown eyes bore into Seb's own.

'Sah, I have no such thoughts.'

'I'm glad to hear it, because I'll shoot you right out of the saddle of that old jade you're riding without a second's worry.'

The Zulu gave him a rueful smile.

'I am certain sure you would do this thing.'

'Good, because I don't trust you.'

'Sah, I do trust *you* – to kill me if you have the chance.'

Seb shrugged. 'Well, it's not something I want to do, you understand, but I will if I have to.'

'Just as we killed many of you on the day of the dead moon.'

Seb's head jerked up at these words. Was the man taunting him with the deaths of his comrades?

'You mean Isandlwana?'

Hot eyes looked into his own. 'I mean the great battle,' replied Thandiwe, with a grim smile on his lips, 'when sun dipped nearly into night.'

The day of the dead moon? Of course, he means the partial eclipse, thought Seb. Yes, he's trying to needle me about our defeat. But I won't be baited. Let him think his jibe has missed its mark because I'm a dull fellow and don't understand what he's talking about.

Seb changed the subject. 'You look uncomfortable on that horse.'

'I never ride a long ways before.'

'No?'

'No, sah – I run. I run faster than this horse, that's most certain sure. He has a lame leg, yes? And he only stops from falling over by having four of them. Also, I think he sleeps while he walks.'

So, thought Seb, the Zulu has a sense of humour.

'He's good enough for you,' he told Thandiwe.

'No, I am deserving of a big white horse, for I am a chief.'

'Well, maybe they'll give you one if you tell them what they want to know when we get to Helpmekaar.'

'Yes, I think they will.'

Seb left the square and returned to his preferred position at the back of the column. Even though they were heading into Natal, he still kept his eyes skinned for signs of any rescue attempt. Mostly it was open country, with no visible habitations. There were rocky, dusty patches and there were grasslands, and on occasion, scrubland. The landscape was broad and long. Sometimes it took on a mesmeric form that could drug a group of slow riders with its sameness. One hour, two hours, three hours, and for the most part the scene remained unchanged.

Sometimes on the edge of the world the silhouettes of people appeared, and the cutouts of animal figures, going who knew where from who knew whence. Sometimes a wild creature excited the horses with its scent, or a snake slid across their track making them start. These interruptions were more welcome than annoying. They broke the trance for a while.

Flies. They gathered around Seb's face, no doubt after the moisture that was running from his brow. Ugly little beasts that would not let a man alone for a second. They drove some soldiers crazy. The flies also troubled the horses a great deal, swarming in their scores around mouth, eyes and nose. Sometimes the air was black with their buzzing bodies. Insects and their cousins were the bane of a soldier's life, out here in the semi-wildernesses of Natal and Zululand. Mosquitoes, flies, scorpions, millipedes, spiders. They crawled into things, flew into things, bit, stung and got into the flour. The only things worse were the unseen ones that made a soldier sick and sometimes killed him stone dead.

'Let's pick up the pace a bit,' he ordered, wondering if all cool breezes had vacated the region for good.

The sun continued hot on Seb's back. He developed a headache, which started at the base of his neck and went up over the top and came crawling down into his eyes. His whole pate felt as if it was being squeezed in an iron vice. By midday the pain was almost unbearable and he ordered a halt at a ruined farmhouse. He could hardly keep his eyes open now, for any light was extremely distressful to him.

'Are you all right, sir?' asked the corporal. 'You look a bit peely-wally.'

'I feel very overheated, Corporal. We'll rest here for the night. Can you post sentries for me? Are these walls unsafe?' Seb nudged one with his foot and it felt solid enough. A lizard scuttled out of a crack, running for the cover of the stones below. 'I think we can trust them. They won't fall on us, I'm sure. We'll camp in here. No fires. No drinking either. Have any of your men got hard liquor on them? If they have, take it away from them.'

'Yes, sir, but they won't like no fires, sir. We're in Natal, sir. They've been looking towards a hot meal.'

Seb closed his eyes and tried to concentrate through the pain.
'I don't care what they like or don't like. We don't know who's
crossed the border and may be following us. I'm – I'm going to
lie down now, Corporal. My head is falling off. You take over . . .'

'All right, sir. But you drink a lot of water, eh? That'll flush you
through.'

Seb just wanted someone to cut his head off at the neck and
throw his skull away. The corporal was right, though, it was probably dehydration. He had been concentrating so hard on the horizon
he had forgotten to take on water throughout the day. So now
indeed he did manage to drink almost two pints before he curled
up in a corner of the ruin and after an hour miraculously went
to sleep. In the night a wind sprang up, whispering through the
grasslands. He woke in the dark with the stars glittering overhead.
His head was somewhat better, but the headache had not gone
completely. Now it was a dull throbbing pain which was at least
bearable. Seb was aware that two troopers were talking in whis-
pers not far away from him. One was smoking a pipe, the smoke
being swept past him on the back of the wind.

'Put that out,' he snapped.

The two troopers stopped talking.

'Sir, it's deep in the bowl. You can't see it,' came the reply.

'Perhaps – but a Zulu can smell smoke from ten miles away.'
Seb's rebuke lacked rancour. He could not summon any genuine
severity to his tone now that the pain in his head was subsiding.
All he could feel was relief that the agony was leaving him. He
thought of something and raised himself on one elbow. 'By the
way, where is the Zulu?'

'Here, sir – asleep,' came a voice out of the darkness. 'I've got
'im, don't you worry none.'

'Good. Well done, soldier.'

He fell into a drugged sleep again, shortly after this exchange.

They reached a farm on the edge of Greytown the next day.
Seb went to the farmhouse to seek permission to water their
horses. He was met by a young woman in her early twenties. She
was pretty enough to cause his tongue to knot for a moment: dark
hair, dark eyes, trim figure and no shoes on her small feet. Seb
stumbled out a greeting and then managed to release the question
he had locked in his mouth.

'Ma'am, we would appreciate some water for the horses.'

'By all means.' There was a soft east-coast-Scottish accent in her voice which immediately charmed Seb. 'For yourselves, use the spring water rather than the water out of the well. It's much sweeter.'

'If – if you're sure you can spare it.'

She laughed. 'There's no scarcity of water here, sir. Would you like some eggs?'

'Eggs?'

'Yes, they're sort of oval-shaped things that the chickens make for us.' She laughed again at his confusion. 'I've just hard-boiled half a dozen. You can have two, if you wish.'

'That's – that's very kind . . .' Seb signalled back to his corporal that he could begin watering the animals. 'May I know your name, ma'am?'

'Her name is none of your business, soldier,' said a much gruffer Scottish voice from behind Seb.

Seb turned to see an older man with a hoe in his hand. He was lean and stringy, with a beard and hair white before their time. Seb judged his age to be around forty-five. There was no menace about him, just a plain-speaking rigidity. Clearly he did not want his wife or daughter dallying with an officer of Her Majesty's forces. Seb did not blame him for that. Even if it was a daughter, soldiers were there and gone, and would take a daughter away with them. Most farmers needed more hands around the place, not have them taken away.

The man added, 'Jest water the beasts and be gone.'

'Och, Father,' said the girl, answering Seb's question, 'don't be so unwelcoming. These men are protecting us from the Zulus.'

'Weel, they can do it at a distance, can't they?'

'No, they can't,' said the girl with some determination in her voice. She addressed Seb again. 'My name, sir, is Mary. Mary Donaldson. I'm very pleased to meet you.'

She held out a slim hand for him to shake. Seb barely touched it in doing so, for it seemed like sacrilege to grip that silken skin with his rough calloused fingers. He was mesmerized by this young woman. There had been several females in his life. He had always liked the girls, though his shorter-than-average stature did not always mean they reciprocated. The only serious attachment had been to a second cousin, Isabel Stratford-Murray, but they had drifted apart after only two seasons, spring and summer, for it seemed their relationship had not been able to withstand a dreary autumn followed by a long cold winter.

'Mary Donaldson,' he repeated. 'Doesn't it seem strange to you that daughters take on the suffix *son* without a murmur of complaint?'

'Whut the hell are you talking about, Lieutenant?' snapped the father, as he shouldered past Seb. 'Have ye got rocks in yer head, or whut?'

Seb did not correct the mistake in rank, because in truth most of the regiments now called their ensigns 'second lieutenants'.

'On the contrary,' said Seb, always very good at charming the ladies and staring straight into Mary Donaldson's dark eyes, 'I feel rather light-headed at the moment.'

She smiled at this compliment, then turned and skipped into the farmhouse kitchen, returning with two eggs.

'I'm sorry I haven't enough for all your men.'

'That's all right. It's very kind.'

'What's the red scarf thing, on your shoulder? Is that a *favour* you carry for a lassie?'

He laughed. 'No, no, there's no girl waiting for me. This is the scarlet sash of a Provost-Marshal. I'm a military policeman. That's why I'm escorting a Zulu prisoner back to Helpmekaar.'

'Po-lice-man, is it?' called the father from the kitchen. 'Ye'll find no criminals to arrest in this house, *Sassenach*.'

'I hope we meet again,' she said in a low voice, so that her father could not hear. 'You seem very nice . . .'

'Sebastian,' he said, quickly. 'Seb to my friends, though some of my army chums call me South-East, because my surname is Early.'

'Lieutenant Sebastian Early,' she spoke it as if chocolate were melting in her mouth. 'I think that's a very braw name.'

'It's Ensign Early, but no matter. I too hope we shall meet again. Do you ever get up to Ladysmith?'

'Not so often.'

'Then I shall call in here on my way down to Pietermaritzburg, next time I am given the opportunity.'

'Will ye now?' cried a voice from the depths of the house. 'Is that a fact?'

Seb grimaced. 'Your father doesn't seem to like me.'

'Och, don't mind him, he's afraid I'll run off. Mother died just a year ago, you see.'

'Oh, I see.'

Her eyes suddenly shone. 'I shall be looking for you, Sebastian.'

'I will be back,' he said firmly. 'Most assuredly I will, but permit me to warn you,' he pointed to her bare feet, 'you'll get jiggers in your toes if you walk about without shoes.' Seb was talking about the chigoe flea, which burrows into African feet and lays its eggs. 'You'll be digging them out with a needle, which isn't pleasant.'

'Och, these auld feet?' she said in a broad accent. 'They're no worth the trouble.'

'They – actually, Miss Donaldson, they're without doubt the prettiest feet I've ever seen,' Seb stuttered gallantly, 'and should be treasured.'

'Lord A'mighty,' cried the father's tortured voice from the kitchen, 'can I believe the claptrap I'm hearing now?'

When he got back to his men and the Zulu prisoner they were all grinning. He could ask them sternly what the hell they found so amusing, but he felt too light-hearted to rebuke them. If one of them were to ask him now whether he believed in love at first sight, he would have clapped the fellow on the shoulder and said, 'Most assuredly.' After feeling so wretched the day and night previously, with his blinding headache, he now in contrast felt rather sunny. It was amazing what a few words with another human being could do for a man's spirit, especially if that human being was a lovely young woman.

They now rode almost directly north to Helpmekaar. Although it was around forty miles distant Seb wanted to do it in one day. On the way the Zulu began singing a song. He had a good voice and it cheered the men into singing too. At midday the chorus stopped as the heat overcame their desire to carol. However, much later in the day, as a cool magenta evening was floating in, they again began their lusty singing, with the Zulu making up his own words so he could join in. With Helpmekaar in sight, Seb was congratulating himself on getting his man to his uncle without any mishap. There had been no Zulu attempt at freeing the prisoner and Seb now realized he had been wrong in thinking he was being set up for a trap. He rode forward to speak to Thandiwe as that man was letting rip in full voice with his own version of '*Cheer, Boys, Cheer*' when the Zulu suddenly toppled from his horse.

The sound of the rifle shot came just a second later.

Seb looked around. There was an outcrop of rocks several hundred

yards away. A flash of metal told him that was where the assassin
was hidden. Drawing his sword he yelled for some men to follow
him and charged towards the outcrop. The thunder of the hooves
on the hard ground would have warned any killer. By the time
the mounted police reached the spot any rifleman was long gone.
There were tracks in the grass, which could have come from a
galloping horse, but they disappeared on bare rock after a few
dozen yards. Seb took out his binoculars and surveyed the area
beyond the outcrop. Nothing. No sight of a human at all. There
were some eland grazing in the distance, but the calm of a beautiful African evening had fallen on the scene and the only sound
came from the awakening crickets in the grass.

'Damn it to hell!' yelled Seb, thumping his saddle. 'Who in Jesus'
name did that? Did anyone see anything?' he asked hopefully of
his police troopers. 'Anything at all?'

He was given shakes of heads for an answer.

'What about the prisoner?' he then asked, riding back. 'Any
hope?'

'Couldn't be more dead,' said the corporal, who had dismounted
and had the black man's head on his knee, the eyes staring and
the lower jaw flopping open. 'Dead centre through the heart, sir.
Those Zulus have got themselves a sharpshooter all right. And we
was almost home, sir. Another mile and we would've been supping
beer and sayin' how well we'd done.'

'What makes you think it was a Zulu rifleman?'

The corporal looked puzzled by this question.

'Why, we was takin' this man back for questioning, wasn't we,
sir? Who else would want him dead? Seems to me they wanted
to stop him talking, eh? That's how it seems to me.'

It was a desultory patrol that entered Helpmekaar just a short
time later, with Ensign Early at its head. He thanked the men for
their efforts and told them it was not their fault the duty had
ended in failure. He wondered whether they would care anyway.
The officer would have to shoulder the blame and it was just
another job to them. Indeed, it was *not* their fault the Zulu had
died. If he had escaped it would be a different matter, but who
could have predicted there would be an assassin waiting to kill the
prisoner? Probably only Seb and he had not allowed the idea to
enter his head. Seb knew a man who was determined to kill a
Zulu chieftain! Surely to goodness it was coincidence that had

brought that chieftain and his mortal enemy within sight of each other this gentle evening, where the most dangerous thing at the time had seemed to be the mosquitoes that were abroad in the picturesque twilight.

Miserably, Seb went in search of his Uncle Jack and found the one-handed major speaking with Colonel Glyn.

'Ah,' cried Jack, 'Mr Early! You have my man?'

'No,' replied Seb, dully. He was aware of the presence of his commanding officer, so he did not presume on his relationship with Jack. 'At least, sir, I have him – but he's dead.'

Jack frowned. 'Dead?'

'Shot just a short while ago, as we were approaching the town. A single rifle shot from a group of rocks. Took him clean out of the saddle. I charged the place where the assassin was hidden, of course, but found no one when we got there.'

Jack pursed his lips. Clearly he was very displeased. Colonel Glyn's expression was akin to a sky threatening a thunderstorm.

'Ensign?' he snapped. 'How could you let this happen?'

Seb was immediately stung into putting some steel into his reply.

'Sir, I fail to see how I could have prevented it. I had no notion of an assassin waiting for us. So far as I am aware the knowledge that I was collecting a prisoner from Fort Tenedos was secure. I take it, Major Crossman, that this was not general knowledge in the camp?'

'No, Ensign, it wasn't,' said Jack, in a softer tone. 'There were those who knew of it, but it was not general knowledge.' He sighed. 'Well, Colonel, there's no point in blaming anyone. I too had no idea that the Zulu would kill him to prevent him talking.'

Colonel Glyn blinked, clearly not expecting that it was a fait accompli that the Zulus were the assassins. However, he seemed to accept it without further argument and left Jack and Seb to go over the details of the failed mission in private. Jack asked to see the body and was taken to where the corpse was draped over his horse, hands and feet tied under the beast's belly to keep it from slipping off. Jack inspected the wound and nodded.

'A very good shot, or a lucky one. How far away?'

'Seven hundred yards, I would say, Jack.'

'Yes, a very good shot. No assassin would count on luck at that distance. He'd get closer if it was that important. However, we have many men around who can shoot that well, do we not? This is an army of shooters, with auxiliaries who can shoot even better. Farmers, Boers, gentlemen adventurers, cattle drovers, stockmen. Many of them can take the pip out of an ace of hearts at two hundred yards.'

'You don't think it was a Zulu sharpshooter, then?'

'It may have been. Who knows? No sense in crying over spilt blood now. Can't bring the man back, can we?'

Seb was downcast. 'I can see you're disappointed in me, Uncle.'

Jack shook his head. 'No, no – not in you, Seb. I don't see how you could have prevented this happening. I should have had better intelligence myself. That's my job, to know things before they happen. But there was no whisper on the wind with this one. I somehow doubt that anything we got from Thandiwe would change the course of the war, so I wouldn't lose a great deal of sleep over it.'

'A man is dead, though, killed while in my hands.'

A hand came down on his shoulder. 'You'll have more upsets than this one during your army career, Seb, so I suggest you put it behind you. I'll speak to Colonel Glyn. He's got his own worries at the moment. He hasn't lost one man – he's lost a whole regiment and he's feeling wretched, though it wasn't his fault either. Things happen in war which tend to buckle our plans. I'll see you again before I leave, but I want you to get on with your job now.'

'Thank you, Uncle.'

Jack was about to walk away, when he turned and asked, 'I suppose you would have told me if he had said anything of significance to you before he was killed? Thandiwe?'

Seb bit his lip. 'He wanted to, Jack – but I didn't listen.'

'Ah. There's a lesson for the next time, then. Never mind. It was no doubt only confirmation of what we already know.'

There was no more reproach than these words from his Uncle Jack, but Seb felt as if he had been torn open. Of course he should have listened to the Zulu. That had been very stupid of him. Jack was probably thinking he was an idiot of a nephew. At this moment Seb would have done anything to go back in time. But that was impossible of course, so he had to take his foul medicine.

'I'm sorry, sir.'

'No matter, Seb. I wish I had a gold coin for every mistake I have ever made.'

Seb watched the older man limp away. Major Jack Crossman had scars on his face and neck, a leg that did not function fully and only one hand. Wars – the Crimea, India, the Maori wars in New Zealand – had taken bites out of his body. He still had the tall dignity of an aristocrat, which he was, and his spirit was still strong, but the years had battered him like a craft that has seen many storms. He was coming apart at the seams and his joints were wobbly. Jack had no need of the army. He came from a wealthy family: his brother was a baronet in Scotland with healthy estates. What was more, the two men were close. And Seb's cousin Jane was the daughter of a rich merchant. But the army had been Jack's life and at one time his only family. He was a soldier through and through, once a private and up from the ranks. He had earned his commission on the battlefield rather than purchased it. Some of his own class sneered at him, despised him for lowering himself into what they regarded as the scum. Cavalry officers especially. But young ensigns and lieutenants of foot like Seb saw him as a hero figure, a man with more grit than ten cavalry men put together. A towering model of courage.

Eighteen

Seb scoured the place for Pieter Zeldenthuis and was not surprised to find him out of camp. When he failed in his search he went and arranged for the body of Thandiwe to be given to local Zulus to do with as was their custom with the dead. Seb knew that for the most part the Zulus believed in a divine creator called Nkulunkulu but he was not sure what form this god took. Once, when he had asked Sam about it, Sam had merely pointed towards the sky. However, Seb also knew the Zulus mainly worshipped their ancestors and put great store into keeping their dead relatives happy. If the spirits were angry there was chaos in the land. When things went wrong, it was because the ancestor spirits were angry. Had he had more time he might have tried to study their rituals and customs a little more deeply.

He had given Thandiwe's shield to Sam and told him to keep it safe.

Just as he was walking away from the group of friendly Zulus, he saw Jack Spense, the photographer, lugging his equipment across the parade square.

'Jack!' he yelled. 'Can you do me a favour?'

The bespectacled Spense struggled over to him.

'What?'

'Good God, man,' said Seb, shocked, 'you look awful. Are you ill?'

'I'm not long back from taking photos of the field at Isandlwana. Had to sneak there with a small patrol. Ghastly, Seb. Utterly horrible. The stink alone . . . and the bloated bodies. Animals too. Depressing scene. I must have thrown up all the way back to Helpmekaar.' A grim look of satisfaction underlaid the pale pallor of his face. 'I got my photos, though. I'll show them to you when they're ready.'

'Did you manage to bury the dead?'

'No, this was a quick in-and-out thing. I have no wish to join those poor beggars lying there with bellies tight as drumskins, covered in flies, and scavengers tearing what's left of them. We saw small parties of live Zulus around, but kept clear of them.'

'Would you do a photo for me now?'

'What, you?' Jack began unloading the heavy camera and its wooden tripod from his shoulders.

'No . . .' Seb signalled to his bunch of friendly Zulus. 'Another dead man.'

Thandiwe's corpse was carried to a baobab tree and propped up against the trunk. His shield was placed alongside him. A photograph was taken.

'I'll let you have it in an hour or so,' said Jack.

'Many thanks,' replied Seb.

Seb spent a night tossing and turning, his head full of the things he should have done to guard his prisoner. He was woken the next morning by Tom, shyly bringing him breakfast of something darkgrey and unrecognizable that lay at the bottom of a wooden bowl.

'Some porridge,' said Tom. 'Never mind the black bits, sir, they ain't ants, them's bits o' charcoal from the fire.'

'How are you faring, Tom?'

'Best as can be, sir,' said Tom, with a sigh, 'knowin' me brother's not coming back.'

Seb took a spoonful of the porridge and found it tasted better than it looked. Probably one of Sam's concoctions. They tended to look ghastly and taste not too bad.

'We must do something about you and your farm. What was supposed to happen there while you and your brother were away at the war?'

'A neighbour, Mr Johnson, he's doin' it along with his own.'

'But you want to go back there, don't you, Tom?'

'Not all on me own, sir.'

'No, I see your point. That wouldn't do at all. But what we can do is contact any relations in Britain. Perhaps someone there might want to come and help you? A cousin or an uncle? We'll see. In the meantime, you're quite comfortable?'

Tom grinned. 'Me and Sam and Corp do lots of things together, sir.'

The boy left him alone and Seb found two letters on the sandmat by his bed. He saw that one was from his father. He guessed that the other would be from one of Peter's parents. Indeed, the second letter was from Mrs Williams, who expressed her heartfelt thanks that Seb had ensured the fitting of a breathing tube to her son's grave '. . . though we would know by now if indeed my dear

Peter had been mistakenly buried alive and must assume he has gone from us forever.'

Seb had a rush of guilt for not telling the truth.

There was a short note enclosed with the letter, folded in two, which had a faint smell of perfume. It was from Peter's sister, Gwen, who had been left to seal and post the letter for her mother. The note on lilac-coloured paper again expressed thanks for the kind service Seb had performed, though there was a hint of 'Is this really true?' Also she thanked him for being such a good friend to her brother and hoped that now that Peter was gone Sebastian would not cease to visit them completely. 'We look forward to seeing you again, once you return to England, for you know you are always welcome in this house.' Reading between the lines Seb got the distinct feeling that he was being regarded by Gwen as more than a family friend. It gave him a little unease, for he felt nothing more than gentle friendship towards Gwen, and he hoped she was not developing deeper feelings for him.

'It's probably just gratitude,' he told himself, 'for being her brother's chum – and the fact that I'm here in Africa, an exotic country to be sure, and therefore a romantic figure in the eyes of those who live in mundane circumstances.'

He had found that girls back in England took it into their heads to turn young men fighting abroad into Greek gods. They wrote passionate letters to soldiers while the men were on overseas duty, but once they returned to England the ardour cooled. They were no longer handsome heroic figures fighting for the empire on foreign shores. They were ordinary youths with the same clusters of boils and spots that plagued the boy who had stayed at home and was training to be a farmhand or a vicar.

Once up, Seb did his ablutions, then collected Evans. The pair shared a horse to ride out to the outcrop of rocks where the assassin had fired from the previous evening.

'What are we looking for, sir?' shouted Evans.

Seb signed, 'Anything. Footprints. Hoof marks. *Anything.*'

They inspected the area yard by yard. There were indeed marks in the dust, but nothing else of any significance. No cap button, or rifle shell, or bridle bit. Clearly someone, or some animal, had been here and disturbed the ground a little, but if Seb had been hoping for a decent clue as to the attacker, he was disappointed.

'Nothin' here, sir,' said Evans, loudly. 'Not a blessed thing, eh?'

'You're right. Let's get back to camp.'

Once amongst the tents and the bustle of the army going about its daily business Seb again went searching for Pieter, this time armed with a photograph. He found the Boer cleaning his rifle outside a small ragged ridge tent. Pieter raised his eyes on the approach, but tellingly there was no smile of greeting on his face.

'So,' Seb said, 'getting rid of the evidence?'

'Ag, what's that supposed to mean?' asked Pieter, avoiding Seb's gaze.

'You heard about the shooting yesterday, I'm sure?'

'No – what shooting?'

'A man was assassinated – here, just outside camp.'

Now Pieter raised lazy eyes up to meet Seb's.

'Oh? What, one of your lot?'

'A Zulu by the name of Thandiwe. A local chief. He was coming in to give information. Now anything he had to tell us died with him.'

'That's a shame. Didn't you question him when you had him captured?'

Seb thrust the photo in Pieter's face.

'Recognize him?'

Pieter's expression hardened. 'Don't do that to me, boy – push that thing at me like that. I'll break your neck for you.'

'Do you recognize him?' shouted Seb, incensed by the Boer's attitude.

Pieter glanced at the photograph.

'No.'

'What about the shield? The pattern? Those two white blotches? Mean anything?'

'Not a thing.'

The two men stared steadily into each other's eyes.

'I could arrest you now and throw you in the stockade,' said Seb. 'I know you did it. I found the shell from a Mauser rifle out there this morning. You probably saw me ride out.'

'Is that so? And you recognize it instantly as having being fired from a Mauser rifle, even though other weapons use a .43 calibre round. Show it to me.'

Seb's shoulders collapsed. 'I haven't got it – there was no cartridge shell. You know that.'

'Do I? Why would I, since I don't know what you're talking about, boysie . . .'

'It's Ensign Early to you, scout. I'm an officer in Her Majesty's army, the army that employs you.'

'Not any more,' said Pieter, 'I've thrown it in.'

This stunned Seb for a moment, realizing that if Pieter had finally got rid of his father's killer, he had no need to be roaming all over Africa looking for him. However, he was more than a little angry with the Boer and was certain the law had been severely broken – the law he was supposed to help maintain – and the perpetrator was probably going to get away with it.

'Zeldenthuis,' he said, 'you will remain in the British army until I say you may leave. You joined for your own ends and now those ends have been achieved you want to leave us in the lurch. Well, it doesn't work like that. You will serve out your time . . .'

'Will I?' snarled Pieter, slamming home the bolt of his Mauser with a loud *clack*.

'Yes. If you do not, I shall cause the most unholy stink for you. This was not just another Zulu. This was a traitor who had valuable information for the intelligence service. Information of which the British army was robbed by your criminal action. No, I haven't got any hard evidence that would definitely convict you. We both know that. But you'd be dragged several times through field courts martial, because each time you were found not guilty, I would discover yet another person who had heard you say you were going to kill the man who carried this shield.' Seb tapped the photograph in his hand. 'Lord Chelmsford doesn't like you and is highly suspicious of you. He would be only too willing to let me throw you in jail pending a trial. You want to rot in a British stockade? They're not very pleasant, military prisons.'

For a long time Pieter simply stared at this young officer threatening him with imprisonment. Seb had no idea what was going through his head, whether Pieter was assessing his chances of avoiding all this unpleasantness, or whether he was deciding whether to strike the officer concerned and make his escape. Certainly the Boers would not care about such crimes. Zulus and Britons were fair game for a people who felt they were the rightful inheritors of Africa. They would hide any one of their kind who flouted British law.

'I'll finish the war,' said Pieter at last, 'because of my own reasons, not yours. When it's over, you and I will have a reckoning, soldier. Be prepared for that.'

'If we're both still alive,' muttered Seb. 'You frontiersmen – so melodramatic. I assume you're talking about a duel? We don't do that any more, I'm afraid. The days of pistols for two, coffee for one, are over for good. I'll give you a round or two behind the sheds, but fists are all you're going to get from me, Zeldenthuis.'

Pieter laughed, genuinely amused. 'I'd break you in two.'

Seb admitted to himself this was true. Pieter Zeldenthuis was bigger, harder, tougher and more able than Seb in many ways when it came to raw strength. A boxing match between them would be a one-way slaughter. However, a British gentleman does not consider such things when his honour is at stake. He would rather be slaughtered, and thus subsequently humiliated, than turn from a challenge.

'I might surprise you,' he replied.

'Nooo. Not at all, bru. Look forward to a thrashing.'

With what he felt was a dignified exit, Seb spun on his heel and walked away, his heart burning for revenge. He sat in his tent and fumed for a while, trying to sort out in his mind what to do about Zeldenthuis. One piece of evidence he did have, if it could be called evidence, was the incriminating shield the Boer had recognized. He might be able to shame Zeldenthuis into a confession if he confronted him with the actual artefact, rather than a photograph of it. He left his tent and went to where Sam was sitting by a cooking fire, humming.

'Sam, the shield I gave you. I need it.'

Sam did not look up. He continued to poke the logs on the fire and hum to himself.

'Sam Weary? Did you hear me? Don't say you've gone deaf on me too.'

'Gone, boss,' said Sam, still not looking up. 'Shield gone.'

'Gone? Gone where?'

'Gone up in smoke, boss.'

Seb stared at the fire. 'Good God, man, you didn't use it for fuel for cooking?'

'Not me, boss. Them Zulu come. They want the shield.'

'What Zulus?' Seb was losing patience.

'Them friendly Zulu who go bury that dead Zulu.'

'What? Damn it, why did you give it away?'

Sam replied, 'They need 'em, boss. Us, and them Zulu, when

we die we have to burn everything. Burn all things belonging to dead person. That's the law, boss.'

Not actual *law*, but custom. Burial rituals. Laws indeed to the local people. Seb did recall being told this now, by someone or other. Probably the padre. The dead person is buried wrapped only in a blanket, all jewellery, clothing and ornaments removed from his corpse, and all property belonging to that person burnt on a ritual fire.

Sam added, 'I knew you'd be angry, sir. Please don't send me away. I had to do this thing. It is our way.'

Seb sighed. 'It's all right, Sam. Not your fault. It's mine. I'm a very stupid officer, sometimes. What's for lunch?'

Sam looked up now, his face covered in a creased smile.

'Goat, boss. Very good. Very, very good.'

'Oh well, that's a comfort anyway. Dish it up, man.'

Nineteen

'Evans, how many thatchers did you find me?' asked Seb. 'Three, sir,' shouted Evans. 'All from the 24th.'

Seb made the deaf-sign for 'quieten your voice' at which Evans nodded, and replied with a croaky, 'Sorry, didn't realize.'

Seb asked, 'When can I see them?'

The pair were standing on the corner of the parade square, Seb with his back to it, Evans facing it. They had agreed earlier that Seb would interview all and any ex-thatchers who had been amongst the personnel in or around Ladysmith the night Captain Brewer was killed. Evans had been making enquiries and looking at such records as there were available on campaign and had discovered some thatchers. Two more had been at Isandlwana and obviously Seb would be unable to interview these unless he joined them before the end of the war.

Corporal Evans, tall and swaying like a reed in the wind, did not answer Seb's question. The reason was not because he was being insolent, but because his eyes had not been on his commander's lips. They had instead been studying a gun-carriage team on the far side of the square as the team practised limbering up.

Evans' eyes grew narrower and narrower as he watched, causing his officer to become alarmed.

'Evans!' Seb waved a hand in front of his corporal's face. 'Are you still with us?'

Finally, the Welsh ex-shepherd looked down into his commander's face.

'Got it!' he yelled, slamming his right fist into his left palm. 'By cracky, I've got it, sir.'

'Got what?'

Evans signed, '*The major's half-hunter gold watch. I know who took it.*'

Seb's eyebrows went up and he too reverted to sign language. '*You do?*'

'*Look just there, sir.*' Evans pointed to the gun-carriage team. '*The postilion.*'

Seb stared hard at the postilion in question, but still could not see what Evans was getting so excited about.

'*I see him. So what?*'

Evans smiled, gleefully. '*Look at his boots, sir – particularly at his right boot, if you please.*'

Seb inspected the postilion again and then finally he realized why Evans was excited. Postilions are troopers who ride the near-side horse of the pair or four that pulls a gun carriage. In this case it was a pair. Because the postilion's right leg is between the horse's right flank and the shaft of the gun carriage it is protected by a reinforced boot. This piece of footwear is always considerably larger than its left companion boot, due to the thickness of its armour.

'*The unequal footprints,*' signed Seb. '*The thief is a postilion!*'

Evans nodded, thoroughly pleased with himself.

'*Sir,*' he signed, '*all right to interview postilions? There's not so many of them as would concern me. That's as while you do the same with the thatchers, eh?*'

'*Yes, Corporal. You've earned it. I suggest you take Sam with you, in case you have trouble with your deafness.*'

'*They won't like a black man sitting with me, on an enquiry, sir, but if I take Thomas too, that'll dilute any unpleasantness, if you know what I mean.*'

'*Do as you think best, Corporal.*'

'*Thank you, sir.*'

Evans stalked off, presumably in search of Sam Weary.

Evans did not have much faith in interviews, or indeed in inter-rogations of any kind. Soldiers could be stubborn beasts and no matter how many questions you asked them, they would come up with plausible lies to cover themselves. Also there was a code of silence amongst them, regarding their comrades. You did not split on a fellow soldier, even if it meant you got into trouble over it. It was unwritten school law carried over into adult life. So inter-views tended to be rather shallow affairs, where the interviewer knew he was going to get very little out of his interviewee, and the latter knowing he was bulletproof, unless the man questioning him had more than just a hunch going for him. Evans cursed the day when thumbscrews had become illegal.

In the end, the corporal devised a very sly scheme. He did not need Sam for this plan, but he took Tom with him. They went to where the gunners were eating their midday meals. Evans held back, looking as if he was just out for a stroll admiring the scenery while smoking his pipe, while Tom approached the separate groups of troopers sitting outside their tents.

'Please, sirs, can anyone tell me the time?'

Some shook their heads. Others reached into their pockets to retrieve their watches. Evans watched keenly as they were taken out, but almost always he saw a flash of silver. There were one or two brass watches, but soldiers on campaign do not polish their personal items, having enough bull to do without fussing over things like that. The brass was dull enough to tell even at a distance that it was not gold. In any event, nearly all the watches Evans perceived from the sidelines were full-hunters, with protective lids that needed to be sprung open for the time to be read.

After three groups, Evans was beginning to wonder if his plan was going to work. After all, the half-hunter could have been sold on, or even be amongst those gunners in the other two columns, out in the field. Or even in the hands of a Zulu warrior, if it had been taken at Isandlwana. So many variables, yet still the patient ex-shepherd was hopeful. He was ever thus, believing that hope was the centre-post of life, that it held up the whole canvas of existence.

Finally, Tom approached three gunners sitting eating stew in a small circle, with one postilion amongst them.

'Please, sirs, does anyone have the time?'

All three men shook their heads.

'Oh, I'm going to be late I think,' said Tom, looking distressed. 'Thank you anyway, gentlemen.'

'Hey,' growled one of the gunners, 'Talbot, go an' get that fancy watch you got in Ladysmith and look out the time for the lad, eh?' The same man reached up and tousled Tom's hair. 'He's upset.'

The postilion first looked annoyed, but then shrugged and got up, went into his tent, and returned with a watch. It glistened gold in the noonday sunlight. It was indeed a half-hunter, a watch without a face cover, just the glass shining as the man read the time. Evans' heart began beating faster. Here was his man, indeed. A lucky strike when the fellow could have been elsewhere. Corporal Evans decided that sometimes luck was a necessary part of detection.

He let Tom get away from the group, then marched over and confronted the postilion.

'You are under arrest,' he shouted into the man's face, startling all three troopers. Evans pointed to his red sash. 'Assistant Provost-Marshal, if you please. You will come with me.'

'Bugger if I will,' replied the postilion wearing the incriminating boot. 'Piss off, you Welsh bastard.'

Tall, pale and willowy, but tough as driftwood, Evans struck the man a blow on his chin, knocking him high off his feet. The postilion went down with a thump on his back, spraying dust. He lay there on the ground, groaning, and squirming a little. His two comrades had leapt to their feet and were squaring up, ready to wade into Evans. The corporal stared them in the eyes and held up his right hand.

'Strike me, lads, and you'll go to the stockade with this man. I am an officer of the law, an' this red ribbon tells it, see. That there gold watch belongs to a major on the staff, right. That there trooper stole it from his quarters. You two can go to jail with him, see if I care. Cause any trouble and I'll go and get a squad to drag you all off by your ears and you'll find yourself on the sore end of the lash.'

They dropped their fists after a few seconds more and then stared at their comrade still on the ground.

'Stole it, did he? Never knew that.'

'Thought he'd bought it from a local.'

Yes, I bet you did, mused Evans, a bloody gold watch and him on a penny a day? But he let this go. He had his man and he had the stolen goods, that was enough for one day.

'Get him to his feet and bring him along,' he ordered the two gunners, even though one of them was a sergeant. 'My commanding officer will take care of him.'

'Well done, Evans,' said Seb, genuinely pleased with his corporal. 'I never thought we'd find this watch.' He inspected the timepiece. It was indeed a handsome gold item, with an etching of a rampant lion on the back and yes, of savonette style, with the seconds dial at six o'clock and the winding stem at three o'clock. There was also some filigree work around the edge of the case where it met the glass. 'Yet here it is.'

Their first case, solved. It was a landmark.

The prisoner was taken away by guards and Seb and Evans went together to proudly present the watch to Major Parkinson.

He found the major talking with another officer and both seemed irritated to be interrupted. When the gold watch was produced, the major's eyes lit up, but he was not as ecstatic as Seb had expected. The major took back his property without any real show of emotion and with the minimum of gratitude.

'Oh, my gold half-hunter, thank you, Ensign, now as I was saying, Welbech, we need to . . .' The major continued his broken conversation with another officer.

Seb was a little indignant. 'It is your watch, sir?'

'What? Yes, man, it is my watch.'

'Sir, have you inspected it closely? It might after all be the twin of the one you had stolen. There are many watches . . .'

Irritably the major took it out of his pocket and studied it.

'Yes, this is *my* watch. Here's the lion, and the design of this pattern around the edge is unique. I am sure this is my property, Ensign, so if you wouldn't mind I'd like to finish my discussion with Captain Welbech.'

'Only I was told you were fonder of that watch than you are your favourite hound,' persisted Seb, with some grit.

'What?' The major blew into his moustache, making it billow like a sail in a gust of wind.

'I was informed by my predecessor that you regarded your watch as your most precious possession.'

'Good God, man, are you mad?'

'A little mad, sir, but not as mad as Mad Henry, of course, who takes some beating in that field. I just thought we'd get a little more praise, since you pestered me a great deal to discover the thief and recover it. The thief is by the way a postilion and is in custody. Perhaps you'd like to hear how we – that is my corporal – devised a plan to discover the thief? It's quite ingenious.' Captain Welbech was doing his best not to burst out laughing. Seb could see him desperately trying to get rid of a grin that was spreading over his face. 'It was like this . . .'

'Dammit, Ensign, do you want to be hauled up in front of your colonel, or what? I won't stand for insolence, sir, I tell you that now. I have the watch, I'm happy to have it back, but I also have a great deal of work to do. Praise, is it? Do I get praise when my paperwork is perfect to the point of being art? Not a bit of it. I am merely doing my job. You have merely done *your* job. Now please leave me in peace.'

'You will mention the recovery of the watch and the arrest of the culprit to Lord Chelmsford, sir?'

'Go, Ensign. Now!'

Seb went, with the captain attempting to cope with a coughing fit, spluttering and croaking into his fist.

'Any luck with your interviews, sir? The thatchers?'

Seb sighed and replied to Evans, 'No, not a blessed thing. I'm beginning to wonder if I was wrong. One of those men said it could probably be done, but not with old thatch. He said you couldn't disguise a disturbance of thatch that had been laid more than a year, because of the change of colour on both sides. The weathered side and the protected side that forms the ceiling of the building.'

'Oh, well, maybe we'll get some luck later?'

'Perhaps.'

Everyone was talking about Trooper George Mossop.

Seb came to the conclusion he rarely heard the word 'miracle' used when referring to battlefield escapes from certain death. For some reason 'luck' or 'good fortune' was preferred. Was it because God was not expected to intervene once the battle had begun? It wouldn't be right, he decided, to have supernaturals interfere with a modern battle once it was in progress, or the credit for any triumph would not go to the generals and their troops. It *was* fair to ask God for victory *before* the battle started, to get Him on the right side. But if something extraordinary happened while the fighting was in progress, well that was Lady Fortune.

Trooper Mossop, of the Frontier Light Horse, had survived a leap on horseback over a high cliff into a deep gorge full of trees and boulders. He had walked away with scratches, or rather rode away, for the injured horse was still able to bear his weight. Had he survived a terrible illness that had been expected to carry him to his grave, it would have been called a miracle. But since it was an event that occurred in the middle of a fierce battle, men looked at Trooper Mossop and said to their comrades, there goes a very lucky man. Yes, said the recipients, adding their own highly original sage philosophy, it's better to be lucky than skilful in war. After all, skill doesn't stop a bullet, does it? Thus Lady Fortune got the credit for Mossop's escape from certain death, not the dear Lord or any of His angelic host.

'The gullies and chasms was choked with dead men an' horses,' George told listeners. 'We was being cut down on all sides. My pal couldn't stand it and he put the muzzle of his rifle in his mouth and blew his brains out. They spattered all over me, along with blood and bits of bone. I panicked then and left Warrior, my pony, and slid down the hillside, but the officer at the bottom gave me a cuff and told me to go back up and get my horse, which I did o' course. But that's when we was overrun again and I urged Warrior over the cliff. We fell separate and Warrior got his withers cut up on the rocks. He got me safe back, he did, that lovely Bantu pony, but he died in my arms the next day . . .'

That morning news had come in to the camp that caused morale to fall and confidence to drop even lower. There had been another distasteful defeat of the force invading Zululand, at Hlobane, twenty miles south-east of Khambula. This time it was the cavalry that took the biggest hit, under Lieutenant-Colonel Redvers Buller and Lieutenant-Colonel Cecil Russell. Buller's force had been made up of Wood's Swazi Irregulars, the Frontier Light Horse, Border Horse, Transvaal Rangers and some Dutch irregulars under the command of the famous Voortrekker, Piet Uys. Russell had led the Mounted Infantry, Natal Native Horse, Kaffrarian Rifles and a detachment of Zulus allied to the imperial forces under a disaffected prince called Hamu. These two columns had converged on Hlobane, a wide plateau that could be reached on one side by a dangerously steep pass.

Waiting for the British, who numbered just over a thousand men, had been the whole Zulu army. The pass ended up being clogged with dead horses and dead men, both black and white. Colonel Weatherley and his Border Horse were decimated and both Weatherley and his fourteen-year-old son, who rode with him, had been killed. Also dead were another prominent officer, Captain Ronald Campbell, late of the Coldstream Guards, and a political adviser, a civilian by the name of Llewellyn Lloyd. No one at this moment knew how many officers and men were gone, but the word 'massacre' was being passed around camp in a hushed tone.

But of course, depressing as this main news was, everyone continued to talk about Trooper Mossop.

*   *   *

Just as with Isandlwana and Rorke's Drift, good news followed bad, to rub balm into the wounded pride.

Khambula was attacked by the same Zulu army the day after the disaster at Hlobane and this time it was a British victory. Twenty thousand Zulus went on from Hlobane to attack the camp at Khambula and were slaughtered. Everyone agreed that the Zulu warriors were among the most courageous of enemies that the British army had ever fought. Their bravery under fire was unimpeachable, worthy of any warrior that had seen battle. They ran at guns and rifle fire mostly with spear and shield. They threw themselves at strong defences with little regard for their lives. Their battle chant as they did so was 'We are the boys from Isandlwana'. Unfortunately for these young men in their prime, they were not able to repeat their famous victory, but suffered horrible losses.

On the coast, Colonel Pearson's column, besieged at Eshowe by the Zulu army for many days, was relieved by Lord Chelmsford, who achieved his first personal victory in the war at Gingindlovu.

Within a day of several battles, off-duty soldiers were back to playing cricket. Since the Grand Combination Match of 1877, between England and Australia, cricket had become an immensely popular sport. It was a comforting sound, the sound of bat hitting ball, or ball hitting stumps, and the subsequent cheers. Men in undershirts ran back and forth, collecting runs or gathering up the ball. Shouts such as 'Catch it!' or 'Howzat?' carried on, right into the evening, when a man could hardly see his hand in front of his face and another kind of cricket was taking over the grasslands where a ball had run. Seb wondered at the mental resilience of the troops, many of whom had lost close friends in the last few weeks and who yet might lose their own lives.

Twenty

Seb was waiting for replies to his letters regarding Thomas Tranter. Letters sent to England. It would be several weeks, perhaps months, before he heard back. In the meantime he contacted Mr Johnson, who had taken over the management of Tom's farm. Johnson proved very cagey and seemed reluctant to admit that the farm had belonged entirely to Tom and his brother. In fact Johnson believed that in working Tom's land he had acquired a stake in it and was sure that he could not just let it go back to the original owners. He said he was willing to pass on an allowance to Tom, out of the goodness of his heart, but since the cattle and crops were put there by his hand, the greater percentage of the income was his alone.

'Did Mr Johnson graze his own cattle on your land?' asked Seb of Tom.

'No, it was our cows. Jack bought 'em.'

'With what?'

'With money Dad left.'

'And did you have seed for your crops?'

Tom nodded. 'We sowed 'em ourselfs.'

After this conversation, Seb rode out to the Natal farm. He did not take Tom with him, because he wanted to assess the situation without the boy getting hot under the collar. Johnson seemed an amiable enough man, with a pleasant wife. The pair greeted him and asked him to stay for some cake. The two men sat at a rustic table outside the farmhouse while a happy Mrs Johnson went enthusiastically into the house to make tea for the unexpected guest. The yard underfoot was covered with dung and goose drop-pings. A foul smell hovered in the air and Seb was aware of the mess on his boots. When the question of the farm came up, Johnson's attitude hardened perceptibly.

'I come here from Norfolk, England,' said Johnson, 'to make a better life, an' I don't intend to work for nothin'.'

'How long have you worked the Tranter farm?'

'Six months on my own, but I helped young Jack Tranter a good deal of the time for a year afore that.'

'Still and all,' said Seb, 'you can't just take another man's property without his permission.'

'Tom Tranter an't a man, he's a boy not full grown and to my mind an't old enough to have any rights.'

'It's still his farm.'

Johnson's expression was fixed firm. 'That farm were abandoned by Jack Tranter, who's now dead and gone to his maker. It's mine now by right of a settler. I've occupied it an' I intend to keep it. I'll see the boy's all right in the pocket, but the land's now bin added to mine. I took down the shack they lived in. It's gone.'

Seb's eyes widened. 'You demolished the farmhouse?'

Johnson seemed to be unaware of any wrongdoing.

'I've got the stuff here, when he wants it. A few sticks of furniture and pers'nal effects and such. Bedding and the like. We'll keep 'em safe until he wants 'em.'

'Mr Johnson,' replied Seb in an even tone, 'you have performed a criminal act here. You may not be aware of it, but this red sash on my shoulder is the symbol of a military policeman. I am the Provost-Marshal for Lord Chelmsford's army.'

'You can't do anythin' to me. I'm not in the army.'

'The civilian authorities might think differently.'

Johnson, still seemingly in an amicable mood, picked up a long-barrelled shotgun resting against a tree stump behind him. He pointed it across the table at Seb.

'I'm goin' to have to ask you to get off my property, soldier-man.'

'Are you threatening me with a firearm?' yelled Seb into the farmer's face.

Johnson's face remained impassive. 'You are trespassin' now and I've a right to shoot trespassers. If'n you don't leave afore I count to ten, I'll squeeze this trigger and take the consequences.'

Seb could see by Johnson's eyes that he meant what he said. The ensign turned on his heel and unhitched his horse from the fence. It was pointless saying anything else. As he rode away Mrs Johnson came bubbling excitedly out of the house with a tray of cakes and tea. The chatter died on her lips as she stared bewildered at the retreat of her first guest in several months. Johnson said something gruffly to her and she burst into tears. Seb rode off feeling both angry and guilty, the first he felt towards the man he had left behind, the second because of his bad manners regarding the hospitality of the woman.

When he got back to camp he was surprised to find an abashed Corporal Evans waiting for him with some news.

Evans shouted, 'There's been a girl here lookin' for you, sir. Pretty, she was. Said she'd be back later, when you returned.'

'Keep your voice down, man.' Seb looked around to see if there were any smirking rankers. *'Girl?'* he signed.

'Yes, sir, one of them delicate creatures what wear dresses.'

Seb ignored the sarcasm, which he actually felt was becoming far too frequent these days.

'Did you know her? What did she look like?'

'Like a lost princess, if I can be so bold.'

Seb was halfway through a wash in the open air, the basin perched on a tripod in front of his tent. He was stripped to his vest on the upper part of his body and his braces were dangling down at his sides where he had shrugged them off his shoulders. His boots were still covered in foul-smelling faeces from the farm animals.

'Hello!'

Seb splashed the soap off his face and then wiped it with a rag that served as a towel.

It was Mary Donaldson.

'Oh – sorry – look, I'll just get properly dressed.'

'Och, dinna fash yerself. Are you no pleased to see your new friend?'

'Absolutely delighted,' said Seb, mirroring her smile. 'What are you doing here?'

'I thought to be of some help. I've come to nurse the wounded and the sick.'

'That's very admirable of you. But what about your father? What did he say?'

Mary smiled again. 'He didna like it, but that's no matter. I'm a woman full grown and don't need my pa's permission. You look better than you did when I saw you last. Not so pale.'

'It was a headache, now gone of course,' he said. He pulled his braces up over his shoulders and began to pull on his red coat. 'It's very good to see you again, Miss Donaldson.'

She laughed. 'You Englishmen, you're so correct.'

'Well, I know a few Scotsmen who are equally, as you put it, correct. Some of the officers of Highland regiments would put my manners to shame. It's only good etiquette to try to be at one's

best for a lady visitor. Please,' he gestured, 'would you like to sit
down?' He took the basin from the tripod, threw the water down
the side of the tent, then flattened the tripod to half its height
before placing a wooden tray on it. 'This is the best seat in town,
I'm afraid. You'll have to use your imagination to turn it into a
proper chair.'

She took the seat, saying, 'You know, you remind me of home
– of Scotland?'

'I do?'

'Yes, you smell like an Aberdeen Angus bull.'

He grinned and then proceeded to wipe the sides of his boots
on the grasses well away from the tent.

'There, is that better?'

'A little more fragrant.'

Seb was absolutely entranced by this farm girl from the Highlands
of clan country, though he knew his parents would be disappointed
that he was having a dalliance with such a woman and would be
utterly horrified if they thought it would lead to an alliance. His
mother especially had fond visions of being reunited with her own
class. She looked forward to her Sebastian marrying a girl like
Peter's sister Gwen, who could wear crinoline dresses to advantage, paint watercolours and play the pianoforte, and whose parents
would smooth the way into Eton for his mother's grandchildren.

'So,' continued Seb, 'you're a trained nurse?'

'No, no proper training – but then Florence Nightingale had
none either. She was just good with soap and water, and at putting
quartermasters in their place. Mary Seacole too, who was also at
the Crimea, was a good nurse but never went to nursing school
as such. A soft kind word and a sweet smile go a long way to
healing a man.'

'Indeed yes,' said Seb, in an unguarded moment, 'why I remember
when I had a shoulder wound . . .' He stopped abruptly.

Mary laughed. 'You fell in love with your nurse?'

'An infatuation,' he confessed shyly, 'along with several hundred
other officers and men.'

'They all do it. It's better than medicine, I'm told.'

Seb turned to comb his hair in the mirror that dangled from a
guy line, when he heard a shuffling sound. He turned back again
to see Tom had arrived and was gawping at Mary with his mouth
wide open.

'Tom, say a polite hello to Miss Donaldson.'

'Ummmrrahh,' murmured Tom, not taking his eyes from the pretty lady on the stool.

'So, it seems you've got yet another beau, Miss Donaldson. Do you go around capturing hearts for the fun of it?' Seb asked in an amused tone.

'Oh,' she smiled as she spoke, 'another beau? Have I captured your heart too then, Ensign Early?'

Seb blushed to the roots of his hair and Tom giggled. Again Ensign Sebastian Early looked around to make sure this remark had not been overheard. Soldiers could be as cruel as schoolboys with their taunts. He was terrified that Evans was listening. It would have been even worse if Pieter Zeldenthuis were within earshot.

Mary saw the look on his face and dropped her head.

'I'm sorry, that was very forward of me – I was not brought up that way. My father would be horrified. I'm not really a hoyden, you know, sir.' Then presumably to cover her confusion, she added, 'You men – you grow such long whiskers here in Africa. Why is that?'

Seb tugged on the strands of his moustache and grinned. 'It's the climate. Lots of warm rain and warm sunshine. It's conducive to a good harvest of hair.'

'You think it makes you look more manly.'

'Ah well, you know us men, we're such shallow creatures,' Seb replied, 'and vain, too. Will I see you again soon? I'm not sure where I'll be.'

'Going out to get hisself shot, so's you can nurse him,' cried Tom, with remarkable insight. 'That's what he's thinking.'

The pair, who had now turned a little more serious, studiously ignored this remark from the youngster.

At this moment Sam announced that supper was ready.

'Come quickly, boss. And you too, Master Thomas. It gets cold.'

'My servant,' murmured Seb. 'At least, he thinks he is, but he gets more like my mother every day.'

Mary rose to go, remarking, 'You've got yourself a nice wee family here, Ensign Early, what with your servant, young Tom and that tall man who's hard of hearing.'

'Corporal Evans? He's my assistant. He used to be a shepherd.'

Mary nodded, smiling. 'A nice wee family,' she repeated.

Seb would rather his small group was thought of as a tight military unit, but he did not correct her.

The following morning Seb was ordered to report to Colonel Glyn.

'Ah, Early. Yes, I called for you, didn't I?' The colonel was sitting at a trestle table dealing with a batch of papers. 'Well done on the major's watch, by the way. Now, the thing is, I have another similar case for you. Well, not so similar, more of an expansion of the same. The quartermaster has reported a theft to me.'

'Sir?' said Seb.

'Thing is, the quartermaster found a nest of clocks and watches the other day, in one of the old storerooms. The door had been padlocked and not having remembered ordering such a lock, he forced an entrance. Have you any idea what he found inside?'

Seb swallowed, having a very good idea. 'No, sir,' he replied, innocently.

'Clocks and watches. Over two dozen of them. He has no notion of where they came from, but someone obviously owns them. It's possible they were stored there after we went into Zululand.'

'Yes, sir, very possibly.'

'Thing is,' the colonel picked up a block of papers and began banging them into the shape of a paving stone. He seemed quite fussy about getting all the edges straight. 'Thing is, they've all been stolen. The quartermaster relocked the shed and it was broken into the following night. All the clocks and watches were taken.'

'Good God, sir!'

'Indeed. Well, as Provost-Marshal it's your job to recover them. Find the thief. Bring the man, or men, to justice. That'll be all.'

Seb saluted. 'Sir, I shall do my best.'

'I have faith in you, Early.'

Seb left the colonel's hut with his mind spinning. Who the hell had taken all those timepieces? Here was a fine thing. Evans collects all the clocks and watches from petty thieves by offering them an amnesty. Then some fiendish robber goes in and steals them all again. It was a circular nightmare. Evans and he were making a maze for themselves. Would it ever end? What if they found the timepieces and locked them up safely again, only to have them stolen for the third time? What a can of worms!

He confronted Evans and using sign language asked the corporal if he had anything to do with the latest theft.

'No,' signed Evans. 'Not him.'

'Him?' said Seb out loud. 'What do you mean, *him*?'

'Sorry, sir,' shouted Evans, 'got the wrong sign – I meant *me* – I'm only still learnin' the finger-craft, same as you.'

'Where do you think they'll be? The timepieces?'

Evans said, 'I expect one of the men who took advantage of the amnesty followed me when I carried 'em to the shed. He'll have got rid of them by now, I reckon. Sold 'em to a black, probably, who'll take them to Ladysmith and sell them again. They're gone now, sir. They're too hot to hold on to now that you're on the case, eh?'

Seb was inclined to think his corporal was right and he just hoped the colonel would have too much on his mind to remember about the theft of a shedful of clocks and watches.

'By the way,' said Evans, his voice under control for once, 'guess who I ran into on his way to Ladysmith?'

Seb was only mildly interested.

'That Private Waters.'

'Private Waters?' Seb strained his memory. 'Who on earth is Private Waters?'

'You remember, sir – Rorke's Drift? The battle? He was the man who blacked his face and laid among them dead Zulus. Stood up, he did, next morning and nearly got himself shot by us.'

A recollection came to Seb. 'Oh – yes, that man.'

'Hid in a wardrobe in the hospital, didn't he? Zulus never found him. Then he did that blacking thing and crawled between the bodies. Pretty harrowin', I would have thought, to spend the night like that amongst a pile of corpses. Can't say I'd enjoy it, like. I spent one night in the hills at home with a dead sheep on me, to keep myself warm, like. Had to use it as a woolly blanket to keep the frost from freezin' my bollocks, see. It was bloody January and froze the bugger's tail as hard as a carrot. Had to snap it off, I did, since it was digging into my ribcage. Not a pleasant experience, though, and that was just an old ewe, not a dozen dead men, eh?'

A ray of light had suddenly penetrated Seb's mind. He stared at Evans as if he were looking at an angel. His face must have been suffused with some sign of his enlightenment, for Evans took a step back in alarm.

'That's it!' Seb cried. 'Wardrobe!'

'Eh?' said Evans, who was obviously concerned for his officer's state of mind. 'What's that?'

'The murderer, man. Captain Brewer's killer. He was in the wardrobe all the time. In the bloody *ward-robe*! I knew that Rorke's Drift held a clue. I just couldn't grasp what it was before now. So simple, really. So very simple. Not through the thatched roof. He never left the room at all. He was there the whole time, all night, until they broke down the door. We've done it, Evans,' Seb cried, elated. 'We've solved the problem of *how*. Now we just need to find out *who*.'

Twenty-One

1. Thatch: possible escape route for a murderer?
2. Three shots fired, the first from a different weapon.
3. (From Peter's notes): No powder marks on victim's chest.
4. Door to DOQ double-locked.
5. Martini-Henry used to kill victim.
6. ~~The bullying of Private Craster.~~
6. The wardrobe.

Seb rode to Khambula Hill to interview Colour Sergeant Murray, the NCO whose company had broken down the door to the duty officer's quarters and found the lifeless body of Captain Brewer. The colour sergeant was not overly pleased at being dragged away from his duties at the camp and complained to his commanding officer, who demanded to know what Ensign Early was playing at, interviewing his soldiers, when the camp was on high attack alert.

'Playing, sir? I have a murder to investigate,' snapped Seb, a little tired of officers interfering with his work.

The captain said, 'Not the soldier who shot the Kaffir? That was an accident.'

'I hadn't heard that one,' said Seb. 'I'll look into that later.'

'You realize of course that there's a war going on?' replied the seething captain. 'Some of us have seen some fighting and will no doubt see more of it, if we're allowed to get on with our work.'

Seb was stung into retorting, 'I've done my share of the fighting, Captain, up until now.'

'Oh?'

'Yes — I was at Rorke's Drift.'

'How peculiar,' said the captain, looking Seb up and down, 'I don't recall hearing about any ensign at that battle. My best information is two lieutenants and a surgeon.'

'I — I was not listed on the strength,' replied Seb, 'but I assure you, Captain, I was there.'

'Really?' murmured the other officer, clearly intimating that Seb was a liar.

As usual when dealing with senior officers, Seb had to go to untruths and empty threats to get results.

'If you refuse to let me see your colour sergeant, sir, I shall be forced to go to the general. He particularly wants this case solved and any hindrance on your part will be reported to him directly. Do you still insist on delaying my investigation, because I'm ready to leave now.'

'Oh, dammit, see the bloody man.'

The captain stalked off towards the lines.

Finally Seb faced his reluctant witness to the discovery of the corpse of Captain Brewer.

'Colour,' said Seb, 'how many men did you have with you when you broke down the door of the duty officer's quarters?'

'Six or seven, sir.'

'Could it have been eight or nine?'

The NCO looked unsettled.

'Why do you ask that?'

'What I'm trying to establish here is that you don't know how many men you had with you, do you? Precisely what order did you give when you asked for those men to assist you?'

'Och, I can't remember, exactly.'

Seb nodded. 'That's all right, I'm not expecting you to remember *exactly*, I merely want to establish that you did not pick six or seven men from your company. You simply said something like, "You lot on the end here. Come with me," or something similar.'

'Could have done. Not sure. I might've. I think I said, "Corporal Prentiss, grab some men and follow me." '

Seb nodded again. 'And when the door came off its hinges, after the use of your battering ram – what was it, a bench?'

'Yes, sir, a hardwood bench.'

'So – when you entered did you go in one by one, or pile in as a bunch.'

'Well, the – mo-mention . . .'

'Momentum?'

'Yes, sir,' the colour sergeant looked relieved to have the word given to him, 'the mo-mentum of the action carried us crashing into the room. Then when we saw the captain slumped over the table, we crowded round him, wonderin' if he was indeed a goner. I mean, he may've bin sick or gone down with fatigue like some do in the heat. There was a bit of a commotion goin' on. It's not easy to keep order, sir, when you go thumping into a room and find a dead officer.'

'I appreciate that, Colour. No one would expect you to, though given a few minutes . . .'

'Och, after a couple of minutes I had 'em all outside again – don't you worry. It was just the first shock of seein' the captain so pale and . . . dead. But I rallied quick as you like. Then I went outside and spoke to the lieutenant, who dismissed the men, sent them back to their quarters while we got someone down from staff to look at things.'

'Lieutenant Williams?'

'Him too, yes, that being the officer who was shot accidental by a Boer. But there was a couple of other officers. Couldn't tell you their names, sir, 'cause they didn't give 'em to me.'

'Colour,' said Seb, carefully, 'I'm going to ask you a question to which you won't know the answer. But I want you to be honest with your assessment. There's no blame attached, so please be entirely candid with me. *Is there any way a soldier could have been hiding in the wardrobe when you entered?*'

Murray blinked rapidly.

'Hidin' in the wardrobe?'

'Yes, there's a battered old wardrobe in that room, for the duty officer to use for his coat and hat. I have a theory that the captain was murdered by someone the previous night. Someone who was hiding in the wardrobe when the captain came on duty. Looking at Lieutenant Williams' notes I see there was a gap of three minutes between the officer on duty leaving and the relieving officer arriving. During that three minutes a soldier hid himself in the wardrobe. Once he knew that Captain Brewer was settled at his desk he came out of the cupboard and shot him in the chest with his Martini-Henry rifle. However, the captain was not yet dead, so the soldier removed the captain's revolver from its holster and he shot him again, through the heart. The soldier then fired one more revolver shot out of the window.'

'Why would he do that, sir? Fire out of the window.'

'Because the captain had been shot twice. The killer knew if they looked at the pistol afterwards they would see only one shot discharged and two wounds in the captain's chest. The murderer had to make it look as if both those wounds were from the same weapon, the captain's pistol – ergo, suicide.'

The colour sergeant's brow furrowed. 'Ergo?'

'Never mind. Listen, what happened next was that the soldier attempted to leave the room. He turned the key in the lock and tried to open the door. It would not budge, Colour. It remained fast.'

'Did it, sir?'

'Yes it did and do you know why?'

Seb was actually enjoying himself here.

'No idea. Not a clue.'

'Because it's a double-locking door. You have to turn the key twice round, completely, to release the bolt. The soldier didn't know that of course, and just kept tugging at the handle. Perhaps he turned the key back once, or maybe twice, and tried again, but what he didn't do, ever, was turn the key a complete one-hundred-and-eighty-degree circle, *twice*. When he failed to get out he finally realized he would have to stay in the room until someone opened the door from the outside.'

'Is that when he went back in the wardrobe, sir?'

'Colour, you are finally with me.'

'So, when we bust in, and was crowded round the captain, he quietly opened the wardrobe door and slipped in among us.'

'Would you have noticed, Colour?'

'No, sir,' he admitted, 'I wouldn't. I was too shocked by the captain and was busy trying to see if he was breathin'.'

'And the rest of your men?'

'Starin' at the captain's corpse, except for the corporal who was feelin' for a pulse.'

'Exactly,' cried Seb, slapping the table with the palm of his hand. 'The murderer left with your men when you told them to leave the room and rejoin the rest of the company waiting outside. He had to come from your company, you see, or he would have been recognized as a stranger in the ranks. Now, what I want from you are the names of any men who missed roll call that morning. Do you have any record of that?'

There was a satisfied look on Murray's face.

'As it happens, sir, I keep a little black book.'

'Can you fetch it for me?'

'Don't have to, sir. Here in my pocket.'

Seb was astonished to see that it was indeed a little book with a black leather cover. For some reason he had expected it to be some other colour, though he could not tell why. He watched as Murray thumbed through the pages, a thoughtful frown on his brow.

'Here it is, sir. Right, missin' men was Corporal Stenson – he was at the sick bay – Privates Jakes, Welthorpe and Harris.'

'You're sure the corporal was sick?'

'As a pig, sir. He had the yellow shakes and was passin' black water.'

'And the privates three?'

'Drunk on the town. So far as I know, they were all together. They usually are, those three. Private Welthorpe is off duty at the moment, sir. Would you like to see 'im?'

'I would indeed.'

Seb drummed his fingers impatiently, until a harassed-looking private arrived at the tent he was using.

'Private Welthorpe?'

'Yessir?'

'You know who I am?'

Welthorpe glanced towards the scarlet sash.

'Provo, sir. But I ain't bin drunk lately, sir. I ain't done nothin' wrong, not so's I recall.'

'Provost-Marshal to you. I want to ask you some questions. Where were you on the morning Captain Brewer's body was found? You were not with your company.'

'I bin punished for that, sir. Got a floggin'.'

'I asked you where you were.'

The young soldier, who could not have been more than seventeen years, had the grace to go red. 'In a lady's bed, sir.'

'A lady?'

'That's what she called herself, sir.'

'And where was Private Jakes.'

The young man was positively burning now.

'In – in the same bed, sir, on the other side of the lady. She was wery accommodatin' and we was both as drunk as toads.'

'She must have been – accommodating, I mean. So I take it this woman was a . . .'

'Whore? Yes, sir, but a wery nice one. Stayed with us all night. Snored like a porker, but she didn't steal nothin'. I still had a shillin' in me pocket when I left.'

'What was her name? Can you remember?'

'Oh yes,' Welthorpe said with some conviction, 'it was Silwia.'

'Silvia who?'

The soldier looked at him blankly and he said, 'Never mind, I take it Private Jakes will substantiate your story? I mean, he'll agree with the tale you've just told me?'

'Positif. Ask 'im, sir.'

The young man looked sincere and Seb had no need to doubt him, because he was indeed going to interview Private Jakes.

'Now, Private Welthorpe. Private Harris.'

'Yessir?'

'Was he with you that night and the following morning?'

Welthorpe blew out his cheeks and shook his head violently, 'Oh no, sir, there was only two of us in bed with Silwia – I'm certain positif three would've bin too much for the lady.'

Seb stifled a smile at this.

'Do you know where he was? Harris, I mean?'

'Not with me and Fred, anyways. True, we all went out together that night, all three of us, but went separate after gettin' drunk on squareface. Willie – that's Harris – said he slept off the gin on the porch of the tin tabernacle. Then there's Pete, Private Sarke, but Pete weren't with us at all that evening, 'cause he had duty and couldn't get nobody to take his place. No, we didn't see Willie till we was all up in front of old Woody . . . sorry, sir, the colonel that is.'

'Harris – friend of yours?'

'Was, yes – Pete Sarke too. We all got recruited at the same time, four of us in Worcester, and stick together, you know, English in a Scottish regiment, sir? Not that we're the only English in the regiment. But we all come from Worcester.'

Seb suddenly sat bolt upright as he remembered an address on a letter from Captain Brewer's wife to her husband.

'Wasn't the captain from Worcester too?'

'Captain?'

'Captain Brewer.'

Welthorpe laughed. 'Oh, yes sir, him. Yes, he was. The captain's father owns all the mills thereabouts. Well known, he is. Most of the folk round about Worcester work at Brewer's. My dad works there, an' Fred's too. Harris's father used to, but he got laid off, not for wery much – just comin' in late to work once or twice. He could quaff a pint or two could Harris's dad and the drink was his undoing in the end.'

'And Harris — Private William Harris — what did he think of Captain Brewer, considering what his father's firm did to his dad?'

'Hated him,' replied Welthorpe frankly. 'You see, the family went hungry after that. The two little ones — Harris's baby sisters — they starved to death. Wasted away, so he told me. I was there when Willie got the letter from his mum. Broke down, he did. Cried like a bairn. Who wouldn't, sir? Your own baby sisters? After that, Harris hated all the Brewer family, though the captain weren't aware of it. Didn't know Harris from a jack rabbit. When the captain was found dead on duty, though, Willie laughed. Did a jig round the cookin' fire.'

Seb studied the backs of his own hands, which he had placed on his knees to stop them from shaking so much.

'You can go now, Private Welthorpe, and could you ask the colour sergeant to send Private William Harris to me?'

'Yes, sir. Thank you, sir. But . . .'

'But what?'

'Can't get Willie Harris for you.'

'Why not?'

'Killed here at Khambula. Shot to death by the Zulus.'

Twenty-Two

Seb was sitting in a damp canvas garden chair outside his tent thinking deeply and smoking a pipe jammed so tightly with tobacco it would not keep alight unless he sucked on it continuously. The ground was wet and covered in deep puddles after a ferocious downpour which had lasted twenty-four hours. Many tents had leaked and men were wringing out their bedding and clothes. Seb did not care about the spongy character of the world. He was struggling vainly with a nasty dilemma: whether or not to report his findings to the general. A man had been murdered. He was now fairly certain he had the name of the murderer. Yet if he did tell Lord Chelmsford there would be a hearing and if the results of that hearing bore out his conclusions the murderer's parents would be told of their son's crime. That sort of news could tear a family apart. A family that had suffered enough.

Yet there was Seb's pride and ambition at stake. He was an officer of Her Majesty's army. Like any other officer he desperately desired recognition of his abilities. He wanted promotion and respect from the powers that moved in high places. 'Well done, Ensign,' he needed to hear, 'you have done a magnificent job. You will be mentioned in dispatches and are hereby promoted to lieutenant, with your captaincy just around the corner.' He wanted to hear words of this sort, or something similar, from General Lord Chelmsford. He ached to hear an apology from his own colonel, for impeding his investigations and dismissing his theories on the murder. These were sweet rewards he was loath to give up for a few grubby people he had never met.

'Not grubby,' he muttered to himself, tapping his pipe on his boot to loosen the tobacco. 'That's not really fair. I don't know them at all. They may be a good and righteous family who don't deserve to be shattered forever by the knowledge that their son and brother is a ruthless killer.' It was hard, very hard, to make a decision on the matter. In the one hand he held his duty. In the other a moral weight. Sebastian Early was a young man of principles and compassion. He knew the right thing to do according to his heart, but there was also this driving force within him that made men the aspiring creatures they are. Progress, such as it is, does not take place without this hunger for glory.

'Cock-a-doodle-do, South-East, my young rooster!'

Seb looked up. Mad Henry was approaching, with something large rolled up and tucked under his left arm.

Henry was wearing a velvet burgundy smoking hat embroidered with gold thread and sporting a golden tassel which hung over his face. He also had on a burgundy smoking jacket, that too embroidered with gold thread. A pair of jodhpurs and hessian boots completed his outrageous attire. In his right hand was a pizzle stick made from a bull's penis which he spun with the deftness of a drum major practising for a parade. Added to this Mad Henry's beard was so long now it reached halfway down his body. He had tucked the end of it into the waistband of his jodhpurs.

There was a smoking clay pipe in the corner of his mouth, which he managed to control by speaking out of the other corner.

'You look strangely worried, young rooster,' said Henry, sticking with his metaphor. He planted himself firmly in a puddle right in front of Seb's chair. 'What appears to be the trouble?'

'I'm on the horns of a dilemma,' confessed Seb.

'Better to be on the horns of a dilemma than inside the horns of the buffalo,' replied Mad Henry. The deep shock of the defeat at Isandlwana was still present within most soldiers. 'This might cheer you up.' He unrolled a hide, holding it up high by its edge to keep it out of the mud. 'An impala skin. Shot it myself. Thought of you. Said you wanted a hide to send home to your ma and pa.'

'Oh yes, a very handsome skin,' said Seb, admiring the characteristic black M mark at the bottom of the reddish-brown hide. 'What do I owe you for it?'

'Gift, young rooster. Yours for nothing but friendship. Was going to charge you, but hate to see a fellow officer in the dumps.'

'Oh, I must give you something.'

'Tell you what, then, settle my gambling debts for me.'

Seb stared at Mad Henry for a full minute before that man burst out laughing, the tassel on his hat bouncing with his mirth.

'Just joking, young rooster – you'd need bloody estates and a fortune to do that.'

'What's all this *young rooster* stuff?' asked Seb.

'Ah, well, it's been said that you've been seen with a nice feathered hen recently, a young thing up from the farm.'

He meant Mary Donaldson, of course, so Seb was not inclined to reply to this.

'Well, I thank you for the gift, Henry.'

'Perhaps you could do my portrait one day? I've heard you're a wizard with the pencil and brush.'

'Happy to.'

Henry then said, 'Pity you fell out with Zeldenthuis – he shot a remarkable leopard. Best skin I've seen since we arrived in Africa. Offered for it, but he refused.'

'Oh well.'

'Shot a Zulu too, but that's by-the-by.'

Seb frowned. 'Zeldenthuis killed a Zulu?'

Mad Henry took a draw on his pipe to keep the tobacco alight. Seb's had already gone out.

'While we were out hunting,' replied Henry. 'Attacked by a party of Zulus. About seven of them. Should have run but the Boer saw one of the shields and turned back. Felt obliged to accompany him. We shot at them and fortunately they ran off. Zeldenthuis got the one he wanted. Said the fellah had killed his father. Knew him by his shield.'

Seb was stunned by this news. Was it possible he had misjudged Zeldenthuis? Then who had shot Thandiwe? Perhaps it had indeed been his own people, to stop him from talking? Good God, thought Seb, I've been a bloody fool. I've jumped to conclusions and accused the wrong man without proper evidence. That was unforgivable in a Provost-Marshal, who really should go on hard facts.

'By the by, young rooster,' Mad Henry interrupted his thoughts, 'need some advice. Been put in charge of training some new recruits for the Natal Native Horse. Staff are probably trying to keep me out of their hair. They're always giving me jobs like this. There's over two hundred of the beggars. Need somewhere to do it. Any ideas?'

As it happened, Seb did have an idea, and over the next ten minutes passed it on to Mad Henry.

'Thank you, now cheer up, moon-gazer. You're an officer in one of the most distinguished regiments in the army. Not a very *grand* officer yet, but your time will come.'

'Will it? I have no connections, you know. My father is only a schoolteacher. I'm not from an eminent family, like you or Harford.'

'Ha! What about Captain Cook? A farm labourer's son. Or Field Marshal Sir Colin Campbell? Offspring of a Glaswegian carpenter. Buck up. And speaking of Harford, he won't get far. He's more interested in becoming a Fellow of the Royal Society, what with his bees and beetles. Me? Well, you can see how far my family background has got me – though I have to say it's not their fault I swim against the tide.'

Seb grinned. 'You're right. Thanks, Henry.'

Mad Henry twirled his pizzle stick.

'Welcome, young rooster. Toodle-pip.'

Seb went directly to see Pieter Zeldenthuis. The Boer was sitting drinking with some friends. He eyed Seb lazily as the ensign approached him.

'Zeldenthuis,' said Seb, 'I owe you an apology.'

The other men, all in the buckskins and wideawake hats of scouts, looked at Zeldenthuis.

'Do you?'

'Yes – you were wrongly accused.'

'Well then, sit down and have a drink.'

'I would, but I have things to do. I just wanted to get things straight between us.'

'All right. Don't let it weigh on you.'

'Thank you.'

Seb did not feel he could say any more. He felt humiliated enough in front of these Boers and British colonials. They were a rough-looking bunch and no doubt would have a great laugh once he was out of earshot – perhaps even before then. Anyway, Seb was not going to beg forgiveness of a man like Zeldenthuis, who would regard such a speech as a weakness of spirit.

Before he walked away, to save a little face he said, 'I solved the murder, by the way.'

'Good for you, policeman,' Pieter Zeldenthuis replied. 'That's what they pay you for.'

'That – and killing Zulus.'

'Oh yes, that too.'

Seb took a long walk back, around the camp once or twice, looking up at the stars occasionally. By the time he reached his tent he had made up his mind. He was not going to tell Lord Chelmsford about Private Harris. It would mean more victims in a war that already had enough of those. There were hundreds of dead soldiers still lying out on the plains, unburied. And thousands of young Zulu warriors, with mothers mourning and fathers bleak of soul. There was a local government in chaos and a general who had so far one of the biggest military disasters ever borne by a British commander to carry on his shoulders for the rest of his life. Who was to blame? Not the courageous Zulus, definitely. They had been betrayed at the Ultimatum Tree, where their fate had been told them by arrogant white politicians. Not the ordinary soldiers of the Queen, for they had as usual fought with great bravery. Someone, some people, were responsible for this mess, but Seb did not have to give them names. History would do that.

'Sam? Tom? Evans? I'm going to write a letter, then I'm going to bed.'

A chorus of voices from the next tent bade him a good night.

He was still working on the letter, the moths batting the yellow glass of the lamp, when Jack Spense came to him. Words for this particular missive had not come easy and Seb had been feeling the beginnings of one of his headaches crawling up his neck when Jack poked his head around the flap.

'Saw the light. Got a minute?'

'Yes, of course, Jack.' Seb put his pen into the ink bottle and left it there. 'Step inside.'

'I – I thought you might like to see this.' Jack Spense put a photograph on Seb's makeshift table. 'It was taken this afternoon.'

Seb stared at the monochrome picture and as he studied it a chill gradually crept through him causing his headache to increase in vehemence.

'I see,' he said, at last. 'It's – it's a – a little sinister.'

'Indeed, yes. That's why I brought it. I'll leave it up to you to do what you will.'

'Thank you, Jack.'

Jack Spense left. Seb sat in painful silence and stared at the grainy picture. Then he went to his sealskin case and took out another photograph, laying it alongside the new one. The one he had retrieved from his case was the photograph of Thandiwe in death, with his shield propped beside his corpse. The second was of Pieter Zeldenthuis holding another shield with a very similar pattern to Thandiwe's shield. Very similar. But they were not the same. There were minor differences, in the size of the white blotches on the dark background, and in the shape of those blotches. Not much, but some. They were most definitely different shields. Seb had no doubt the newer picture was of the shield taken from the Zulu Pieter had shot when Mad Henry was with him on the hunt.

Something very dark was occurring on Seb's watch.

Joseph Johnson recently sowed further crops on the Tranter land – land which he now considered his own. When told of the invasion by his black workers, he went riding out to find a regiment of mounted soldiers charging back and forth in columns over the very ground he had ploughed and sown just a few weeks before now. His seedlings were strewn every which way and hoofprints littered the fields. Johnson, enraged, galloped up to an officer who looked like a peacock in a feathered hat and bright red jacket above startlingly tight yellow pantaloons. Milling around the officer's horse were about a dozen fox hounds. The dogs looked up at Johnson expectantly.

'What the hell d'you think you're doing?' he roared. 'Get those bastards off my land.'

The dogs cringed and the officer sitting on his horse directing the exercises of these horsemen looked Johnson up and down in contempt.

'*Your* land, sir? I am of the firm belief that this land belongs to Mr Thomas Tranter, who has given his express permission for me to use this area as a training ground. And if I were you, sir, I should curb this tendency to generalize as to the marital status of the parents of my troopers. There will be one or two natural births amongst them it must be true, for passion can occasionally get out of hand in young unwed couples, but for the most part, sir, these recruits are from morally unimpeachable families.'

Johnson ignored this speech, some of which he did not understand anyway. He was more concerned with what was happening around him than falling into the trap of debating ethics with a university graduate. In the near distance, Johnson could see some military engineers erecting a building with remarkable speed and efficiency.

'What in hell are *they* doing?' he asked, exasperated.

The brightly coloured officer replied, 'Not that it's any of your business, but they're constructing temporary staff quarters.'

'Looks more like a farm dwelling to me.'

The officer tapped the bridge of Johnson's nose with the end of a leather-covered stick he had in his right hand.

'My dear old cockerel,' said the officer, 'I wouldn't give two blind baboons to know what you think. You are interfering with Her Majesty's troops involved in the exciting exercise of learning how to kill people from the back of a quadruped. I advise you to leave this area as soon as possible, before it is decided to use you as a drag.'

'A what?' cried Johnson.

'Not a *what*, a drag. Have you never seen a drag hunt, old cockerel? And you a Norfolk man by your accent. Similar to a fox hunt, but of course there's no live fox involved. Most drag hunt masters lay a scent using a marked lead horse for the hounds to chase, but in my home county we drag the carcass of an animal over the landscape as a trail for the dogs to follow. If you stay around long enough you might very well become that carcass.'

'There'll be hell to pay for this,' yelled Johnson, incensed by this officer's facetious attitude. 'I'll go to the governor.'

The officer laughed. 'My dear old cockerel, feel free. I have, by the way, been to the land registry office. I'll send the governor, who I have to inform you is a not-so-distant cousin of mine, a copy of the deed. Now you, sir, are in my way. You are interfering with important exercises of men who serve their Queen and country. Have the good grace to vacate the space which you occupy before I have you physically removed.'

Despite the jocose tone being used by the officer, and his peculiarly colourful attire, Johnson could see by the man's face that this was no idle threat. There was something about this lieutenant, or whatever he was, which seemed more than a little mad. His strange uniform proclaimed him to be unhinged, and his expressions and his uncanny eyes, when you looked into them closely, were quite unnerving. Johnson had no doubt this man would act irrationally, with impromptu lunacy, without considering the consequences.

Clearly, Johnson decided, his life was in danger here. He rode away in haste, leaving behind the thunder of yet another brilliant mock charge by the Natal Native Horse. Weeks of work were being churned into the soil behind his back, but he had decided the fight was not worth it. Thomas Tranter had the whole force of the British army at his beck and call, and he, Joseph Johnson, had been outmanoeuvred.